TRUCK STOP
TITAN

KRISSY
DANIELS

Published by Kiss Me Dizzy Books

Cover Design by:
Damonza.com
www.damonza.com

Editing by:
Madison Seidler
www.madisonseidler.com

Proofreading by:
E-book Formatting Fairies
www.marieforce.com

Formatting by:
Elaine York
www.allusiongraphics.com

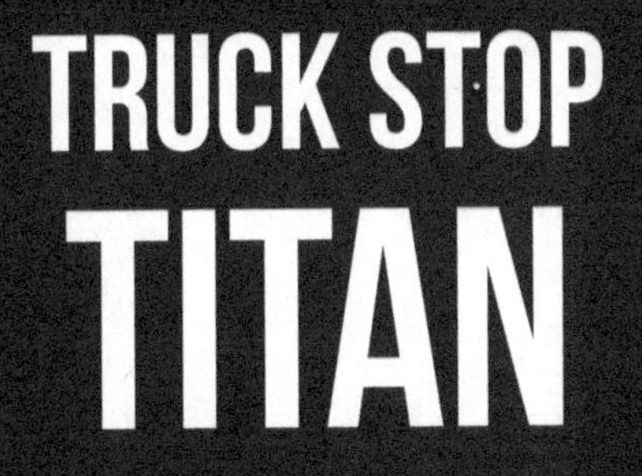

TRUCK STOP
TITAN

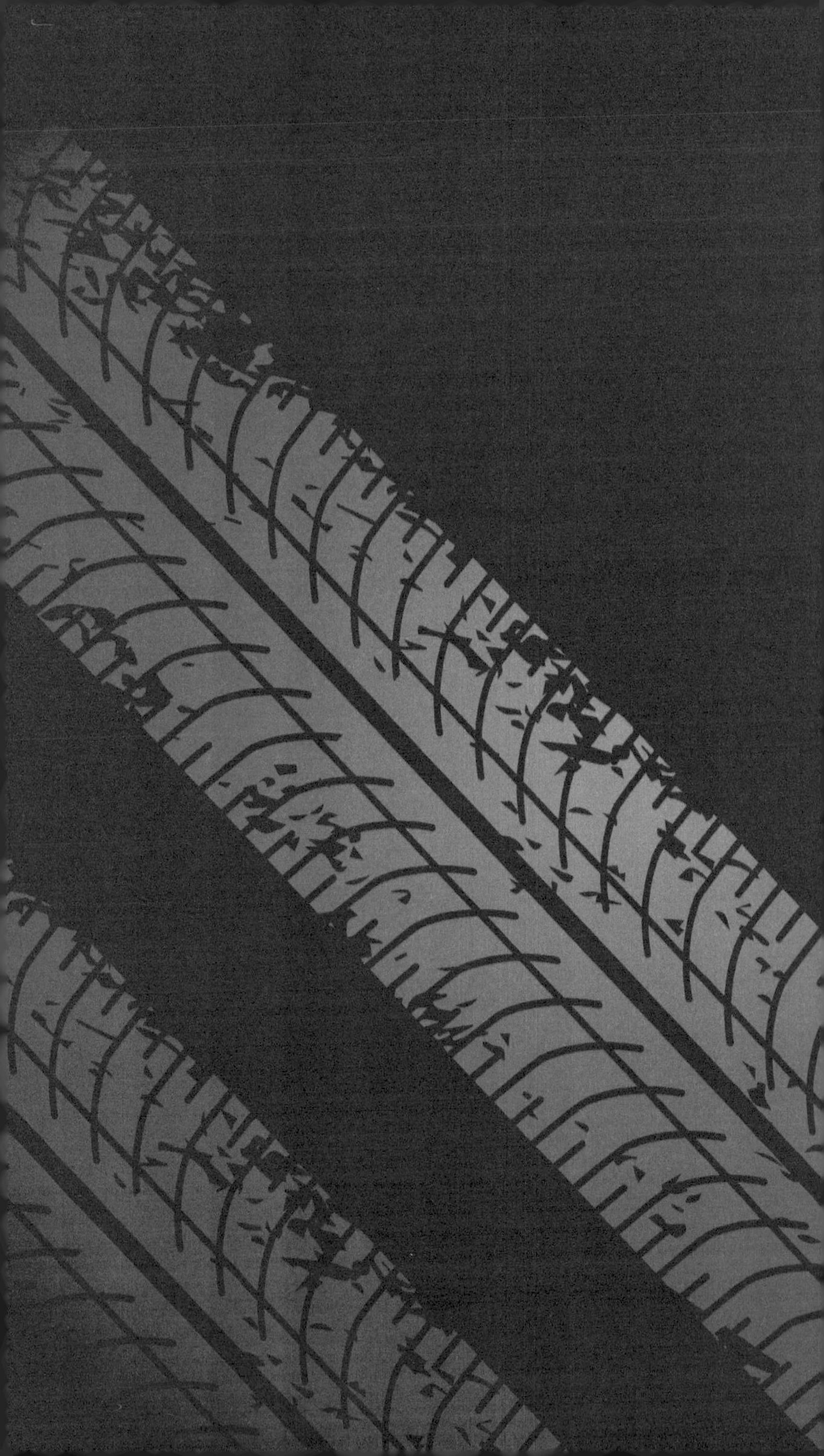

For those of us who
are not so easy to love

CHAPTER 1

"HOLD STILL." HAMMER GRIPPED my hair in a tight fist, his rank breath blowing across my face.

"Jesus." I shifted my ass on the hard stool, gripping my knees to keep from punching the bastard. "Just get it done."

The ugly fucker sneered, peering down at me, his gaze unsettled. "You want that piece of glass outta your forehead, or not?"

"I wanna get this fuckin' show on the road."

"Then maybe you should'a shot that tweaker instead of wrestling him through the window." He jerked my head back. "This is gonna hurt. Close your eyes."

Hammer yanked. I winced, blinking against the pain. Glass clinked in the sink. An unholy fire burned above my right eye. The stench of alcohol seared my lungs.

Pinching the wound closed, he got busy with the liquid stitches, then held my skin in place while the glue dried.

Screams echoed through the house, terror laden cries of a child, amping my adrenaline to dangerous levels.

"What are we doing here?" I growled, rising to stand.

Hammer hadn't offered details as to why we'd come to Wilson Kyle's cabin, other than we were collecting a debt.

Clearly, he'd visited before, as he knew where to find the spare key.

"You're here for backup." He pointed a bloody finger in my direction. "Not to ask questions."

I turned to check the damage, meeting my own eyes in the mirror, hating what I found in their depths, hating what I'd become. "What's with the girl?"

"Not your fucking business." Hammer tossed the bloody cotton balls in the trash, then stomped toward the back room shouting, "Jesus, kid. Shut the fuck up!"

The man in the bathtub groaned, the sound a bubbly gurgle. Good. I wanted him conscious. I tore back the curtain and knelt, pinching his chin to keep his focus on me.

"You're gonna burn today. Hope you know how much it kills me I can't stick around to watch." I patted his cheek.

Pleading eyes bulged, the man thrashing against his binds.

"You know why this has to happen, right?"

He stilled, urine staining his jeans in a slow spread. Yeah. He knew why he had to die.

Still, I reminded the sick fuck. "That girl. What is she? Five? Six? She's fucked for life. She'll have nightmares for years. She'll probably end up in foster care, with more sick bastards. Most likely, she'll end up on the street, sucking diseased cock like yours in exchange for her next fix."

What Kyle had done to that little girl, what I'd walked in on, broke something in me, brought to surface buried memories, the scenes of the Slayers and what they'd done to my cousin, Addy, after they'd thought she'd betrayed them.

I was one hundred percent a Satan's Slayer, from my first ride, my first toke, my first fuck, and my first kill. I'd done time for my brothers. I had scars to prove my loyalty, but the fucker lying beneath me? The pedophile motherfucker? He ruined me. The fact that one of my brothers had stood by watching and hadn't dismembered that piece of shit?

Final nail in the coffin.

I was done.

I yanked the gag from Kyle's mouth, shoved the funnel between his teeth, then poured what was left of the gasoline down his throat, making him swallow.

Then I landed two strikes between his eyes, because I wanted him to hurt, and dragged him down the hall, to the back bedroom, past the woman lying on the floor, and to the hole in the center of the room. The dirt prison that was currently occupied.

"Jesus, Hammer. Get her outta there."

"She ain't moving," Hammer growled, standing hands to hips, looking down at the vacancy in the hardwood. "Ain't no way in hell I'm jumping into that pit."

"Jesus H Christ." I shoved Hammer aside, grunted, "Check on the woman," then dropped to all fours, and ducked my head into the dark hole, covering my mouth and nose, the stench too much for even vermin like me to bear.

My guts protested, twisting into fierce knots. The tiny child wore a man's dirty white T-shirt, the collar sliding off her bony shoulders, the hem dusting her feet. Her head hung low, offering me a view of her wild mane, which had at some point been braided, but was mostly a tangled mess.

One blanket lay bunched in the corner of the five-by-five dirt cell. In the opposite corner, a bucket.

"Hey, Little Lady." I lowered a hand. "Wanna get out of there?"

The screaming stopped, replaced by heavy, erratic breaths.

"This fucker ain't gonna hurt you no more." I sank lower, hoping to get a better handle on her situation.

She shuffled backward, knocking dirt chunks off her newly dug prison walls.

Behind me, grunts, feet shuffling. Hammer yelled, "She isn't breathing. Goddammit. She ain't breathing."

I glanced over my shoulder to find my brother-in-crime inspecting the woman's neck and chest, tearing at the collar of her blouse.

Wilson moaned, then mumbled. "The junkie slut is dead, asshole. Get away from my Dollie. She's mine." At the sound of Wilson's voice, the little one screamed again, backing into the corner, thrashing with rabid sobs.

"Trailer, we need to ghost. You can't save her, she's too far gone."

"Not leaving her here."

Videos played in a loop on Kyle's computer screen. One kid after another, boys and girls alike. Kids he'd filmed at the park, the mall, fucking restrooms. It was only the girl below my feet that stopped me from shredding the molester with my bare hands.

"I'm gonna put this guy in the hole, Little One. I'm gonna drop him in the dirt, and he's never coming out. So, unless you wanna stay down there with him, I need you to take my hand so I can pull you out of there."

Out from the dark corner she scrambled, eyes lifted to mine, wide, red-rimmed, and sunken. I lowered my arm, she grabbed hold, and I raised her out of the god damn earth. The second her feet hit the ground, the child crumpled, then kicked, hands and feet skidding on the floor, scrambling to get to the dead woman.

Wilson cried, "Dollie. My Dollie. Baby, come here!"

One fist to the nose wasn't enough to shut him up, so I struck again. Then again, 'cause damn, there was no better balm to a blistering rage than the crack of bones under your knuckles.

He tracked the little girl, his mouth moving, nothing but bloody gurgles coming out. Sick fuckin' loon.

Hand around the man's throat, I dropped him in the grave, pulled the floorboards back into place, and nailed those fuckers down, keeping one eye on the kid, and one on my brother.

The child curled around her mother's body, hugging her round belly, petting her cheek. It was then I took a good look at the dead woman sprawled on the floor, a dirty needle stuck in her arm. Mick. She'd done a few odd jobs for the club. Cleaning. Cooking. She'd show up for a few months, then disappear. Didn't know she had a kid. Couldn't believe she was pregnant. Killed me, seeing that baby bump. How could a woman so battle-worn and emaciated carry a child?

The house of horrors was about to become ash. I moved to grab the kid, and the grief and fear that bubbled from her throat split my soul into jagged shards. With all the strength she had in that tiny body, she curled around her mother, clinging for dear life.

"We need to go, Little One." I forced an arm around her middle, trying to pry her away.

She stiffened but didn't let go, screaming silent sobs into her mama's hair.

"Please, kid." I bent, pressing my lips to her ear so our convo stayed out of my brother's earshot. "Don't make me leave you here. Your mama's gone. I can't help her. But I can help you."

More with the crying, and snot, and desperate attempts to rile her mother's corpse.

"We go now, Trailer, or you're burning with them."

Fuck. Leaving the girl was not an option. Visions of Addison's final days played through my head, poking the embers of that ever-present burn, leaving an acrid taste in the back of my throat.

The burden of my fuck-all life had never weighed so heavy than it did when I pried that hysterical child's fingers from her mother's body. I absorbed her kicks and scratches and spitting hysteria, eventually shrugging off my cut and cocooning her in the heavy leather to prevent further injury to either of us. Took every ounce of self-control I owned to keep my shit together for that little girl.

With heavy steps, I made my way to the back door, past the overturned furniture, emptied drawers, and smashed electronics. Not sure what Hammer had been looking for, but judging by the trail of profanities following in his wake, he was leaving empty-handed.

I looked down at the girl in my arms, sickened by her pale skin, her bony frame, but awed by her spark, her fight. God damn. Wide hazel eyes. Auburn waves. Freckles. Just like my Addy.

Fuck me. Fuck my life.

"You'll have to do the honors," I told Hammer before yanking open the truck door.

He ran a hand over his bald scalp, took one last drag, then used his cigarette to light the wick sticking out of his glass bottle. He tossed the bomb, hitting the fuel-soaked porch.

We didn't wait for the house to catch fire. We'd made sure it would burn.

Thank fuck we'd brought the Jeep, or the ride down from the mountain would've been god damn impossible. Took both arms and one leg for me to keep that baby still, and a good twenty minutes before she passed out from exhaustion.

Silence hung like a third wheel in the cabin of that vehicle.

"Gonna tell me what the hell happened back there?"

"No." Hammer sucked a final drag from his Marlboro, then chucked it out the window. "And you speak a word of it to anyone, I'll skin you myself."

I'd never had cause to question my brother, but damn, my hackles were raised. "Prez know we were on that run?"

"Yep," he lied, scratching his jawline just below his ear. His one tell.

"That was Mick."

Hammer nodded, then pounded the steering wheel. "Damn shame. She'd been clean for three weeks."

"Did you know she had a kid?"

Jaw clenched, he nodded.

"Kyle Wilson the girl's dad?"

"Don't know. Don't fuckin' care." He jabbed a finger my direction. "You should'a left her."

I didn't question further. Everything about the day had been off. Wasn't like Hammer to keep shit on the down-low, so I figured he had good reason.

The child's body slackened, and for the first time in hours, I relaxed, too. When her head rolled back on my arm, I noticed the chain around her neck, too damn heavy for her tiny frame. The thick silver braid looked new, but the heart locket attached was tarnished, and the key hanging next to it, out of place. I thumbed the piece of metal, then rested my head on the back of the seat and closed my eyes.

We hit the clubhouse and Hammer headed inside, fists clenched, mumbling under his breath. I stayed in the cab, scared shitless I'd wake the kid.

Didn't take long for Prez to storm my way, not a hair out of place, or a wrinkle in his clothes, but wearing a scowl known to set even the strongest men back a step. "The fuck you thinking, bringing a kid out here?"

"Did you know what was going down in that cabin?"

"What cab—"

"She was locked in a damn hole." I cut him off before he could spew any bullshit. I raged, itching for a fight. "The fucker was making movies."

Prez tried and failed to hide his disgust, then covered his tracks with, "You goin' soft, Trailer?"

Fuck no. I was hard as a mother-fucking tank. Hard enough to take down him and everyone in that damn clubhouse. "I don't have a fuckin' clue why you sent us to that cabin. Hammer ain't talking, but I know he'd been in and outta that place, and I know damn well he knew about that fucker's extracurricular activities. And that shit don't sit well with me. She's a fucking baby, Prez."

Prez flinched, seemingly confused, then yanked a hand-rolled out of his pocket. He lit the bud, and drew a deep inhale, eyes aimed over my shoulder, clearly working something out, and apparently not ready to divulge.

His silence spoke volumes, cementing my resolve.

"I've paid my debt to this club. More than you ever asked of me."

His gaze sliced to mine, brows furrowed. "What're you saying?"

Before considering their weight, the words left my lips. "I'm out."

"Out?" Throwing his head back, he released a maniacal, threat-laced laugh. "There is no out. I own you, kid. Every breath, every blink, every kill. Every piss you take, every load you blow into skanky pussy. They're mine. Don't ever forget that. You were nothing but trailer trash, like your old man. Only reason you're not pushing up daisies is because you do the nasty shit others won't. Don't forget what I did for you."

I would never forget. Wore the scars like a god damn suit of armor.

Still, if I backed down, I'd lose respect, and the girl would die. Wasn't another girl dying because of me. "I'm out. Kill me if you have to, but I'm taking this kid somewhere safe first."

The child twitched in my arms, her head jerking back, catching Prez's attention. A long, hard minute passed. Jaw clenched, he gnawed on his bottom lip. I watched him, watching her, undoubtedly thinking about his nieces, one of whom had been taken by sex traffickers only a year ago. With a head shake, he checked over his shoulder where a few of the brothers were spilling out of the clubhouse. On a deep inhale, he met my glare, then pulled his Sig out of its holster, and aimed straight between my eyes. "Get out of the truck."

"Fuck," I growled, shoved the door open, and hauled the girl out of the cab.

"The cut." He gestured to the kid. "It's mine. Hand it over."

Sure as hell wasn't expecting that order. By some miracle, I unwrapped the girl and tossed my leather vest at his chest without waking her.

"Down the road, you'll find a white sedan. It's hot. Keys are inside. Get the fuck outta my sight and don't come back unless I call you back."

He was letting me go, without losing face. The day had gone from strange to downright insane.

Without a word, I turned my back on my brothers.

"And Trailer," he called. "You're not out. You're never out."

I didn't look back. Wouldn't. But I couldn't help my grin. The asshole still had a heart.

And that shattered little girl may have just saved my life.

"Breathe, baby. C'mon." I pulled the tiny thing against my chest, rubbing her back, rocking, fighting my own fucking panic attack because I had no god damned clue how to comfort anyone, let alone a traumatized child.

Purple-faced, she struggled to breathe, silent screams racking her body.

"Please. I won't hurt you. I'm not gonna hurt you." I was so far over my head I feared I'd never see daylight. "The bad man is gone. He won't touch you again."

Her body trembled, but her chest rose and fell against mine. Once. Twice. She managed to suck in oxygen between sobs. Thank fuck.

I held her close but not tight, her body fragile with bruises. She needed words. Solace. I had none to offer. What did I know about that shit? What the fuck did I know about anything?

When her tears slowed, and her breaths turned wet and shallow, I forced a string of deep inhale-exhales. Muscles weary, my bones ached, and my head buzzed like I'd survived a three-day bender.

I held her for an eternity, running my fingers through her long, dirty hair, bile rising in my throat. She smelled like piss and raw earth. How long had that bastard had her? How was she still alive? How had her tiny, breakable body taken that abuse and not shattered?

When she relaxed in my arms, a soft snore coming from her lips, I shifted, eager to lay her down and get back on the road. Tiny fingers gripped my shirt collar, clinging for dear life.

"Listen. I know you're scared. But I have to lay you down. I need to drive. I need you to help me out here, Little One."

She only whimpered, burrowing her face in my neck.

Fuck.

Fuck me.

Fuck it.

I yanked the seatbelt around our joined bodies and pulled back onto the highway. The sky had darkened to black. Nobody would see the multitude of wrongdoings I committed, unless of course I got pulled over. So, like a fuck, I drove the speed limit, maintained a safe distance between passing cars, and sweated rivers for the remaining five hours of my drive.

Thirty minutes from Whisper Springs, I pulled out my burner phone and dialed the number I'd programmed earlier.

"This better be fucking important to wake me at three in the morning." Tango Rossi's voice rattled through the phone.

"It's Reynolds. I need your help." More painful words had never escaped my lips.

"Dane?"

In the background, Slade asked, "Dane? What's he calling for?"

At the same time, the little girl in my arms started screaming, another night terror taking hold. God damn not again.

I pulled to the side of the road, her tiny body convulsing in my arms.

"I need help. Right fucking now."

"The fuck?" Tango growled.

"Need your buddy, Tucker. Need him now, and a woman. Tell him to bring a woman. Someone with a soft touch."

"That a kid?" Tango's anger fizzled.

My voice, however, rose to full panic mode, unrecognizable. "I'm out of my fucking element here, Rossi. She's in bad shape."

To his credit, the pretty boy didn't mess around. I gave him my location, tossed the cell, and got busy with the rock, rock, rub, rub, shh, shh.

"You're safe, sweetheart. Nobody's gonna hurt you," I whispered over and over, until her breathing returned to normal, her body relaxed, and a set of headlights pulled up behind me.

Two bodies came into view, coming to my side of the car at a hurried pace. When I opened the door, a "Fuck me," escaped, because I hadn't expected to see Blondie ever again, and that woman was a sight that never failed to steal my wits.

Slade blinked at me with those wide-as-fuck baby blues, her pretty mouth hanging open. I gave her a minute to adjust to the scene.

"Reynolds," Tucker said. "What's going on?" He stepped around me, inspecting the child in my arms. "Jesus. What the hell happened?"

"Found her about fourteen hours ago. Sick bastard had her caged in a hole. She's hurting. Inside and out."

"Why didn't you take her to the hospital?" Slade asked, no judgement, only concern.

"Not important. Need you to take her. Do that thing you do. Keep her safe. Find her family."

"Name?" Slade asked, brushing trembling fingers down the girl's back.

"Don't know." I swallowed a wave of nausea, bit back a slew of cuss words.

"Okay. Okay." Slade nodded. "Give her to me. We'll get her to Tuck's mom. She's a doctor."

Slade held out her hands, waiting for me to pass the child over. My arms solidified, coiled around the tiny body.

"It's okay, Dane. We're gonna take good care of her." Slade's voice was soft, reassuring, and trembling a little, just like mine.

I whispered in the baby's ear, "My friend Slade is gonna take you now. She's very nice, and she'll take good care of you."

The child shivered, a full body tremble, then crawled up my chest, clinging tighter, her arms and legs hooking around me.

"Kid. They're going to take you somewhere nice and warm. They're gonna help you feel better."

Face buried in my neck, she shook her head, tears wetting my shirt.

God.

Jesus.

Fuck.

Fuck.

Why me? Why fucking me?

"Okay," Tucker said. "Give Slade your keys. She'll drive your car. You get in the back seat with the girl. We can't stay out here."

"Keys are in the ignition." I nodded to Slade before sliding into the back of the sedan and stretching the seatbelt once again around both of our bodies.

Tucker pounded the top of the car. "Go. Go. I'm right behind you."

Blood curdling screams echoed through the hallway, bouncing off the mint green paint and driving deadly spikes through my temporal lobes.

Pace.

Pace.

Pace.

My fist met the wall. The pain jetting up my arm did little to distract me from the feral buzzing in my head. I'd stayed too long already. I should've left the second I'd laid her in that damn bed.

"I can't do this."

Tucker blocked my exit, standing stone still, arms crossed, brow raised.

"I did my part. I got her somewhere safe." My pointed finger met his chest. "Now it's on you!"

The guy didn't budge, but damn, his jaw twitched hard enough to dislocate, the child's pain clearly grating his nerves, too.

I pounded my head, and resumed pacing, the gut-wrenching screams driving me mad. "I need to hit the road."

"Doesn't work that way. We need to do a thorough exam. She's not letting anyone touch her but you. So, whatever you got to do that's so important can wait."

"Jesus fuckin' Christ." I stopped dead, turning to face Tucker, ready to draw blood. "You don't understand. I'm not built for this shit." Then I realized my mistake—showing weakness. Stumbling, I hit the wall behind me and scrubbed the dirty hair out of my face.

The lines between his eyes deepened, his assessment of my appearance slow and thorough. "You look like shit." Arms dropped to his sides, he stalked closer. "The fuck'd you get yourself into?"

"Dane!" Slade shrieked. "Get in here. Now!"

Tucker and I shared a stare down, violent tension stifling the air. He nodded toward the room. I shook my head in a slow *no*. Then turned to leave.

A heavy hand landed on my shoulder, halting my retreat.

Out of instinct I struck, hitting the blond bastard square in the jaw.

Tucker moved fast, landing a jab to my gut, just hard enough to prove he could hold his own in a fight if given cause.

"Get your ass in that room. You assumed responsibility the second you pulled that little girl out of whatever hell she was living. Don't let her down now."

"Fuck you." Tucker was right, but still, I didn't appreciate being told I was wrong. And damn, why was I facing off with the guy? We were on the same side. Her side.

I turned on my heel and entered the room where Tucker's mom, Leticia, attempted to examine the hysterical child while Slade held her down. Slade was wiped, her face pale and stained with tears, her hair a ratted mess, scratches marring her neck and arms.

God, they were gonna break the tiny thing. Two strides and I scooped the baby into my arms. Hands fisting my hair and pulling tight, she buried her face in my neck. Her breaths steadied when I rubbed her back in slow circles.

The women in the room shared nervous glances, and Slade fell into one of the chairs, rubbing blood off her cheek with the back of her arm.

"Okay," Leticia whispered, stepping closer. "We need to get this dirty shirt off and clean her up a bit." She lifted her pale blue eyes to mine. "Can you help me with that?"

"You want me to undress her?" I choked on the words.

"No, Dane. Just hold her. I think she'll let me do what I need to do if you're holding her."

How was the woman so calm?

I nodded, then moved to the bed, settling on the edge and resting the girl's weight on my thigh.

Slow and steady, Leticia lifted the shirt. Inch by inch she revealed the bruises, the sores, and when the child's hips came into view, I pinched my eyes shut.

I'd lose my shit if there was evidence of what I'd suspected Wilson had done to the little girl.

Leticia tapped my arm, then tugged the shirt higher, and we managed to remove the article of clothing.

The next hour was pure torture. We weighed the child. Bathed her. Dressed her in a small hospital gown. And finally. Finally. Thank fuck. Leticia gave her a sedative, and damn, I was jonesing for some of that shit, too.

Even in her drug-induced rest, the child didn't release me. So, I maneuvered into her small hospital bed, lay back, and waited for her body to go limp.

Soon as I could pry myself from her side, I would leave. Hit the open road, and never look back.

"Dane," a soft voice whispered. "Dane." Small fingers nudged my shoulder.

Between my arms, someone stirred, something small and bony striking dangerously close to my groin. I peeled open one eye, and then the other, the dimly lit room coming into focus. Soft hair tickled my nose, my senses waking with the scent of sweat and antiseptic.

"Fuck." I grumbled, my stretch halted by the dead weight on my arm, the small, unconscious child breathing shallow breaths against my neck.

"Dane." Slade and her bewitching smile came into view. "Here. Let me help."

"Don't wake her," I growled.

"A high school marching band couldn't wake her right now. She's sedated. She'll sleep through most of the day." Slade curled the girl into her arms, allowing me freedom to roll off the small bed.

I stretched the kinks from my spine.

"You did a good thing last night," she said, laying the girl on her back.

My stomach revolted, the child's terror too fresh in my mind, my flesh sore where she'd carved grooves with her dirty little nails.

Slade tucked blankets around the sleeping kid. "We called the psychologist. She'll be here first thing tomorrow morning."

"Good. That's good." I nodded, calculating how far I'd be from Whisper Springs by then, the girl nothing but a fading nightmare.

"C'mon." Slade nodded toward the door. "I made you coffee.

"Thanks. But I need to hit the road." Last thing I needed was to hang out with Slade, the woman a blaring reminder of all I'd lost.

"No." Hands to hips, she gave me a motherly scowl. "You need breakfast. Coffee. Then you can go."

"Thanks, Blondie. But I'm good."

"Dane. Please." She dropped her arms, pleading, "Stay."

A thick lump stuck in my throat. Only good thing I'd done in my life was help Slade get my pregnant cousin free of my piece of shit father.

We hadn't saved Addy from the crazy that cursed my family, but her son, Rocky, thrived with parents who would give him the world and who would die to protect him. I couldn't have asked for more, aside from being in his life, which was a no-go because I would die to protect him, too. And he would never be safe if the club knew he was my flesh and blood, or that I'd taken part in setting him free.

I stared at a dent in the newly polished hardwood, the back of my eyes prickling, my throat thick, raw. "Thank you."

Blue painted toenails came into view, and I caught a whiff of something akin to peaches, a scent that suited Slade.

"Thank you for what?" she asked, too damn close for my liking.

I stepped back, meeting her soft gaze. "You know."

"No. I don't."

"Rocky," was all I needed to say. She'd raised Addison's son as her own, giving him the life I never could.

"Dane." She sighed, stance softening.

"I have to go." I stomped out the door and down the hallway, not a fucking clue where I was headed, but fuck me, I needed to blow before my head exploded.

"Dane. Wait," Slade called, flip flops smacking an erratic rhythm behind me.

"Take care of that little girl." I waved a hand over my shoulder and slammed past Tucker, and through a heavy wooden door that led to the kitchen. I dodged the massive island and headed straight for the back door.

I was at the car, so damn close to escape, when I heard, "Reynolds."

The East Coast accent was unmistakable.

I mumbled, "Moretti," over my shoulder, surprised to see the guy, but in no condition to shoot the breeze.

"You takin' off?"

"The fuck's it look like?" I answered, fingers curled around the door handle.

The guy was crazy, like me. Didn't like him much, but we shared a mutual respect, the kind only two twisted fuckers could share, so I turned to face him.

His glower spoke volumes, his silent assessment rattling my nerves. "What? You expect me to invite you out for coffee or some shit?"

He snorted. "Yeah. Good one." Tito came closer, a thousand questions in his eyes.

"Fucking hell man, what?"

He rested a hip against the car and tilted his head, the scarred side of his face in full view. "Where are your brothers?"

Yeah, I was done with the chit-chat. "I gotta go."

"You fuck up?"

Every muscle in my body coiled tight. "Stay out of my shit."

"You did." He pushed off the car, came toe-to-toe, a shit-eating grin on his face. "You fucked up for that little girl."

"It fucking matter?" Christ, I needed a cigarette.

"I couldn't give a shit."

"Great. Then I'll be on my way."

Tito stepped between me and the car door. "Just saying. This place is off the grid. You need to ghost. You can haunt this house for a bit."

"Yeah, yeah. Thanks, but no thanks."

"Fine. But before you disappear, I need details about that girl."

Jesus. The girl and Whisper Springs needed to be in my rearview. "I'm sure you can figure out what she's been through without hearing the gruesome details."

Tito's voice wavered, just a tick. "I need to find her family, man. Anything you can give me helps."

Fuck. I needed to be done. "Her mama's name was Mick. She'd dead. That's what I know. Lived in and out of shelters. Frequented the Prairie Point Women's Haven in Missoula. Check there first... They should be able to give a full name."

"Anything else I should know?" He moved away from the car, giving me space.

I reached for the door handle. Yanked it open, then slammed it shut. "The guy I found them with, Wilson Kyle, he's dead, too. Real piece of work, that one, and it was a pleasure doin' that sick fucker in."

"You took care of him?"

"And then some."

"Good." He nodded, looking over his shoulder at the house, then meeting me with a hard glare.

The fucker had something to say.

His hesitation gave me time to blow him off. "Listen. I gotta go." I reached for the door again.

Tucker slammed a palm against the window. "Not yet. You and me got some things to discuss."

CHAPTER 2

Moriah

"DISCUSSION OVER." I STEADIED my voice, considering my surroundings. "I can't make the dinner tonight. I'm sorry, but I don't know how many more visits I have left with her." I bit my lip, fighting the swelling tears.

"Everybody is bringing their significant others, Moe. How do you think that makes me look every time you bow out?"

"Matthew," I warned. "We'll talk when I get home." I ended the call, lacking the energy required to argue with that man.

Three deep breaths, composure gathered, I entered her room. "Mom." I pressed my lips to her forehead, eyes closed, inhaling her scent.

"Baby," came her weak reply, head tilting up in greeting.

"How you doing today?" I asked, tucking the blankets tighter around her frail, weathered frame.

"Mmm," was all she managed.

I scooted the rocker closer to her bed and settled in. "I brought *The Silent Girls* today. I think you're gonna like this one."

Mom loved her horror novels.

I read. Mom drifted in and out of sleep. The nurse came and went. I sat until the sun made its descent, then kissed my mother goodnight. "I'll see you tomorrow."

"Baby," she whispered, voice strained, lips sallow.

"Yeah, Mom?"

"I'm sorry about your sister."

"Oh, Mama." My chest caved. "It's not your fault. You have nothing to be sorry for."

"I couldn't find her for you."

God, my heart. I gripped her hand in mine and brought it to my chest. "I'm sorry I couldn't find her for *you*, Mom."

"She's a good girl, just like you. She just fell in with the wrong man."

Ha, the wrong man. I refrained from laughing. Bless my mother's well-meaning heart. That *man* had led my sister straight to hell. That *man* had convinced her twice to leave rehab because he was lonely. That *man* stole her identity. Her soul. Bled her dry, then disappeared, dragging her deeper into the bowels of hell. That *man* wasn't a man at all, but a monster.

I hadn't seen my sister in over seven years.

"I won't stop looking for her." I raised mom's knuckles to my mouth for a kiss. "I promise."

"It's time to stop. You have to live your life. For you. Promise me. No more looking. No more worrying."

Her eyes fell closed in exhaustion, her chest rising and falling in rapid bursts. I was tired, too. But I would never stop looking for my sister. How could I?

So, I lied to my dying mother. "I promise." I kissed her sunken cheek, laid the book on the nightstand, and adjusted the thermostat.

It wasn't until I was safely belted into my car that I let the tears fall, opening a new box of tissues, tossing the empty box behind my seat where it landed with the others.

When my sobs slowed, I drove home. I crawled into bed. Matthew rolled over, kissed my head, then tucked me against his chest. Always the same routine.

I couldn't sleep, the weight of Matthew's arm stifling. I pried myself free and stood at the open window. The rush of the river outside offered no solace, neither did the rustle of trees, or the drone of cars passing on the highway in the distance.

The heaviness in my heart weighed me down, that tiny organ swelling inside my chest, filling with vile, poisonous worry. Sometimes I feared the only way to make it stop growing was to pierce my heart, release the pressure, bleed out the pain.

Love wasn't supposed to hurt, or make you sick with unease, or fear. God, how I wanted to take a knife, punch it through my breast and release some of the damn pressure.

Matthew moaned in his sleep, reaching for me. "Moe," he grumbled. "Come to bed."

"In a minute."

A long sigh. "How was Liz tonight?"

"She talked more today. But it wore her out."

I could practically hear his eyes rolling, screeching in their dried-out sockets. Although he was obliged to ask about my day, I knew he hated hearing my woes.

"I want to have a baby."

"We've talked about this." He rolled to his stomach, burying his face in the pillow.

"I want to have children, Matthew."

"You want to replace your mom and sister."

Maybe he was right on some level. And so what if he was correct? My childhood had been amazing. I had nothing but beautiful, cherished recollections of our family. I wanted a family, too. I wanted to build those kinds of memories with my own sons and daughters.

Matthew huffed. "You know work is my priority right now. I want kids, too, eventually. But I need to focus on my career first."

And me, I wanted to scream. *You need to focus on me.*

Silence weighted the air between us.

"Are we ever going to get married, or am I just convenient?"

"Moe. It's late. I have an early meeting. Come to bed."

"I need you, Matthew. I need a hug. I need you to make love to me. To make me feel good. I need you to tell me you love me, and that you can't live without me, and that if I want babies, you would do anything in your power to make that happen because that's how much you love me." I gasped for breath, then continued. "I need you to tell me that you're sorry my mother is dying, that you're so, so sorry, and that you wish you could make everything better." Another pause to wipe the tears off my cheeks. "But you don't. You don't ever tell me those things."

"You're exhausted. Come to bed. Everything will be better in the morning."

Defeated, wiped, aching, I crawled back into bed. I didn't fall asleep.

Things were not better in the morning.

"Ready to go?"

"Not yet. Few more minutes."

"Everyone has left." His voice carried a hint of irritation.

"I don't care."

Matthew checked his watch, the gold catching in the rays pouring through the high, stained-glass windows. He sighed, then dropped a chaste kiss on my head. "I'll be in the car."

I sat in the pew, wadded tissues in hand, and stared at the photo of Mom. Her golden hair, the freckles dotting her nose and cheeks. Her crooked tooth that suited her quirky smile. God, I missed that smile. And her laugh. Nobody laughed harder than Elizabeth Peterson.

The church was mostly empty, save a couple of flower arrangements. That crushing weight barreled down on my chest again, overwhelming me from the outside, suffocating me from the inside. What came next? Mom was gone. Mickey was nowhere. My father had passed when I was sixteen. I was utterly alone. Drowning in grief, and I'd never been more ready to throw in the towel.

A throat cleared behind me. Matthew, rushing me along, most likely.

"I said I need a minute."

"Moriah Peterson?"

I turned in my seat to address the deep voice behind me. "Yes?"

A tall, mountain of a man with piercing blue eyes and a kind smile stood behind me in a green dress shirt and dark jeans. A woman stood next to him, barely reaching his chest, her gray hair pulled into a neat bun, dressed for a day at the office.

I stood, used tissues rolling off my lap and landing at my feet.

The woman extended her hand first. "Hi, Moriah, I'm Dr. Leticia Slade. This is my son, Tucker."

Tucker offered his hand, and I gave him a firm shake.

"Did you know my mom?"

Dr. Slade looked over my shoulder, studying the portrait of my mother, her eyes glossy. "I'm sorry for your loss." She cleared her throat. "And we're sorry for coming to you today, but what we need to discuss with you is time-sensitive."

My hands trembled. Mickey. Their untimely visit had to be about Mickey.

"Is she alive?"

The doctor raised her face to meets her son's worried expression. "You know about her?"

The knocking in my chest grew painful. "My sister, Mickey. This is about her, right?" I clutched my chest, tears welling. "Is she in trouble?"

The sadness in the woman's eyes told me all I needed to know. I fell into the chair behind me, curling into myself, the truth turning me inside out. I'd known deep down that she was gone. I'd known, but I'd clung to faith, the pathetic hope that someday I'd get my sister back.

The man coiled his arms around me—strong, warm, comforting. He held me while I cried silent, painful sobs. He held me against a solid chest while I bled, the grief pouring out of me, the pressure releasing, finally releasing.

When I was coherent enough to speak again, I pushed out of his arms. He held tissues at the ready.

"Thank you." I wiped my eyes, blew my nose. "How did it happen?"

The man, Tucker, cleared his throat, scratched the back of his head. "Drug overdose. But that's not why we're here."

"Why then?"

"Her daughter."

My heart stopped beating. The world stopped spinning. "What do you mean, her daughter?"

"You don't know about your niece?"

"I haven't seen or heard from my sister in over seven years."

"Moriah." Dr. Slade sat next to me, pulling my hand into her own and settling it on her lap. "Your niece was found a few days ago. She's in bad shape."

"Where's her father?"

"We don't know." Tucker growled.

"Wait. I. Um." I rubbed at the pinching pain in my temples. "I don't understand. She was found. Where is she?"

"That's the, um, sensitive part." Mother and son exchanged glances. Tucker nodded for his mom to continue.

I listened while they explained how my niece was brought to them. How she hadn't spoken a word since they'd found her. How she'd bonded with her rescuer, and he was the only person she'd allow near. They explained that my niece needed me, and how there was no legal record of her birth, nor of my sister's death. They explained that if I came to claim my sister's child, more laws would be broken.

They spoke as if they were giving me a choice. As if I might not want Mickey's daughter. Because, of course, there were people who wouldn't take in a troubled child even under normal circumstances.

"When can I see her?" I asked, my heart a thousand pounds lighter, despite the heaviness of the day.

"Moe," Matthew's voice echoed through the room. "We need to get going."

Protective instincts welled inside me. I didn't want Matthew knowing anything about these people, or anything about my niece. And God, that spoke volumes about our relationship, didn't it?

"Go." I waved him off. "I'll Uber home. Be there soon."

"You sure?"

"Yes. I have a few things to take care of here," I lied, knowing he didn't care enough to question.

"Okay." He eyed Tucker, then Dr. Slade, offered a smile, then turned to leave. "See you in a bit."

"When can I see her?" I asked again.

"How fast can you get to Idaho?"

"As fast as I can book a flight."

"I'm so happy to hear that." Dr. Slade pulled me into a hug. "Come on, we'll give you a ride home. I can answer any of your questions on the way."

"What's your poison?" The bartender asked, tattooed arms planted on the bar, twisted grin lighting his features.

"Whiskey sour," I said without hesitation because that's what Mom used to drink, and I needed to drink in her honor.

"You new in town?" He snatched a tumbler from under the counter and got busy mixing my drink. "Don't think I've seen you around."

"My first time in Idaho."

"Yeah?" he asked, cocking a brow, like everyone had been to Idaho. "Where you from?"

"Shelbyville, Illinois."

"Well." He slid the yellow concoction my way and offered a killer smile. "Welcome to Whisper Springs, Shelbyville. First drink is on me."

"Thank you." I noted the playful lilt of his smile. A well-practiced grin, for sure. That Hollywood mug had to earn him a killing on tips. "What's good to eat?"

He made a quick assessment of my figure. "Buffalo sliders. You could use some meat on your bones." His insult could've been mistaken for a compliment, paired with that show of white teeth and that heady gaze, so I gave him a pass. Besides, he'd hit the nail on the head. I'd lost more than thirty pounds since Mom got sick. I'd neglected my health worrying about hers. "Perfect. I'll have the Buffalo sliders."

He nodded and headed to the service window. I looked around for a table. When I found none, I claimed the closest barstool. My phone buzzed the moment I sat down.

Matt: You left?

Me: Yes

Matt: UR flight was scheduled for tomorrow

Me: Couldn't wait another day

Matt: We need to talk about this

Me: Nothing to discuss. She needs me

Matt: What about us?

Me: Us ended when u made me choose

Matt: We'll talk when U get home

Nothing more to talk about. I had a niece to take care of. Matt wanted nothing to do with the bastard child of a drug addict. I wanted nothing to do with a man who would abandon a child in need. So, I'd left a day early. Gave me time to get my bearings before meeting my sole living relative.

"Here's to you, Mom," I mumbled to myself before taking a sip of my drink. Ah, so good. "Here's to you, sis." I chugged two more swallows. "And here's to finally kicking Matt to the curb." Which reminded me...

Me: In case UR unclear. We're done. Have UR
things out of my house by the time I get back.

He didn't reply. Then again, I hadn't expected a response. Matt had never fought for me.

My cell hit the counter with a dull thud. The glass touched my lips, liquid scorched my throat, fire hit my gut. The burn helped clear the static from my head.

Glass raised to the sky, I mumbled, "Eff you, Matthew." I took a long swallow, then another. "I don't need you. I can do this by myself."

A deep chuckle came from my left. I turned to find the profile of a large man. His shoulders were so broad they left no room for anyone to sit on either of the stools flanking him, and the glower he wore expressed he wanted it that way. His hair was shaved on the sides, the top long and fallen to the left, blending with a full beard that nearly reached his broad chest. His jeans hugged what looked to be a great ass and thick thighs, and the sleeves of his black T-shirt stretched tight around lumberjack, solid arms.

Forcing my gaze to his face, I found the same hard edges. "What's funny?"

"Nothin', sweetheart." The man brought his glass to his lips, sipped, then set it down, without so much as a glance my way.

Rude.

"If you're gonna laugh at someone, you can at least look them in the eye."

Not a grunt, a huff, or a subtle blow-off. Although I was pretty sure his jaw clenched.

Men sucked. Okay, not really. I liked men. A lot. Especially the bartender because he made a damn fine whiskey sour, but the beefy dude? He could kiss my ass.

I threw back another long swallow, twisted to face the guy, and released my ire. "You know what? Eff you, too."

That got his attention, and he shot me a sideways glance. "Eff you? Really?" He gestured to the bartender for another drink. "You're gonna insult me, at least do it right. Don't give me that half-assed shit."

"Half-assed?"

"That's what I said, baby."

"Baby?" That just made me angry. Matthew didn't even call me baby. "'Eff Matthew, and eff you."

"Is this a joke?" he asked the bartender. "You got hidden cameras or something?"

The bartender shook his head, gaze dancing between the two of us, then hustled to the other end of the bar. Smart guy.

"I'm not being funny," I assured him, leaning closer, certain that if he actually gave me the courtesy of eye contact, he would see the magnitude of my seriousness.

The man ignored me and stared at the plethora of bottles decorating the wall behind the bar. When he lifted his drink to his lips, the muscles under his colorful arms bunched and coiled, doing all kinds of crazy things to my insides. Or maybe the alcohol was doing its job.

Regardless, I pretended to ignore him, too, while I picked at my food and ordered another drink. I drank for Mom, I convinced myself, not because I'd rather sit next to grumpy guy than sit alone in a hotel room and fret over my future.

Two sips into my third drink, a tall man shuffled beside me, leaning one elbow on the bar, resting his free hand on the back of my stool.

He told me I was beautiful, asked if I would join him for a drink. I politely shot him down. He persisted, scooting closer, caging me. "C'mon sweet thing. You and I both know if a woman comes to a bar alone, she's looking for company."

I readied to protest and give the dickhead a piece of my mind when a thick voice came over his shoulder. "She isn't alone, Bub. You wanna keep your head attached to those bony fuckin' shoulders, you'll walk away, right the fuck now."

Dear God, that voice, thick and dangerous, like he gargled shards of glass just to prove he could, just to show the world he was badass.

Bub raised an eyebrow at me, straightened his spine, turned to face Mr. Grumpy, and shrank two sizes when he got a good look at his "competition."

Hands raised in surrender, he backed away. "Hey, man, sorry. I thought she was alone."

The bartender made his way closer, watching for trouble. He nodded, silently asking if I was okay. I smiled and gave him a nod back.

Grumpy's eyes, weary and red-rimmed, but lethal nonetheless, finally met mine. He seemed to glare right through me at first, but his focus moved from my hair to my lips, then lingered on my freckled nose. A warmth softened his stone-cold features, as if he were seeing an old friend for the first time in ages.

Toes to scalp, every muscle that was capable clenched. Even my skin joined the party, vibrating in response to his feral power.

Beautifully brutal. Hard edges. Dangerous. The man was terrifying in size and aura. Unapproachable but mesmerizing. Fading bruises on his cheek, angry scar above his brow. A hot heap of sexy trouble.

Oh, God, I was staring.

And blushing, my cheeks blazing hotter than my grandfather's old pot belly stove.

"Thank you," I mumbled, my throat too dry considering the amount of liquid I'd consumed.

He only nodded, one corner of his lips pulling to the side.

Was that an invitation? Did I care? "Bartender, I'd like to buy this man an effin' drink."

Grumpy smiled and shook his head. "You're killing me, sweetheart."

"My name's not sweetheart." I offered a hand. "It's Moriah."

"Tell you what," Grumpy said, sliding to the stool between us. "I'll buy the next round, you do one thing for me."

His thick, warm voice was like an orgasm for the ears. "What would that be?"

He nudged his empty glass out of the way and turned to face me. "Give me one proper fuck you."

"I don't like that word."

"Jesus. H. Christ. Are you for real?"

I couldn't help myself, the guy was too damn serious. "Fudge yes, I'm for real," I said, unable to stifle a laugh.

"Fudge," he huffed. "Not even close." He gestured to the bartender for another round. "Come on. Just one good, old fashioned fuck you."

I shook my head.

"Okay. Okay." Grumpy perched one elbow on the bar, leaning closer. "Who's Matthew?"

"Why?" I asked, not missing Matthew one iota.

"Because you said his name earlier, and you seemed upset with the guy."

"He's my ex."

"Okay then, obviously he's a douche if he let you slip through his fingers. So, for Matthew, let's hear it." He tilted his head toward mine, drawing out the words. "Fuck. You. Matthew."

"Oh, God. You're not gonna relent, are you?"

"Not a fucking chance, sweetheart."

"Okay. Fine." I lifted my glass toward Grumpy and waited for him to clink, because for some reason, the moment seemed monumental and toast-worthy.

His scowl bounced between our glasses, then back to me. "I don't do that shit."

"Fine." I reached over, our shoulders bumping, and tapped my tumbler to his, then raised it to my mouth for a long swig before slamming it on the sticky wood.

I winced through the burn, cleared my throat, and shouted, "Fuck you, Matthew!"

"Fuck yeah," Grumpy growled, raising his glass in salute. "Good girl." He chugged his drink and hooked his finger at me. "Keep 'em coming."

So, I did. "Fuck you, Matthew. Fuck you, cancer. Fuck you, drugs. Fuck you, douchebags who prey on women in bars..." And I continued with my list of grievances.

Grumpy started to laugh, and *oh sweet Jesus,* what a beautiful sound.

"See?" He chuckled. "Feels good, right?"

Perhaps it was the overindulgence of libations, or the release of pent-up frustration, or maybe the company, but the weight on my shoulders lifted, and I did feel better.

"Feels great." I straightened my spine. "Thank you."

"You're welcome." His hand landed on my thigh, an innocent gesture between two people sharing a laugh, but the heat his fingers ignited was anything but moral.

Obviously, we were both drunk. Had my head been in the right place, had I not just buried my mother, dumped my boyfriend, and agreed to take-in my dead sister's daughter, I would've chosen that moment to say goodnight. Knowing that could very well be my last moment of freedom, my last chance at wild abandon, I threw caution and sanity to the wind.

I leaned into the large man's warmth, and confessed, "I don't want to be alone tonight."

Strong fingers curled into my thigh. He tossed a look over my shoulder, made a tsk sound, and shook his head before meeting my gaze. "Then you won't be, sweetheart."

He dug into his back pocket, retrieved his wallet, then threw a handful of bills onto the bar.

"Let's go." He slid off the stool, his heavy boots thumping on the wood floor, his thick fingers lacing with mine like we were seasoned lovers.

Holy shit, the man was huge, at least two hundred pounds of mean, unforgiving muscle.

Hand in hand, we made our way outside. I led him down the block and around the corner to my motel room. The second the door closed behind me, he flipped the lock, and caged me against the wall.

"Tell me you're sure about this, 'cause my dick's been hard since you walked into that bar, and the second you give me the go-ahead, I'm gonna wreck you."

Oh. God.

Before reason could settle in, I kicked off my shoes, and attacked his belt buckle. That was all the go-ahead he needed.

In one swift move, he lifted me, then pinned me against the wall with his hips, both hands cupping my face. The man attacked. Forgoing gentle persuasion, exploring and tasting, and kissing me dizzy. He sucked on my tongue and oh my Lord, that tug reached all the way down to my belly.

"Gonna fuck you hard, sweetheart." He rolled his hips, rubbing his erection between my legs, then gripped my butt with a painful squeeze and turned toward the bed.

Like a vice, I clamped arms and legs around his thick body, holding tight, holding him close, craving that connection. Loving the taste of whiskey on his breath.

I landed on the mattress, bouncing, with no time to recover before he was over me, blocking the light, claiming my mouth once again before moving down to my neck, then my chest. A few grunts and tugs, and my shirt was gone. My bra didn't stand a chance, and he didn't bother removing my skirt, opting to bunch it around my waist before tearing my panties down my legs and tossing them across the room.

I was breathless but doing none of the work. The man... "Wait." I grabbed his head, halting the kisses he planted on my stomach. "What's your name?"

"Does it fucking matter?" he growled, lips curling in a sneer.

Did it? I would never see him again. Our tryst was a one-time thing. Not knowing added mystery to what was quickly becoming the fantasy I would forever play in my head.

Settling broad shoulders between my knees, he rubbed where I needed it most, then pierced my folds with thick fingers, making me arch in pleasure.

"No. God no. It doesn't matter."

With that, the man smiled, ducked his head, and attacked me with violent urgency. Lips, teeth, tongue. My hips curled, thrusting against his mouth, riding the storm of pleasure.

I'd never felt dirtier or more used. More wanton, more passionate. More...free.

And when I came, thighs clamped around his head, fingers tangled in his hair, I let go and whimpered all kids of dirty, lusty words.

Boneless, I melted into the mattress, sweaty and spent, and riding a high I'd never thought possible. Grumpy kissed my thigh, pushed to stand, then dug into his pocket.

With a "fuck yeah," he tossed three condoms onto my stomach, then turned off the light.

When he fell next to me, he was naked, and he settled me against his side, hands wandering to all my sensitive parts.

For hours he followed through on his threat, wrecking me with his body, his words, his foul mouth. "You're so fucking beautiful. Sweet, tight cunt. Gonna fucking ruin you for anybody else. That's it, gorgeous, come for me. My cock, take my cock. Yeah, like that."

And before he came inside me for the last time, me face down on the bed, his chest heavy on my back, his cock thrusting between my closed legs, he coiled his arms around me and breathed into my ear. "Fuck, sweetheart. Could fuck you like this every day."

His whole body shuddered with his release, and when he thrust his tongue in my ear, I came again, too. He rolled us to our sides but never let me go, our bodies tangled until his phone rang hours later, waking me from a deep sleep.

My mystery man rolled out of bed, pulled the comforter over my naked body, then answered the call. "Yeah." Heavy breaths. "Shit. Yeah. I'll be there."

He stomped to the bathroom. Ran the water. Returned. The mattress sank, and rough lips landed on my cheek. "I have to go. Lock the door behind me."

I nodded, stretched, then watched his shadowed form dress. My head spun, liquor taking its revenge, but I felt compelled to say, "I've never done this before."

"No?" He tugged his jeans up those thick thighs.

"No. But I'm glad it was you." I'd met my yearly quota for orgasms in a few short hours.

He huffed, then scooped his shirt off the floor. "Hope you're not gonna ask for my number."

I should've been hurt by his brush-off, but I knew better. Besides, my life was about to change forever. I had no time to pursue a relationship, sexual or otherwise. "I was just thinking how lucky I am, that's all."

"'cause of my monster cock, or my mad tongue skills?"

I laughed, despite the lack of humor in his tone.

"Both. Definitely both. And seriously, have you looked at you? Every girl's fantasy come to life."

He dropped his ass on the mattress and worked on his boots, our thighs and shoulders bumping, my skin coming alive all over again. "I'm no fantasy, gorgeous. Nightmare would be more accurate."

His words were meant to be a warning, or maybe a shield.

"Definitely fantasy."

He tied his laces, then rested his elbows on his knees. Head cocked my direction, voice thick with gravel, he said, "Trailer. My friends call me Trailer."

"Trailer," I whispered. My new favorite word.

He leaned closer, then kissed me hard and fast before pushing off the bed. He was halfway gone before he turned and said, "Moriah, promise me something."

"Yeah?"

"Let me be your last one-nighter, okay? There are a lot of dangerous fuckers out there."

CHAPTER 3

I WAS DANGEROUS ENOUGH on a regular day, but add zero hours of shut-eye, a hangover, and a raw dick to the mix? Better steer clear by at least three states.

"When's the aunt showing up?" I asked, blinking the muck from my eyes, my jaw cracking with the force of my yawn. I hadn't slept a fucking wink, the little girl waking all through the night, trembling, crying, screaming.

For reasons I couldn't fathom, she only calmed when I held her. Only let the doctor inspect her while she buried her face in my chest. Me, of all people. How fucked was that?

"She'll be here soon. Thanks for coming back," Leticia whispered, tucking warmed blankets around the child.

The mansion had become a prison, the girl my steel cell. Last night had been my first venture out, and even then, I'd been snagged back into the child's hell.

Tucker entered the room, coffee mugs in hand. "She finally sleeping?" he asked, kissing his mom on the head, then handing her a java.

"Yes." She took a sip of her coffee, gaze meeting mine over the rim of her cup, a plan forming in her squinted eyes.

Oh, fuck. I knew what was coming next.

She swallowed. Smiled. Tilted her head. "Dane. You're great with her. I know you don't want to be here, but would you consider staying another day or two?"

"I can't."

I rolled, sliding my arm out from under the girl's head, and waited, holding my breath, to make sure I hadn't woken the sleeping angel. When satisfied she was still unconscious, I inched my way off the bed.

If my brothers saw me, they'd have me tarred and feathered.

Mother and son watched while I stretched the kinks from my weary bones, both eyeing me with suspicion.

"She needs you," Leticia said, a sugar-coated attack on my heartstrings.

Lady was wasting her breath. I didn't have a heart.

"And I need to get the fuck outta this prison," I snapped, agitation, nausea, and dehydration getting the best of me.

Leticia's eyes narrowed, face reddened.

Aw, fuck. "Sorry, Doc. Didn't mean to bark at you."

The sweet doctor shooed me away like my short fuse was no big deal.

"Dane." Tucker shot me a glare and gestured toward the door. "Outside."

I followed the lug, too tired, and too fucking hungover to put up a fight. I did, however, snag the cup of coffee he'd left on the table on my way out.

I followed him down a narrow hallway, then up a set of stairs, another hallway, more stairs. He opened a door and led me into a massive, fully furnished studio apartment. "Listen. I don't wanna know your business, but if you need a place to crash for a while, we've got spare rooms. No one will bother you."

"Thanks, but no thanks." I didn't need anybody's help. Although the bed was huge, and tempting, and damn, how I needed to crash into something soft and sleep for days.

"Fine. Fine." He stomped to the window and yanked the curtain, making way for the rising sun. "Could you at least wait until the girl settles in with her aunt before you disappear? She needs you right now."

I'd given too much of my time already. But that girl had my guts wrapped around her tiny fucking fingers. I couldn't walk away. "Only until she's settled. What's the aunt's name, anyway, and when can I meet her?"

"You know damn well you can't meet her, and you can't know her name. Keeps everyone safe."

"How do you know she's not an addict like the girl's mother, or a sadistic fuck like the asshole I found her with?"

Tucker smirked, and had I not been so exhausted, I might've knocked that dimple off his face. I shot him a warning glare instead.

Tucking hands into his pockets, he cleared his throat, then said, "Tito did a full work-up. She checks out. The woman's squeaky clean."

I nodded, not wholly convinced anyone would be good enough for the girl. Then again, what did I know? Tucker and Tito did the rescuing shit day in and day out. They were the good guys. Me? Heh. I ate pansies like them for breakfast.

Tucker nodded toward the bed. "Room's yours. We don't have any other kids at the moment, so you can come and go as you please."

That four-poster frilly shit called my name. As much as I needed to ghost, I also needed a good night sleep, needed time to think. Change my game plan. "I'll stay tonight. Not sure what's gonna happen tomorrow."

A phone buzzed. Tucker yanked a cell out his pocket, read the screen, stuffed it back into his jeans. "I'll leave you to it then."

My stomach protested, reminding me I hadn't eaten in too damn many hours. "Don't suppose you've got a car I can borrow? The one I drove here needs to disappear."

"Pull the sedan behind the barn. We'll help you ditch it later." He yanked a set of keys out of his pocket, tossed them my way. "There's an old Ford parked around back. She'll get you where you need to go. Just bring her back. She was my first love."

"No problem."

I shot him a nod, then headed out, missing the hell out of my bike.

The Truck Stop Diner hadn't changed much since I was a kid, even after a recent remodel. The same rusted three-tier sign still stood tall above the pines, visible for miles from any approaching direction on the highway. Fresh gravel had been laid in the lot in lieu of pavement, which somehow suited the landscape, and the million-dollar view was still a sight under-appreciated by those of us who'd squandered our youth in the small town of Whisper Springs.

A cowbell rattled when I entered. A feisty redhead greeted me and pointed to the only empty table. "Grab that one. I'll be with you in a sec."

I sat, my bones protesting, my muscles screaming, my weary head perking back to life when I spotted a wild head of auburn hair.

Moriah.

Damn if my mood didn't shift.

The beauty who'd given me a rigorous workout mere hours ago sat alone, facing the window, gaze on the lake in the distance. She seemed eons away, lost in thought. My thoughts drifted to those creamy thighs, her soft moans. Her damn smile. She'd been a great fuck, best I'd ever had, but more than that, she'd made me laugh.

I'd thought she was gorgeous in the bar, a little sex kitten with an attitude, but damn, in the light of day, the sun hitting her skin, those freckles dotting her nose and cheeks, the girl was downright edible.

The thought of another go 'round had me shifting in my seat.

"Hey," came a soft voice behind me.

Blondie.

The one woman I would lay down my life for.

My throat clogged when her son, my only living relative, bounced to my side, held out a hand, and announced, "I'm Rocky James Mason. Welcome to The Truck Stop."

Fuck if I didn't smile like a kid on Christmas morning.

I gave his hand a good shake. Nice to meet you, Rocky."

"Do you want a milkshake?" he asked, nodding, as if willing me to say *yes*.

A fuckin' milkshake of all things. My stomach grumbled, but hell if I'd turn the kid down. "You gonna make it for me?"

The little tyke stood taller. "I make the best milkshakes. Be right back." Off he sprinted, leaving me alone with his mother, Slade Mason, the chick responsible for my first boner. The only woman I'd ever set sights on and hadn't boned.

"How's the girl?" she asked, sliding into the seat across from me, setting me on edge.

"Sleeping. Healing." I considered the child's night terrors and roughed a hand over my aching scalp. "Physically, anyway."

Slade tilted her head, seeming to study me. "You heading home today?"

Home. What a fucking joke. Home was a refuge most people took for granted. Although Blondie had been present for most of my youth, and she knew damn well what "home" had looked like for me and Addy, I held back any sour retort. Wasn't Slade's fault, the cards I'd been dealt.

Blondie shook her head, soft coils of hair falling over those huge blue eyes. "I get it. You don't have to say a word. Just know that I'm here if you ever need anything."

"Pretty Boy'll skin me alive if he thought you and I were back to being friendly."

"Tango knows you're here. He knows what you did for that little girl. He'll never forget what you did for Rocky, or his father. He might beat his chest a bit, but he couldn't do a damn thing to stop us being friends. You're Rocky's family, whether that little boy knows it or not, you're his family. That makes you my family."

Blondie's eyes welled with emotion, and damn, her words hit like a bat to the chest. I offered the only gratitude I could muster. "Rocky looks good."

Her smile sliced me to shreds. "He's got Addy's nose. He snorts like she used to do when she laughed, too." She sighed, eyes losing focus. "I see her in him all the time."

My dead cousin was the last person I wanted in my head. Her death was on me. *Me*. And the little bitch haunted me on the daily.

"He's the spitting image of his dad, if you ask me."

Slade shrugged, a look of pure bliss softening her face. "Can't argue with that."

Rocky barreled through the swinging doors, plopped a drippy cup on the table, then pulled a straw out of his back pocket and dropped it next to his concoction.

"Mom, can I have a milkshake with...wait." His head bounced, attention shifting from his mom to me. "What's your name?"

Slade bit her lip, brows quirking in apology, then pushed from the table to crouch next to her son. "Rocky. This is Dane. He's an old friend of ours."

"Cool. Do you play football, too?"

Definitely his father's son. "No, kid. No football for me."

"Rocky, time for school." Slade roughed a hand through his already messy hair. "Go grab your things out of the office."

"'K, Mom!" With a hop and a skip, the boy sprinted off again.

Seconds later, he was back, a Seahawks backpack slung over his shoulder. "Bye, Dane!" he yelled, jetting by, and rattling that damn cow bell on his way out.

Slade leaned forward, hands splayed on the table. "It's really good to see you, Dane. Take care of yourself, okay?"

"Yeah, Blondie. Take good care of that little shit."

She nodded, then turned to leave, a light sway to her steps. I watched, unsure I'd see the two of them again, and fuck if that didn't make me nauseous.

I chanced a glance at the beauty in the corner. She'd spotted me, her mouth tilting in a shy grin, her cheeks glowing pink.

I raised my hand in greeting, and what the fuck? I didn't wave at people.

Moriah laid cash on her table, stood, straightened her skirt, and came my way. Her green dress hugged her chest and showed off the perfect amount of leg, skin dusted with freckles like on her nose. Pretty shoes and pretty feet. Hair the color of vintage leather. She glowed, and damn, she was far too clean and shiny for the likes of me.

Shit.

"Fancy meeting you here." She laughed, shrugging her purse tighter up her shoulder.

"Yeah. What a coincidence." Those eyes held me captive, rendered me speechless.

"I have a meeting to get to." She shifted foot to foot, then offered her hand. "It was nice meeting you, Trailer."

I took those soft fingers in mine and swear to Christ a cluster of bombs detonated in my chest. I cleared my throat, found my voice. "It was an *effin'* pleasure meeting you, Moriah."

Her laugh soothed my aches, and I held her longer than necessary, captivated by those gorgeous, fuck-me eyes.

The girl leaned closer, her soft lips parted, and she whispered, "Best night of my *fucking* life." She pulled her hand free, winked, then turned on her heel and sauntered out the door, that damn cowbell clanging, an ugly reminder she was gone.

Best night? *Mine, too,* I thought to myself. Mine, too.

"The fuck you grinning at?" Tito parked his ass in the chair across from me, and looked over his shoulder, following my trajectory.

Moriah had disappeared behind an SUV.

"Not a damn thing."

"You putting us in danger being here?" Tito slapped two envelopes side by side on the red Formica, then waited for my response, not a lick of emotion or judgement on his face.

"Wouldn't be here, that were the case."

He eyed my shake, shook his head, smirked. "Any Slayer's gonna be rolling into town looking for you?"

"No."

"Club making a play for Whisper Springs?"

"Not in the mood for an interrogation," I warned. "Ain't a damn thing you could do to stop them, that were their intention." And because my bones were too damn weary for a fight, I threw in, "But no. No play for Whisper Springs."

"Good to hear." With two fingers, he slid one envelope my way.

"The fuck's this?"

Tito rested his elbows on the table, crossing his forearms. "Hasn't gone unnoticed you're not wearing your cut."

"Your point?"

"Could use your skills, if you're in the market for a job."

"Skills?" I pounded a finger into the manila casing, thick with what I assumed was a stack of Benjamins. "You mean of the criminal variety."

"Maybe."

"Enough with the games, Moretti." I leaned over the table getting right up in that scarred mug, half-cocked for a fist to face.

To his credit, he didn't bow.

"Sit down, you're scaring the children." Again with that dam smirk.

I fell back on my ass, glared, waited for further explanation.

He picked up the second envelope, rapped the edge against the table. "You no longer have a criminal record. These are yours, regardless you take the job or not. Consider it a thank you, for helping me out last year."

"How'd you pull that off?"

Tito merely shrugged those huge fucking shoulders. "I know a guy."

Bullshit. He was the guy. That smug mug told me so.

Shocked damn near speechless, I shoved that flimsy straw into the chocolate mess and sucked hard, my mouth watering something fierce before that first sickening sweet glob of chocolate hit my tongue.

A white-haired, angelic little thing bounced up to our table, planted a kiss on Moretti's cheek, and tossed an overstuffed backpack on the table.

The guy fuckin' melted right before my eyes, morphing from wild monster to docile pet.

"Bunny," he rasped, sliding over, making room for her to sit. "You remember Dane?"

"Dane?" Her brows quirked, right before her eyes widened to the size of hub caps. "Dane. Right. Hi." She shot a hand my direction.

I gave her a quick shake. "Tuuli, right?"

She responded with a nod, then said, "You look different."

Not sure what she meant. Regardless, I said, "So do you." Last time I'd seen Moretti's lady, she was half-naked and bloody, holding a rifle to the racist, pedophile motherfucker I'd had the pleasure of dismembering, limb by limb.

Her beige sweater upped the wattage on those crystal clear, ice-blue peepers. The blonde beauty shifted in her seat, her gaze dropping to the table, then bouncing back to meet me head on. "You brought in that poor girl." The look she gave me was pure adoration.

I only nodded, foreign feelings washing through me like acid. Was that little lady still sleeping? Was her aunt in town yet? Nerves jetted through me, agitation prickling my skin. Why did I care? Kid wasn't mine. Wasn't my responsibility. Fuck. I needed sleep.

"Listen, uh." I hooked a finger on the first envelope, shoved it Moretti's direction. "I don't need a job. How much I owe you for the other thing?"

"Nothin' man. Just consider my offer." He grabbed the money, shoved it in the front pocket of his sweatshirt. Then handed me the other envelope. "Take this."

I took his offering, waved it, testing its weight. "This being?"

"New name, new life. In case you ever find yourself in a jam."

Fucking guy was doing me a solid. A way out in case any demons came back to haunt me. I hadn't a clue why. He owed me nothing.

A *thank you,* or *much appreciated* would've been the proper response, but I was Dane fucking Reynolds, asshole extraordinaire, social misfit, deviant, criminal, and I was suffering one pisser of a hangover, so instead I grunted, "fuckin' prick" while I slid from the table and made my exit before all the damn shit going on in my head erupted like a geyser.

"See ya 'round." Tito laughed.

Not if I could help it. Whisper Springs and her fucking residents belonged in my rearview.

After I caught some shut eye.

CHAPTER 4

Moriah

"YOU JUST NEED SOME shut-eye. A good night's sleep."

"I'm afraid it's going to take more than that." I slumped against the wall, afraid I'd crumple into a heap without the support.

"You're right. It's going to take time," Dr. Slade consoled, wiping my cheek with a tissue. "But she's warmed to me, and she'll warm to you."

"She's terrified." Raw scratches decorated my arm, red and angry, evidence of my failed attempt to connect with my niece.

"She needs more time. You did good today, talking to her, telling her stories about her mother and grandparents." Leticia pulled me into a much-needed embrace, rescuing me from my reverie. "The man who rescued her is coming to help us with lunch. Why don't you head back to the hotel for tonight? Get your bearings...and some rest. Tomorrow, we'll start fresh."

God, how I wanted to stay, ached to assure that child I would die to protect her. But the doctor was right. Healing took time. I whispered a goodbye to my niece and followed Leticia down the back hallway, so the man who'd given me

Mickey's daughter could come to the rescue, his presence being the only shelter in her storm.

Disheartened, bearing the weight of failure, I retreated back to town and locked myself in the lonely room.

The mattress caught my weight, bouncing me twice then stilling, offering meager comfort in what was undoubtedly the most physically, mentally, and emotionally challenging hours of my life. I studied the welts on my arms, the angry grooves carved by a traumatized child—my own flesh and blood who couldn't stand the sight of me. My vision blurred, and I briefly considered a revisit to the corner bar, to drown my sorrows and numb my spinning brain. Although, I doubted nothing short of a lobotomy would wipe the images from my head. Her tiny body, sunken cheek bones, the dark circles consuming her eyes. Eyes like her mother's.

The tears I'd refused to acknowledge finally fell, sobs ripping loose. I cried. For my sister. My mother. My niece. I cried until I had nothing left.

A heavy knock yanked me from dead sleep to the upright position, fuzzy-headed, overheated, and for a few scary seconds, unsure of my whereabouts. Until the EXIT sign over the door came into focus.

My cell told me it was almost midnight.

Pound. Pound. Pound.

I padded toward the intrusion, heart racing, and peeked through the tiny hole, my body heating at the sight. Trailer's face filled the space, eyes red and swollen, from drink or lack of sleep, I wondered, not that it mattered, because the raps in my chest propelled me to action, the barrier between us a horrible nuisance that needed to be removed.

I tore open the door without considering the consequences.

His perusal, deliberate and maybe a bit hesitant, lingered at my mouth before licking every inch of my skin, waking every nerve, all the way down to my bare feet, and back up before our eyes met. As if he couldn't help himself, he leaned into me, stopped a hair's breadth from my face, bracing himself with one hand on the doorjamb.

"Tell me you don't want to be alone tonight," he commanded. That voice. Thick and jagged. A promise. A warning.

"I don't want to be alone."

"Good fucking thing I'm here then." He shoved through the door, all whisky breath and sex eyes, scooped me up by my ass and kicked the door shut behind us.

The man vibrated, every muscle strung tight with raw power, need, but mostly want. God, what a heady feeling to be wanted. He didn't kiss me. He didn't need to kiss me. Our eyes locked, his burning through the darkness, searing me with their intensity. My back hit the mattress. Trailer crawled over me, then gripped my thighs, spreading me wide. He shoved a hand between my legs, and attacked, shoving my silk thong to the side, and diving deep with one finger, then two, his thumb brushing my clit with a nasty tease.

"Oh. Yes. Yes. Shit, shit, shit," I groaned, meeting his intrusion with greedy thrusts.

With a sharp tug, my panties disappeared. A rough tongue replaced his fingers, shoving into me over and over, then retreating. A short pause, then he captured my clit between his teeth and sucked hard, shoving his hands under my hips, supporting me while I bucked off the bed, high off the pain and the dizzying pleasure.

With urgency, the man pleasured, nipping and licking, taking my assaults as I tossed, and writhed, and scratched at his head, reaching for something to ground me, desperately searching for an ounce of control.

I dug my heels into the mattress, trying to scoot away from the violent pleasure. He gripped me tighter, pulling me back against his mouth, like a ravenous beast fighting for his only meal, taking me like I was his to ruin.

"Wanna hear you, gorgeous. Fucking scream for me."

Again, he forced his tongue between my folds. So dirty, so wild, so brazen. My body bowed, and I slammed my hands around his head, fingers digging deep as I pounded my hips into his face, that stranger's face. That man who seemed to know my body better than even me. Lost in pleasure, I shed all inhibition, and I came, my body splitting in two, grinding against that dangerous mouth. I came so hard a white light exploded behind my eyes. Tears erupted. The mattress dampened beneath us.

Allowing no time to recover, Trailer flipped me to my stomach, shoved my skirt over my ass, and forced my legs together, his knees bracing my thighs. I panted through the long pause, impatient through his heavy breaths, wiggling beneath him while he readied. A handful of condoms landed on the pillow—a promise of what was to come—before he fell over me, his heavy chest on my back, hot breaths in my ear, and he shoved in, taking me from behind. Rapid, forceful thrusts, pounding me into the mattress, stealing my breath, stripping my sanity, overshadowing my worry.

The dark room filled with moans and dirty words, the rhythmic drum of bed frame beating wall while flesh pounded flesh.

He came, cursing into my hair, his weight crushing me, warm and possessive. We lay together, unspeaking but touching, panting, groping, working each other into another frenzy of lust. He took me against the wall, then again on the bed, and after I rode him on the hard floor, my knees ruined, my thighs burning, he ordered me to bed.

I crawled between the sheets, limbs heavy with exhaustion, and watched his shadow move through the room, dressing in the dark, my phantom lover.

"I'm checking out this morning," I rasped, still catching my breath.

"Okay." He grunted, tugging on a shoe.

A heavy air filled the space between us, silent torture.

I didn't want our torrid affair to end on a negative note.

"So, don't come-a-knockin' again. You might scare the shit out of some elderly couple."

He snorted, and the tension eased.

"Trailer?"

"Yeah."

"Thanks."

"For what?" He came closer, enough I could make out his features.

"I needed you tonight."

His shoulders slumped, head falling back. "Fuck," he yelled to the ceiling. "If circumstances were different." He cussed again. Shook his head. "Never mind."

More than anything, I wanted to know what he was thinking. I didn't push. Wouldn't matter. I would never see him again, that man who made me feel more alive than I'd ever thought possible.

"Moriah," he rasped, snagging his keys from the counter. "Gorgeous fucking Moriah."

With the soft click of the door, he was gone.

I couldn't remember ever feeling so worked over, so sated, so relaxed. Multiple orgasms and hours of no-strings, dirty, sweaty sex with a tattooed stranger would do that to a girl apparently. Too bad I couldn't have penciled Trailer in for a few more nights. I had a feeling I would need the release if my first meeting with my niece was any indicator of how the rest of the week would play out.

I checked out of the hotel early, then drove through the streets of Whisper Springs. The downtown area was quiet, the quaint little shops still closed but all the more charming in the splendor of morning. Floral baskets hung from every ornate street lamp, purple, pink, and red flowers spilling over. Brick buildings, mixed with newer construction, lined the street, leading toward a lake, diamond studded and blinding under the rising sun. A street sweeper whirred past, heading the opposite direction, and the man commanding the rig tipped his hat as he passed.

I found the city beach and parked, awestruck by the full view of the lake and the surrounding mountains. Early morning joggers passed, heading toward the park, and I decided to follow, not ready to face my impending future just yet.

I strolled the clean pathway that led to the public beach, and found a spot in the sand, ignoring the cold, wet bite on my tender underside. A shiver tore through me, tiny ripples of pleasure, aftershocks I supposed, from the man who'd made me quake in more ways than one.

I watched the water tickle the shoreline, a peaceful ebb and flow, and I thought of Mom. She would have loved the little gem that was Whisper Springs. She would have been overjoyed to meet her granddaughter, no matter the circumstances. She would've chastised me for being careless enough to allow a strange man into my hotel room, but she would've been so proud that I finally gave Matthew the boot.

Matthew. Ugh. Wasted years. Not once had he brought me to tears during orgasm. Not once had he gripped me with enough passion to leave bruises. Dear God. Two nights with a strange man, and my whole existence had been upheaved. Flipped. Smashed to bits, exposing corners of me long hidden. I was more than a daughter. More than a caretaker. More than just an administrative assistant, or a girlfriend.

I was beauty. I was passion. I was raw, uninhibited sex.

And thank God for that bar. Thank God for whiskey sours. Thank God for hotel rooms, and one-night stands, and for Trailer. God. Trailer. The man with the funny name who made me feel, for the first time, like a desirable woman. Thank God I'd met him before my world turned again, and I could never again be so reckless, my sole focus, from that moment forward, being that tiny, broken girl who needed me to be her world.

I rose to my feet, dusted my rear, and headed back to the car, then toward the mansion, leaving my past behind, and hell-bent on embracing the future.

My suitcase wheels rattled and squealed as I dragged the purple beast over the newly polished hardwood floor.

"We've made up the room next door to your niece." Tucker pushed open the door, revealing a large furnished bedroom, with a huge bed, a lush couch, and a large screen television perched above a stone fireplace. Soothing powder blue coated the walls, while bright pinks and pale yellows made up most of the accents.

"Thank you, Tucker." I moved past him, and stood center, taking in the large space, and the perfect view of the lake through the picture window. "This is perfect."

"Good." He nodded. "The bathroom's fully stocked, but if you need anything at all, let us know."

A lawnmower roared to life outside. I peeked through the sheer curtain to see a tall man riding a bright red Toro. "You have a groundskeeper?"

Tucker laughed, his smile full of pride. "That's my dad. You'll meet him soon enough." He rapped on the door. "I'll let you get settled. I'm heading down to make breakfast, so feel free to join us whenever you're ready."

"I'd like to see my niece. Is she sleeping?" I forced confidence into my question, hoping to hide my reluctance, my jumbled nerves.

Tucker shook his head. "Dane is in there. He got her to eat a little bit more this morning. Now he's helping my mom with her exam."

Faint voices traveled through the walls. A deep male voice, and Lettie's, but no cries from a frightened child.

I hated that a stranger could soothe her when I couldn't. Make her feel safe, when she shied away from me. "Oh, good. I'd like to meet our hero." I headed for the door, anxious to get in that room, give the man a hug, or a kidney, or a lung perhaps. Pretty much whatever he needed.

Tucker slid to the left, casually blocking the door. "That can't happen, I'm afraid. I have to protect his identity, as well as yours."

"But he saved her life. I owe him so much. I would like to thank him."

"It's better for everyone this way." His voice lowered, and he pushed the door closed behind him. "The guy doesn't operate on our side of the law. You're better off not seeing his face."

"Is he a criminal or something?"

"Something."

My insides seemed to shift, settling like cement in my gut. "But you've left him alone in a room with a little girl?"

"Yes." He scratched above his eyebrows, glanced out the window, then back to me. "She's safer with him than anyone."

I rubbed my aching stomach. "How do you know?"

Tucker cleared his throat, and his words came strained. "Because I know what he sacrificed to save her."

Then he hit me with those piercing blue eyes, and they were sad, but sincere, and I understood there was a story he couldn't tell.

"Oh. That's too bad. I really would love to give that guy a hug, ya know?"

"Not sure he's much of a hugger. Honestly, I'm surprised he's stuck around to help. But enough about Dane. How about some breakfast?"

"Breakfast sounds great. I just need to wash up, then I'll be down."

"Perfect. How do you like your coffee?"

"Strong."

He chuckled. "All right then. See you downstairs."

I nodded, shoving my hands into the back pockets of my jeans, and waited for Tucker to let himself out.

When the door clicked shut, I wiggled, shaking off the nerves, then made my way to the wall, and pressed my ear against the cold blue surface. I couldn't make out their conversation, but someone left the room a minute later, the door clicking shut, heels clacking on the hardwood floor outside.

Heavy footfalls made their way across the room. The bed creaked. A low male voice started to hum. Oh, God, my heart. He was singing to her. Emotion got the best of me, and I made my way to the bathroom to dab my wet cheeks.

Didn't feel right, leaving her, but down to my bones, I knew my niece was safe with that man, criminal or not.

I made my way downstairs and joined the Slade family for breakfast. I met Leticia's husband, James, Tucker's wife,

Aida, his daughter, Lucia, and their dog, Lola, who managed to position herself between me and the baby, no matter who held the little angel.

We ate. And I readied myself for the challenges ahead.

"Good morning, sweetie."

I laid the bag of toys down on the chair, then stood a few feet from the end of her bed, gauging her response.

My niece sat upright, clutching a doll to her chest. A pink hue dusted her cheeks. Her eyes shone brighter. She didn't make eye contact, but she didn't shy away, and that was progress.

"Lettie told me you ate some breakfast this morning. That's wonderful. Breakfast is my favorite meal. I love pancakes the most. But only with peanut butter and real syrup. Maybe someday we can make pancakes together." I moved closer, steps measured, and smoothed a hand over the bedspread, keeping to the corner.

She tracked my movement, hugging the doll tighter.

"What would you like to do today?" I retreated to the chair and rifled through the bag, pulling out a puzzle, a couple of books, drawing pads, and crayons.

I looked around the room. "We could read, or we could draw, or maybe you could help me put this puzzle together." Her eyes darted from the doll to me, then she quickly turned her head.

"You like puzzles?" I asked. Paused. Continued. "I love puzzles. This one here..." I held up the box so she could see the picture, the bright spring flowers with kittens poking their heads through cheerful petals. "I've tried and tried to put it together, but I can't seem to make the pieces fit. Then I realized that this is a two-person puzzle. Did you know there was such a thing? A two-person puzzle. Silly, right? Anyway, I was hoping you could help me. What do ya think?"

I searched her face for a sign, any hint that she would allow me close enough to put the puzzle together. She lay back down, rolled to her side, and brushed her fingers through the doll's hair.

My heart ached. "Maybe we can do the puzzle later." I laid the box down on the small table, settled for a book, curled up in the chair, and started to read *The One and Only Ivan* out loud.

Three chapters in, the sleepy little girl hopped out of bed, padded to the bathroom and closed the door. The toilet flushed. The water ran, and a few seconds later, she came out, ran to the bed, and curled under the covers, tucking her hands under her cheek just like my sister used to do.

I continued reading until her breaths turned into faint snores. Then I let my own lids fall shut.

Whisper soft humming lulled me from a dream, and the room came into focus, the sun bright and unrelenting. I was drenched with sweat and covered to my waist by the comforter that had been on my niece's bed.

She sat at the table in the corner of the room, the puzzle half put together, her head down, freckled face covered in wild waves of auburn hair.

I stretched, letting the blanket fall to the floor, and watched the little girl rifle through puzzle pieces, twisting and turning each one. No doubt, she would have finished the puzzle in record time, had the heavy stomp of boots not sounded outside the door.

The child gasped, ran to the bed, and buried herself under the sheet.

Male voices came from the hallway, footfalls moving at a fast pace. I waited for them to pass, then whispered, so as not to startle her, "Thank you for the blanket. Can I put it back on your bed now?"

No response.

"If you want me to put it back, you need to tell me." I waited. Not a peep. "Or you could shake your head, or wiggle your toes."

I watched the sheet for signs of movement. Her leg twitched, then straightened, and seconds later, her little foot wiggled under the sheet. I held back the laughter that bubbled inside me. Joy. Pure joy. We'd made a connection. I didn't think I'd ever been happier.

"Okay. Here it comes."

I gripped the edge of the comforter, stayed to the end of the bed, counted, "One. Two. Three," then shook the cotton out in a wave, high above the bed so it billowed out and floated for a brief moment before landing on top of her tiny body.

God, how I wanted to jump into that bed with her, curl her into my arms, and hug her forever.

Instead, I watched her wiggle more until she peeked her head out for oxygen.

I picked up the book and continued to read.

Come lunch time, my niece wouldn't touch her food. Lettie suggested we give her savior a shot at getting her to eat. Reluctantly, I agreed, retreating to my room next door, ear to the wall.

The next three days continued at the same pace. I'd spend the day with her, excluding meal times. Come bed time, I'd listen through the wall while the man named Dane hummed and sometimes sang her to sleep.

By the fourth day, my spirits were bruised. I had hoped to make better progress, but every time she made a breakthrough, something happened to set her back. A bad dream. A spilled glass of orange juice. A loud noise.

When she was scared, the only person to calm her was that damn stranger. And as the hours rolled on, the little green monster sank his claws deeper into my chest.

CHAPTER 5

IGNORING THE ACHE IN my chest, I stretched, then winced, my body protesting even the slightest movement.

The girl sat next to me, her tiny body curled into my side, my ass wedged into a too-small chair.

I looked down at the puzzle piece she held, then pointed to the corner where I thought it might belong. She shook her head, then set the piece in the opposite corner, clicking it into place.

Her body jiggled with silent laughter, her head shaking as if chastising my incompetence.

"Oh, you think that's funny, huh?" I couldn't help my grin. She still hadn't spoken a word, but the girl didn't need words to communicate.

Five puzzles in three days. Fucking puzzles. Fuck me. My back was wrecked from the damn mini-chair. And I silently cursed her aunt for bringing those God damned toys into the room. I had it my way, we'd've had an Xbox hooked to the television. Hell, I'd even take watching cartoons for ten hours straight over putting those fucking pieces of cardboard together.

But the little one was happy. The happier the kid, the faster I'd be able to blow town.

Outside, the world moved on, boats and skiers littering the lake, the summer heat bringing everyone outdoors. The last summer I'd spent in Whisper Springs was a lifetime ago, chock-full of memories better left buried.

Looking across the lawn, I noticed a swing hanging from a high branch.

"Hey. Think you might want to go outside today?"

She ignored me, studying another puzzle piece.

"There's a swing out there, by the beach. Looks like fun."

No response.

I shrugged. Wasn't my problem. My days at the mansion were winding down, my soul itching to hit the open road.

Soon, the pesky little kid would be nothing but an unpleasant memory.

"I brought lunch." Lettie knocked on the door. "Can I come in?"

"Yeah," I grunted, shifting my numb ass.

Little One tightened against me, then made a mad dash for the bed.

Lettie came through, tray in hand. I pushed to stand, my hips locking, and fell back, landing with a hard thud, knocking over the table, sending puzzle pieces in every direction.

Profanities escaped my lips before I had time to check myself. Lettie gasped.

Little One giggled. Fucking giggled. Filling the room with the sweetest damn sound I'd ever heard.

Lettie joined in, laughing, not at my expense, I assumed, but out of sheer joy that the girl had shown an emotion other than fear.

I pushed to stand. "Oh, you think that's funny, too?"

Little One shook her head, sucking her lips between her teeth, then smoothed out the blanket, making space for Lettie to set down the lunch tray.

I claimed my spot by her side, and together we ate peanut butter and jelly sandwiches, apple slices, and chocolate milk. I showed her how to blow bubbles with the straw. She giggled again before making a game of whose bubbles could reach the top of the glass first. I let her win, of course.

After lunch, I turned on the flat screen and muscled through an hour of those damn rescue dogs.

While Little One watched TV, I mostly dozed, my mind drifting to Moriah. That cute as sin, crazy woman I couldn't shake.

Shame we hadn't met under different circumstances.

Voices drew my attention out the window. Rocky and his dad tossed a football back and forth in the yard, the little boy throwing taunts. Tito soon joined the party. Before long, the three of them wrestled in the grass, Rocky's squeals infectious.

Little One sat up on her knees, peering over me to see outside. She glanced my way, brows lifted high, then hopped off the bed and ran to the window, rising on her toes to get a good look.

I moved the wingback chair closer to the window, lifted her by the waist, and settled her on the cushion. She leaned forward, hands and nose pressed to the glass.

"You wanna go outside?"

No response.

But damn, she was interested in those boys. One in particular, I suspected. I pulled out my phone and dialed Tito's number. He dislodged himself from a headlock, pulled his phone out of his pocket, then looked up at the window where we stood.

"Reynolds, what's up?"

"You see us?"

He nodded. "Yeah."

"Think maybe you and that pretty boy can ghost for a few minutes. I'd like to bring her down, see if she'll take to Rocky."

"Worth a try."

I watched Tito fill-in Tango. Tango looked my way, scowled, nodded, then squatted to talk to his son. Rocky looked up, noticing us for the first time. He waved, then jumped up and down, saying something to his dad.

Tito waved me out. The men headed for the garage.

"All right, Little One. See that kid out there? He's just about the coolest little boy I've ever met. We're gonna go outside, say hi, maybe he can show us around the beach or something. Yeah?"

Crickets chirping silence.

Then again, I didn't wait for an answer. I scooped her against my chest, the way she liked to be held, then headed out the door, down the hallway, down a set of stairs, then out the front door, nodding to Lettie and James. The early summer heat hit with a blast, but damn that fresh air was a welcome sensation.

Rocky barreled our way. "Dane! Dane!" He crashed into my thigh. "I didn't know you were here. Did you come to play football?"

"Nah." I squatted, resting Little One on my bent leg. She leaned her head against me but didn't hide her face. "I have someone I'd like you to meet."

The damn kid smiled, putting Pretty Boy's mug to shame. "Are you her dad?" Rocky asked.

"No. Just her best buddy."

"Hi." Rocky held out his hand. "I'm Rocky James Mason. Nice to meet you."

Little One didn't budge.

Rocky's brows crinkled.

"Rocky makes the best milkshakes I've ever tasted. Maybe he can make us one later."

Little One sat straighter.

"Do you like to swing?" Rocky asked, pointing to the tree. "I helped build that one. It goes super high, but if you're scared, I can push soft, so it only swings a little bit."

She didn't make a sound, but her body vibrated against mine.

"Why doesn't she talk?" Rocky asked, an innocent question from a curious mind. "Does she have automism? My friend in school has automism. Some kids make fun of him, but I don't."

"No, Rocky, she doesn't have autism. She just hasn't found anything worth saying yet." I gave Little One a squeeze. "What do you think? Wanna try out that swing?"

She inched off my leg, her toes dusting the grass, then scooted more, until her feet lay flat. I mentally urged her forward. Excruciating seconds passed before the girl let go of my shirt and took a step toward Rocky. That damn mini lady killer took her hand and bolted for the swing, and fuck me if she didn't follow, looking back only once to make sure I was still there.

Swear to Christ, a lump swelled in my throat.

I followed them to the swing, hoisted her up, then stepped back, letting Rocky take charge.

"Hold on tight," he ordered, gearing up for the first push.

And when she gasped at the first rise, and smiled on the drop, that lump popped like a bubble and came out a choked laugh.

Fucking hell, why were my eyes watering?

God damn allergies.

"That's my grandson," Lettie crooned. "That boy makes friends with everybody." She put her hand on my back, rubbing small circles. "She's smiling. Do you see that?"

I nodded, crossing my arms over my chest to keep from hugging the petite doctor. I wasn't a hugger, but damn how I wanted to squeeze somebody.

Rocky pushed for a good ten minutes, then halted the swing and helped Little One down. He held her hand and she didn't pull away.

"Dane! Dane! Can I show her the beach?"

"Yeah."

"Just don't go too close to the water, Rockster," Lettie shouted. "We don't know if she can swim."

"Okay!" he bellowed, skipping toward the sand.

We followed, giving the kids their space, my gut a rumbling mess.

Tito and Tango watched from the top floor of the garage, both assuming the same stance, arms crossed, chests puffed. I almost laughed, until I realized they mimicked my pose.

The kids ran up and down the length of the beach, finding rocks, and sticks, sitting for a few minutes to draw in the sand, then getting up to run again.

Lettie excused herself. When the kids finally settled in the shade of a willow tree, I joined them, parking my ass a few feet away.

Rocky rambled on about school and football. Little One listened, nodding her head as if in agreement, never tearing her gaze from Rocky's enormous green eyes.

I felt like an intruder, but damn I wasn't ready to let her out of my sight, or out of reach.

Rocky pushed to his feet, then helped Little One up. Protective. Like his father. Like his uncles. Like me.

"Dane, can we get a fruit pop from Grandma? She keeps them special in the freezer for me."

Hell, the thermometer had read close to ninety degrees in the sun. I needed a refreshment myself. I studied Little One to make sure she was okay, half expecting a meltdown, but she only kicked at the grass, her hand squeezing tight around Rocky's.

"Sounds good. Let's go."

The two of them took off again, at a slower pace than before, the heat taking its toll.

We entered through the front door and headed for the kitchen. I stopped short at the conversation ringing through the hall.

"Outside, really? That's good, right? Really good."

That voice sent a shiver through me. A full body jolt that hit me straight in the balls.

"Yes," came from Leticia. "And she smiled. And laughed today."

"And I missed it? Oh, God. I shouldn't have left. I knew I shouldn't have left."

Shit. The aunt.

"Grandma. Grandma!" Rocky bellowed, drawing attention our way before I could duck around the corner. "Can Mim and I have a fruit pop?"

Familiar eyes locked on mine, more gold than green when the light hit them right. Sweet Jesus, her face glowed, those freakin' sexy freckles spread across her sun-kissed cheeks.

No fucking way.

"Trailer?" fell from lips that only days ago had wrapped so perfectly around my cock.

"Moriah."

"Mim?" Lettie asked, halting Rocky's dash to the fridge with a death grip on his shoulder.

Rocky nodded.

"Wait." Moriah shook her head, tearing her gaze from mine. "How do you know her name?"

Rocky wiggled free of his gran's hold. "She told me, at the beach."

"She talked to you?" asked Moriah and Leticia simultaneously.

"Yeah." He shrugged, leading Little One to the freezer, clueless to the bomb he dropped.

"My sister called me Mim," Moriah whispered, watching the kids, tears spilling. "That was my nickname."

Rocky climbed up the stool and dug through the freezer like a pro, Mim at his side.

"Wait." Lettie gripped each side of her head, then pointed first at me, then Moriah. "You two know each other?"

"We've met," I grunted, yet to move from my spot in the hallway, unsure I was able.

"Mim." Moriah choked out a sob, her hand coming to her throat. "She named her daughter after me."

"Grandma, how many can we have?"

"One!" Lettie shouted. "Just one. For the love of Pete." She grabbed the box of frozen treats out of Rocky's grip. "Get down before you fall."

Rocky hopped down and led Mim to the sink, dragging the stool behind him. "Here, Mim. We have to wash our hands first."

Lettie helped the kids, while Moriah broke down in the center of the kitchen, her silent sobs gaining power.

Little One was in good hands. Moriah? A hot mess of trembling bones and devastation. Whatever was about to go down needed to happen in private. I grabbed her hand and led her around the corner to the bathroom, slamming the door shut behind us.

"You?" I grabbed tissues from the shelf. "This is fuckin' crazy. God damn crazy."

Snatching the offered box, she parked her ass on the toilet, then leaned forward, hiding behind her hands, shoulders bobbing.

Shit.

Dropping to a squat at her feet, I whispered, "Let it go, gorgeous." I gripped her neck, pulling her close. "Let it out. Then pull yourself together. That little girl needs you at one-hundred-percent. Whatever you need to purge, do it here. Do it now."

The woman sobbed in my arms, wetting my shirt, fingers curled into my waist, her full weight falling against me.

A good three minutes passed before she drew a long, hitched breath, then blew it out nice and slow.

"Oh, God. I can't do this." She pulled away, her hands moving to my shoulders, red, swollen eyes searching mine. "I can't take any more."

"Take any more of what?" My words came clipped. Flaming daggers pierced my chest, making my blood pump hot. Wasn't sure I wanted her answer, because it sounded to me like she was giving up on her niece, and that was un-fucking-acceptable.

"I buried my mom less than a week ago. That same day, I learned my sister was dead and that I had a niece nobody knew existed. Then I met this amazing guy the same day I dumped my boyfriend. Then I met this gorgeous, broken little girl. And she's the only family I have left, and she doesn't want me, but she wants this man who's a stranger, who sings to her, and makes her feel safe, but who's going to leave. And this guy who saved her happens to be the man I can't stop thinking about, even though I believed I was never going to see him again. Then I leave, to clear my head, and this child who I love more than life, who hasn't spoken a word to me, tells another stranger her name. The very name my sister used to call me. And it's all too much."

Okay. Fuck. That was some shit. I was about to say so, until she slapped my chest.

"And what the eff? Seriously. You? Of all people? You're the man who saved her life? Oh, God." Her face crumpled again. "You gave me my niece. You saved her." She wrapped her hands around my neck and dotted my face with wet kisses. "Thank you. Thank you so much. I can never repay you."

Salty tears mingled with more kisses.

A few hiccups followed.

"Trailer." She cupped my face, her nails scratching through my beard. "Tucker said I couldn't know who you were, that it was dangerous for me to know. Is that true?"

Fuck.

Lying was not an option. She deserved the truth. "Yeah. It's true. I'm not the kind of guy you can afford to be mixed up with."

"I don't understand."

"And I'm not going to help you understand. I'm leaving as soon as that little nugget is good to go. Not gonna soil what happened between us with the dirty details of my life."

"All right." She nodded, still working her fingers through my facial hair like a nervous tic. "I won't pry. I owe you that much."

"Good." That was too easy. She was too God damned sweet. "You okay now?"

"Yeah." She gutted me with a bright smile.

After helping her stand, I offered, "I'm sorry about your mom and your sister. Shitty you've had to deal with those cards on your own." I swiped a tear off her cheek...and... What the fuck? I didn't do that shit.

To save face, I cupped between her legs, squeezing hard because, yeah, that was more like it. "Not sorry about the boyfriend, though. Not one fuckin' bit."

The aroma of slow-cooked roast perforated the walls, twisting my guts something fierce, challenging my decision to stew alone rather than join everyone downstairs. Family dinners were not my thing. I appreciated the invitation, but sharing a table with Pretty Boy? Recipe for disaster. And after my run-in with Moriah, the camaraderie would set my nerves into hyperdrive.

We'd been under the same damn roof for days.

What were the odds?

Hungry, and too damn exhausted to contemplate the turn of events, I sprawled on the frilly bed, flipped through the channels, landing on an old episode of *Fast N' Loud*, and waited to see if I'd be called again to servitude.

Not that putting Little One to sleep was much of a chore. Hell. Favorite part of my day, to be honest.

Which was bullshit.

Sooner I detached myself from the situation, the better.

A soft rap on the door preceded a fit of giggles. With a groan, I rolled my weary bones and aching muscles off the bed, flipped the lock, and then yanked open the door. Rocky and Mim stood side by side, wearing cheesy smiles, each holding a plate of food.

"Mim said you would be hungry, so we brought you dinner. She also saved her roll for you. She said you liked rolls the best."

God damn.

Godfuckingdamn.

Only a monster would turn those faces away. I was a dickhead, but I sure as hell wasn't a monster. I swung the door wider, moving out of the way. "Come on in, then."

The kids made their way to the small table and laid down the plates. Tango and Slade then filled the doorframe.

"Pretty Boy," I grunted.

He jerked his chin. "Reynolds."

"Hey, Blondie."

"Hi, Dane." Jesus. That smile. Voodoo. "Hope you don't mind." She gestured toward the food. "They insisted."

Tango cleared his throat. "Rockster, say goodbye to Mim and Dane. We need to head home. Got school tomorrow."

Fuck, was it Sunday already?

"Aww, Dad. But what about Mim? Who's she gonna play with?"

Mim scooted behind me, her small fingers gripping the back of my shirt, a meltdown brewing. I gave Tango a look, hoping he could decipher my plea for help.

"Hey, little man, Wednesday's your last day of school. Then it's summertime. You can come and play with Mim every day until she goes home, if Grandma and Grandpa say it's okay."

"Yay! Yay!" Rocky threw a fist in the air and then jogged around me, wrapping his arms around Mim from behind. "Bye, Mim." He punched my arm. "Bye, Dane. I'll see you next time!" He bolted out the door, yelling, "Come on, guys."

Tango followed his son. Slade lingered, quirking a brow, shooting a quick glance in Mim's direction. "You gonna be okay in here?"

"Yeah." I'd never been more comfortable with another human being than I was with the quiet little mouse skittering behind me. Probably because she asked nothing of me, aside from sitting in silence and letting her use my body as her personal shield from the big bad world. Perfect set up. "Moriah know she's up here?"

Blondie nodded. "She's coming up after she helps Lettie clear the table." Astute, questioning eyes blinked at me. "So, you two know each other, huh?"

Wasn't in the mood for an interrogation.

"See ya," came out more a warning than a goodbye.

Slade smirked. "Later, Dane."

Leaving the door open, I turned to find Mim on my bed, kicking off her shoes, her feet dangling over the edge. She eyeballed me, then scrambled to the pillows and tucked herself under the comforter. I tossed the remote her way and settled at the table. God damn it was good to see some color in those cheeks. The sun seemed to make her freckles spread. She twitched her nose, just like her aunt, and hell if a spark didn't jet through my chest.

The floor creaked, and I turned my attention to the door. Moriah stood in the jamb, as if waiting for permission to enter. I shoved a forkful of roast into my mouth and gestured to the chair next to me. That slender beauty came my way, those hips of hers swaying something ridiculous.

"Hey."

"Hey," I mumbled.

She passed me and headed to the bed. Mim pulled the blankets up to her chin, eyes glued to the big screen.

Moriah sighed, said, "Hi, Mim," then waited excruciating seconds for a response before giving up and slinking into the chair beside me. She tucked her knees against her chest, heels hooked on the edge of the seat. "So, today was a good day, right?"

Killed me, that look of defeat on her face.

"Hell, she did great."

"She talked."

"Seems so."

She traced a pattern in the wood's grain. "Why to Rocky, and not us?"

"Don't know." I shoved another forkful into my mouth. Chewed. Shrugged. "But progress is progress."

Moriah looked over her shoulder, then back to me, and whispered, "I want so badly to curl up next to her. Hold her in my arms. It's killing me not to touch her."

It was killing me not to pull that woman into my lap, kiss those fucking freckles, hell, kiss every inch until her troubles were forgotten. "She'll come around."

"What if she doesn't?"

She looked so torn, so lost, and she stared at me like I had the answers to life's problems. I didn't have answers. I didn't have a fucking clue.

And because I hated being so helpless in the situation, and there was nothing I hated more than being helpless, I lashed out at the underserving woman. "I look like a God damn shrink?" I whisper growled. "What the fuck do I know?"

That pretty face reddened, eyes narrowed, shooting daggers straight through me. I half-expected a slap across the face. Hell, I hoped for a cold-cock, just so I could feel something other than useless.

She dropped her gaze to the table, shook her head, then swiped underneath her eyes.

Shit. Fuck. Shit. "I'm sorry," I mumbled, shoving a roll between my lips.

The door was little more than five strides from the table. I could go. Just get up. Walk out. Never come back. I had zero responsibility in the situation. No ties to the strangers sharing my space. Stand. Walk. Disappear.

Hell, I was halfway gone, until her voice broke my musings.

"Don't worry about it." Moriah dropped her feet to the floor and leaned closer. Then she grabbed my fork and dragged the tines through my mashed potatoes before stabbing a slab of roast and shoving the damn thing into her mouth. She chewed. Swallowed. Handed my utensil back, then shrugged. "It's obvious you care about her as much as I do, otherwise you wouldn't be here. Neither one of us expected to be in this situation. I've never been around kids. You have kids?" she asked.

I shook my head no.

"So, we are the least qualified people to take care of that little angel." She jabbed her thumb over her shoulder, gesturing toward Mim. "I've considered slipping away in the night at least fifty times since I've met her. I mean, seriously, what do I know about raising a child?"

Huh. Hadn't expected that reaction.

Moriah picked at her nails. I finished my dinner.

When I mopped up the last of the scraps on my plate, Moriah grabbed my dirty dishes and headed to the sink. She returned with two beers, slapped one into my palm, then made herself comfortable on the couch.

I kicked off my boots and settled on the bed, back against the headboard, legs stretched in front of me. Mim wasted no time burrowing into to my side.

"When do you have to go back?"

Moriah shot a glance my way, then settled those weary eyes on Mim. "One week."

Silence fell like a wet wool blanket, suffocating us in the heavy, scratchy truth. Seven days was not enough time. Mim would not be ready by then.

Little One and I zoned out to the big screen while Moriah seemed content watching the two of us. I didn't mind her staring so much.

Before long, Mim was asleep at my side, and Moriah snored on the couch, her legs tucked to her chest, her head at an awkward angle on the armrest. I should've carried Mim to her room, but then I'd risk waking the little thing, and then I wouldn't have reason to keep Moriah in my sights. So, I lay quiet and still, and wondered if the pressure in my chest would ever abate.

Dawn stretched hazy rays through the open window. A heavy weight blanketed my chest. I lifted my chin, wincing through the pain in my neck, to find two legs draped over me, dead weight. Mim, out cold, arms spread across the mattress, hair everywhere, drool wetting her cheek and blanket under her head.

Coffee fumes perked my senses, and I lifted the limbs, inching off the bed.

The clock read 6:38 AM. Moriah was gone. A fresh pot of coffee sat on the counter, still steaming.

God bless that woman.

I stretched. Poured a cup. Made my way to the window.

Blinding bursts of light danced off the lake's surface, forcing me to look away.

A small figure stood on the beach, arms wrapped around her middle, a soft breeze blowing her skirt into a tangle around her legs. The sweater she wore hid her figure, but I knew what was underneath that bulky fabric, and hell if it didn't give me a certain pleasure having that knowledge to store away and revisit as I pleased.

Moriah walked closer to the water, then sat, chin lifted to the sun.

I looked over my shoulder at the sleeping princess. She hadn't budged.

I poured another cup of coffee and headed, barefoot, down three flights of stairs, out the door, then across the lawn, my heart banging my chest like an angry, caged gorilla.

"Hey."

Chin to shoulder, she smiled up at me, content and sleepy. "Good morning." She stared for a moment. "So, is it Dane or Trailer? I'm not sure what to call you."

"Dane," I grunted. I fucking hated Trailer and all that nickname stood for.

I handed her the cup, then planted my ass next to her in the wet sand. "It's *effin'* cold out here," I teased.

"The air is so crisp. I love it." She took a healthy swig of coffee. "Mim still sleeping?"

"Yeah."

"One of us should be there when she wakes up."

"We'll go back in a minute." I couldn't tear my gaze from those damn freckles. Was there such a thing as a freckle fetish? "What are you doing out here alone at the crack of dawn?"

"Got a phone call." Moriah lifted her cell and then dropped it back in the sand, a sad laugh escaping her lips. She stared, gaze aimed across the lake, shook her head, then rubbed her free hand over her eyes.

"What is it?"

"I no longer have a job."

"The fuck?"

"Budget cuts. Great timing, huh?"

"What are you gonna do?"

"Not sure. Not yet. I have a little savings, enough to get by for a few months. The job market isn't great in Shelbyville, and I don't have a clue what's gonna happen with Mim." Her face crumpled. "And I still have to wrap up my mother's affairs, and oh God," she moaned. "I haven't even had time to mourn my sister. And Matthew hasn't called me once. Not once. You would think after four years together he would at least call. I mean, I wasn't expecting him to beg me to stay or anything but…" She turned to look at me, those weary eyes glistening, the dam about to break. "Aren't I at least worth a phone call?"

Jesusfuckingchrist I couldn't hear another word. I dropped my cup and wrapped my arms around her head and shoulders, pulling her against me. She'd lost her mother. Her sister. Her boyfriend. Her job. And now she was saddled with a child who came with her own heavy baggage. Yeah. I was clueless. Helpless. Had nothing to offer but a shoulder to cry on. What else could I do but let her cry? Better in private with me than in front of Mim or anyone else.

That's what she did, sobbing softly, using me as a shield.

I watched the waves licking the shore, my nose buried in her messy hair, and waited for her cue. When she lifted a hand to rub her face, I released my hold. The damn woman wrapped an arm around my middle and squeezed before sitting straight again.

"Thank you." She wiped under her nose with her sleeve and shot a glance over my shoulder toward the house. "I can't let them see me like this. They can't know that I'm unemployed, or that my life is a mess. They might decide I'm not qualified to take care of my niece."

"They're good people," was all I could offer. "They wouldn't do that."

She nodded. "I'm sure you're right. But please, for now, can we keep my current situation between the two of us?"

If she kept pleading with those soft fucking eyes, I'd do anything she asked. And when the hell had I turned into such a pushover? "No problem."

"We should head back." Moriah reached across my legs, grabbed my mug, then her own, and pushed to stand.

I snagged her forgotten cell out of the sand and followed her across the lawn.

"Morning." A gruff voice came over my shoulder when we hit the porch.

I turned to find James Slade, Lettie's husband, Tucker's dad. He held his own mug of coffee in one hand, and the morning paper in the other. He smiled the same damn smile as his son, dimples and all. But in his eyes, I saw Blondie. Big and blue and full of zest.

"Morning," I offered, with a chin nod.

"Morning, Mr. Slade." Moriah said, her voice still shaky. "You're up early."

"Ah, well. Got a ton of ground to cover today. Mower needs a tune-up. There's a faulty sprinkler head out back." He huffed. "But first, got some digging to do. Lettie loves her lilacs. Gonna plant a row of bushes out back, so she can see them out the bedroom window."

"Aren't you the romantic," Moriah practically purred. She patted James on the chest, then headed inside.

The old guy blushed.

I nodded and made to follow her, but James cleared his throat. "Dane."

"Yeah?"

"I know you're not sticking around much longer, but while you're here, if you need a change of pace, I could use a hand. You know, with maintenance and such. Tucker helps when he can, but the place is big, and, well, I'm not as young as I used to be."

"Sure, Mr. Slade." I scratched the back of my head. "Anything you need." I owed the guy, after all. He'd played a major role in keeping Rocky alive. And a little physical activity would do me good.

"None of that Mr. Slade crap. It's James."

"All right, James." I met him eye to eye. "Need me this morning?"

"Why don't we see how the little one does. You get a break, you come find me."

"Sure."

With that, he headed toward the barn.

I made my way inside, shaking my head.

I SHOOK MY HEAD. Pinched the bridge of my nose. Drew a deep breath. "Sure. Sure. I understand. Thank you for your time."

Another dead end.

I ticked off the ninth contact on my job search list.

"It's okay. It's okay. Like Mom always said," I mumbled to Mim, although I knew she wasn't listening. "'God closes one door, he opens another'."

Maybe Mom had been right.

I'd told Matthew I wanted kids, and he shut me down—door closed.

Bam! A child dropped into my lap—door open.

I had always wanted to travel, get out of Shelbyville. Matthew hated traveling, and Mom got sick—door closed.

Boom! An impromptu trip clear across the country—door open.

Although, the unexpected opportunities did seem to pose more challenges than I was capable of handling.

I glanced over my shoulder. Mim stood at the window, fingers pressed to the glass. She hadn't moved for at least ten minutes.

"Hey, Mim." I made a slow approach, careful not to startle her. "What're you looking at?"

She didn't cower when I came to her side, and sweet Lord, that made my heart soar. I pulled the lacy curtain aside and glanced down at the expansive yard.

Sweeping left to right, I found the target of her attention. Dane. Shirtless. Covered in ink. Mostly black and white, with a few splashes of color. Muscles taut. God. I'd been naked in bed with the man, but I hadn't really seen him naked. We'd been in the dark both times he'd... I shook the thought away, my cheeks heating.

He was beautiful, in a tragic sort of way. Thick with bulk that seemed more armor than vanity. A scowl on his face that looked more like contrition than concentration. He forced a shovel into the ground, scooped the grass and dirt, and then tossed it into the pile at his side, his muscles flexing and rolling and bunching and... Oh, God. I had to stop.

"Mim." My breath fogged the glass.

She ignored me.

"It's so pretty outside. You feel like going down to the beach, or maybe I could push you on the swing?"

No response.

"Dane sure does look thirsty. He probably needs a big glass of water. You think we should bring him some water?"

The little girl gasped, then ran to the bed and found her shoes. In a dash, she was down the hall and headed toward the kitchen.

I chased behind, watching her wild hair bounce across her back, unbrushed, untamed, so much like Mickey. We reached the empty kitchen, and she knew right where to go, sliding a step stool across the tile and climbing up to reach the cupboard where the glasses lived.

Vile jealousy rolled through me, and I hated that weakness. Would she ever respond to me the way she responded to Dane or Rocky?

"Hey. It's almost lunch time. I bet he's hungry, too. Maybe we should make some sandwiches." I knew better than to wait for a reaction.

While she filled a glass with ice, then water, I pulled bread out of the cupboard, then dug through the fridge, happy to find sliced cheese and deli meats. Clueless to his palate, I found the mustard and mayo, lettuce, pickles, too, and laid everything on the counter.

"What do you think he likes? Ham, salami, turkey, or maybe all three?"

Mim pushed the stool next to me and climbed up. She seemed to contemplate her choices, then lifted bright eyes to mine, and pointed to the ham.

"Ham it is."

"Think he likes mustard?"

She nodded.

"Mustard it is."

We continued that way until we'd made three sandwiches, all varying combinations, one of them extra heavy on the pickles.

"Three sandwiches should be enough to fill him. Now, what about you?" I laid two slices of bread in front of her. "What do you want to eat?"

She shook her head, then climbed down the stool and headed for the pantry and disappeared behind the door. She came out seconds later with a bag of corn chips and a paper plate.

"Good thinking. Boys love chips!" I piled the sandwiches on the plate, grabbed the glass of water, and together Mim and I headed outside.

We passed Lettie and James on the way. The couple pretended they hadn't been hanging back in the hallway, giving my niece and me our space.

"Hi, guys." I winked. "We're just taking Dane some lunch. We'll clean our mess as soon as we get back, right Mim?"

Mim continued through the door, a healthy spring in her step.

The stench of cigarette smoke permeated the air. When Dane noticed us coming his way, he drove the shovel straight into the earth, and rested an arm across the handle. A white cancer stick hung from his lips. My stomach soured.

Hadn't noticed he was a smoker. Then again, I'd never smelled the vile scent on his clothes, or his breath. Odd. Being extra sensitive to the odor, I could smell that poison a mile away.

"We brought you lunch." I forced a smile, fighting a sudden wave of nausea.

Dane raised one brow, pinched the cigarette between his fingers, and dropped the stub at his feet, smashing it into the newly uncovered dirt.

He couldn't take his eyes off Mim, and that damn green monster pinched my chest again, especially when a grin cracked the hard planes of his face, white teeth showing between his beard and mustache. "Lunch, huh?" he asked, rubbing a forearm across his sweaty brow.

Holding the glass his way, I blurted, "And water, too. Mim thought you looked thirsty."

Mim smiled.

Dane grabbed his shirt and pulled it over his head, covering all that sweaty, beautiful skin, then squatted. "Thanks, Little Lady. How did you know I was starving out here?" He fell back on his ass, crossed his legs, and gestured for us to sit, too.

I waited for Mim to claim her spot next to the hulking man, then I made myself comfortable in the cool grass. A warm breeze blew through the willow trees, and a boat jetted across the lake in the distance.

"Which one is mine?" Dane asked.

I waited a beat, giving Mim a chance to pipe in. When she didn't move or speak, I offered, "All three of them."

He laughed. A deep throaty chuckle that heated me through and through, targeting inappropriate places.

And sweet Jesus, he noticed, his eyes darkening to a lusty shade when they landed on me. My heart responded, its rhythm changing tempo, and I wondered if I was about to dance through another open door.

I listened through the wall while Dane put Mim to sleep, my eyes leaking something fierce. God, how I wanted to be the one holding her. She'd insisted on showering herself. Brushing her own hair. Dressing. But eating or going to bed? Those tasks she couldn't do without Dane by her side.

And my period must've been getting close, because for some reason, her rejection, although expected, had set me on a crying spell I couldn't break. I couldn't fathom the hell she'd been through, or the hell my sister had been through, and maybe I was better off not knowing the horrid details, but how could I help if I didn't know her triggers. How could I help if she wouldn't let me into her little bubble?

I waited for an hour on the floor, my head against the wall, hoping to hear anything, any sneak peek into their world—their private space I feared I'd never be part of.

When I heard Dane sneaking out of her room, I hopped to my feet and waited, hoping he'd not pass my door.

A soft knock made my chest pound, adrenaline spiking, and I took a long, slow breath before facing him.

A breath he stole the moment our eyes met.

"Hey," he greeted me, gruff and sleepy. One hand shoved in the front pocket of his jeans, the other squeezing the back of his neck, that unruly hair falling over his face.

"Hey." I tried to tame my voice, but the quiver gave away my unstable emotions.

"Aw, fuck." In a move so strange coming from a man so daunting, he cupped my face and dragged his thumbs under my leaky eyes. "What now?"

"I don't know. I can't stop crying. Must be that time of the month."

Matthew had always cringed when I brought up the subject of my period, said he didn't need to hear about my lady problems. He often worked late those few days every month I was particularly sensitive and moody.

Dane only laughed, said, "Be right back," and jogged down the hallway.

He returned minutes later holding two beers, a spoon, and a pint of cherry vanilla. "So, what'll it be? Beer or ice cream?"

Oh God. Sweetness overload. I tossed my wad of tissues in the trash, threw myself on the bed, and covered my face with my arm. "I could use your mad tongue skills about now."

Silence. Heavy, thick, palpable silence.

I peeked out from under my arm to find Dane staring down at me, not a lick of humor on his face.

"That was a joke," I whispered, my voice catching.

The ice cream landed on the floor. A beer bottle hit his lips. He chugged. Swallowed. Inhaled. Blew out a breath. "Don't joke about that shit."

I sat up, leaning on my elbows. "What?"

"You heard me." He stalked closer, took another drink, then set the bottles on the bedside table. "Been fucking torture keeping my hands off you."

Oh dear, sweet Jesus, I wanted another go at that insanely beautiful man, but the timing sucked, and my life... my life...ugh. "But I'm a mess. And I'm leaving soon. And you're leaving soon. And Mim. And thin walls."

"Shut up." He growled. Growled. Bared teeth and all, and holy wow did that snarl do dark and dirty things to my insides.

The beast fell over me, palms pounding the mattress, and claimed my lips in a desperate, bruising kiss—hard and fast and with a moan that crept over my skin, making every inch of me tight and tingly. He moved to my ear, giving the lobe a nibble, then whispered, "I'm gonna fuck you now."

"What about Mim?" I managed to ask through my panting.

"Out cold." He shoved a hand under my waistband, found my clit, and teased with a slow rub.

"What if someone hears us?"

"They won't." He sat back on his heels and tugged on my leggings until I was naked from the waist down.

"But—"

"You want my mouth on that pussy, or what?"

"Yes." My core clenched tight at the thought.

He moved to the door, hit the lock, killed the light.

A deafening *thump thump thump* battered my ribcage.

Strong hands gripped my ankles, yanked me to the edge of the mattress, moved to my knees, and spread me wide. His beard tickled my thighs, the only warning before he swept his warm tongue over the length of me, then sucked my clit between his teeth, going straight for the kill, drawing me into mindless pleasure with sharp pulls and soft nips.

Thrashing, I tried to adjust, to find reprieve, slow his pace. Strong fingers curled into my hips, holding me steady, forcing me to lie still, absorb, and feel, and ride that torturous wave to the crest. When I thought I couldn't take any more, he shoved a finger inside me, throwing me deeper into the swirling, pulsing, consuming sea of pleasure.

Silent rasps escaped me, "Oh God. Oh God. Yes, yes, yes..."

Fingers tangled in his hair, I came, the world bursting into blinding light, my body warming, thrusting, bucking against that beard, that face, that tongue, those lips. Devouring what he offered. For that delicious moment I was a greedy, beautiful, warm, wanton woman.

Spent, I relaxed into the mattress, struggling for breath, eyes wet, brain fuzzy. An empty condom wrapper landed at my side. Dane crawled over me, nestled his hips between my legs, and drove his hard length into me, the noise coming from his throat that of raw, unbridled desire. A long pause. His breaths hit my face, lips dusted mine, and then with whispered profanities and dirty promises, he pounded into me, taking his own pleasure, selfish and with no apology, and I melted, absorbing his thrusts and grunts, and shivering under his filthy words, and oh my God, that man... That man...he made me so, so thankful to be a woman.

He cursed his release into my neck. Collapsed at my side. Caressed my skin. Took me again, rendering me boneless, until we both gave way to the pull of exhaustion—spent, sweaty, and tangled.

In that hazy space between wake and sleep, I thought I heard him mumble, "Fuck my life."

I laughed to myself and thought, yeah, eff my life, too, because I knew I'd never meet another man like Dane.

But thank God I'd had him for a few precious moments.

A child's cries carried through the wall, jolting me into a state of consciousness.

I bolted upright, searching the bed for any article of clothing to cover my body.

I found a shirt, shimmied the cotton over my head, kicked my tangled legs free of the sheets, and dashed for the door, crashing into a naked chest.

A strong arm came around my shoulders, steadying me. "Hey. I got her. It's all good."

"But she's my—" I stopped myself. True, she was my responsibility, but for the time being, Mim needed Dane, not me.

I couldn't blame her. The man had a way about him. Arms that made you feel safe. A deep, husky voice that soothed. And despite his large, menacing appearance, on rare occasion, I'd catch a look in his eye that promised he'd destroy anyone who hurt those he cared about, and there was no denying he cared about Mim, although I suspected, a man like Dane would never admit such nonsense out loud.

"Go back to bed," he ordered.

As much as I wanted to be the one to soothe my niece, I knew she wasn't ready. I nodded, whispered, "Thank you," and retreated.

Eventually, I told my wounded ego to be quiet, and trusted that Dane had everything under control.

Morning came too soon. Small breaths hit my nose, coaxing me awake. I peeled one eye open, then the other. Warm hazel eyes met mine. Nose scrunched, Mim brushed hair out of my face, her small fingers tangling in my morning mane.

I smiled. She smiled back, tracing the angles of my face. My cheeks, my nose. My chin. My eyelashes. I waited, heart in my throat, while she studied me.

Mim smiled again, pushed a finger to her lips, warning me to stay quiet, then pointed to Dane, who was fast asleep on the sofa, one leg on the floor, the other cocked against the back of the couch. One arm lay across his chest, while the other was draped over his eyes. Even in sleep, the man was too much, daunting and larger than life.

I looked back to Mim, afraid to move, afraid to scare her away. She tangled her fingers in my hair once again, then closed her eyes.

I stared, my heart so full it overflowed through my eyes. When soft snores escaped her lips, I rolled over, inched myself off the bed, and made for the shower, my skin still tender from the night's activities.

When I returned from the bathroom, Dane sat upright on the couch, eyes heavy with lack of sleep, but bless the man, he held two cups of coffee in his hands.

"Morning," he mouthed, rendering me breathless and tingly.

He tracked my movements, his lids heavy with exhaustion.

I took the offered mug, hitched one leg on the sofa, and sat, facing the mountain of muscle. "Did you get any sleep?"

"Yeah," he lied, avoiding my glare, and gestured toward the sleeping angel on the bed. "She had a rough night, though. Woke up three times after I went in there. Finally brought her in here."

My guts roiled. No child should have reason for such horrible nightmares.

"What happened to her?" I asked, terrified of the answer.

Dane shifted, his attention moving to the floor. "Bad shit, gorgeous. Bad shit."

"Tell me."

"Details won't do you any good."

"How can I help her if I don't know?"

Lifting the cup to his lips, he sipped, swallowed, glanced toward the bed, then met my eyes. "The guy was a predator. I don't know how long he had her. Don't know much other than I found her in a hole."

That awful clench in my stomach pulled tighter.

Dane studied me, brows drawn. "You really don't want to hear this."

"I have to." As much as I wanted to curl into the pain, I forced my spine straight.

"The room she was in had a bed. Cameras and lighting set up. There were toys. Some for kids. Some not. And that damn hole." His breath hitched, and I watched his throat work, the muscles strained. "The physical wounds will heal." He tapped his temple. "It's what's in here that's gonna take work." His eyes glazed over, lips drawn tight, as if haunted by a painful memory.

Oh God. Had he been abused as a child? I knew nothing. Nothing about that man's life, past or present, yet I was trusting him with so much of mine.

"How did you find her?"

Silence.

"Did you know my sister?

"Met her once. She did a few odd jobs for some of my buddies when she was sober enough. Didn't know about Mim, though."

"Mickey wasn't a bad seed. She wasn't. She wouldn't let something like that happen to her daughter. Not my sister." Although I spoke with conviction, the truth sickened me. Mickey *had* let something terrible happen, her addiction stronger than any motherly instinct or moral compass.

Dane set his cup at his feet, sat back, ran his hands through his hair, then laced his fingers at the back of his head. "Men like Wilson Kyle prey on single women. I suspect your sister was an easy target, given her drug habit."

The temperature in the room seemed to spike, my tongue drying, head spinning. "I'm going to be sick."

I rushed to the bathroom, my stomach protesting the flood of hurt, rage, and disgust.

Large, bare feet came into my periphery. The water ran in the sink and he laid a cold, wet washcloth over my neck.

I shooed the hulking beast away, ashamed of my weak constitution.

Buck up, little camper, used to be my father's go-to advice whenever I had a moment of self-pity. He would allow me a few minutes to pout, then tell me to pick myself up, dust myself off, and march on.

If Mim could survive her horrors, then I could certainly handle hearing about them. *Buck up, little camper. Buck the eff up.* I pulled my shit together, brushed my teeth, thanked Dane for telling me the truth, then I crawled back into bed where Mim was fast asleep, arms and legs spread wide.

I needed to touch her, hold her, feel her heat, smell her sweaty head, and hear that beautiful beating heart. I rolled to my side, curled my arms around the sleeping beauty, and fought tears until exhaustion pulled me under.

CHAPTER 7

EXHAUSTION THREATENED TO PULL me under where I stood, but fuck if I was about to back down.

"What I don't get"—Tito threw a right hook, landing a brutal lick to my jaw— "is what that little angel likes about you." Smack. Smack. "You're scary as fuck."

"My sparkling personality, dickface." I swung. He shifted left, avoiding my right hook.

"And you fight like an old man." His next strike came out of nowhere.

I hit the mat, blinked the stars from my vision, contemplated staying down, then shook the thought away.

Moretti stood over me, bare chested and begging for more. Tito wasn't the kind of guy you conceded to, no matter how bad you hurt.

I pushed to hands and knees, ignoring the catch in my hip, then struggled to my feet.

If Moretti noticed my discomfort, he didn't let on, but instead, he backed away, bouncing foot to foot, waiting for my next move. I'd never seen the guy fight, but I'd watched what he could do to a man, witnessed the depravity. He was a survivor, like me. Not trained, but honed. Street. To the bone.

When he'd asked if I wanted to join him in the gym for a spar, I figured we'd pussyfoot around each other for an hour, release some pent-up frustrations, work up a good lather.

Shoulda known better.

The guy came at me, no-holds-barred, and out of sheer survival instinct, I blocked, then stuck. Once. Twice.

He countered. Kidneys. Ribs.

Yeah. Moretti was rabid, maniacal in his approach, but I was a machine, a God damn tank. Get me rolling, I wouldn't stop until the ground was leveled. And I was ready to roll because fuck, I hurt everywhere.

I struck, catching his jaw.

He kissed the mat and bounced right back to his feet. "Now we're talking." The fucker smiled. "Haven't had a real fight in ages."

And so went the back and forth. We ended the verbal taunts and dove straight into beating the shit out of each other.

Bloody, bruised, we continued, neither of us backing down. God. Damn. I fucking loved the adrenaline rush.

"Boys!" a husky voice shouted, drawing my attention to the curvy woman in the doorway.

The distraction was enough for Moretti to land a final blow. Somehow, I managed to stay upright, although on my knees.

Tito cracked a smile. Bent to my level. "Thanks, bro. I needed that." He offered a hand to help me up. Before turning to face the woman in the doorway, he said, "Mim is lucky you stumbled into that cabin. Doesn't matter why she's taken to you. Doesn't matter you're a bastard. She feels safe with you, so make sure she keeps on feeling that way."

I had nothing to offer but a, "Fuck off," while I slapped his hand away.

I was sick of people telling me what I needed to do. Like I didn't feel the weight every time Mim looked me in the eye, or wrapped her little fingers around my hand, or those tiny arms around my neck. My bones cracked under the pressure.

And Mim wasn't the only one weighing heavy. Moriah. Fuck. That woman had me twisted.

Tito slapped me on the back. "Same time tomorrow?"

"Yeah," was all I could manage.

He laughed. "Ever want a real challenge..." He pointed over his shoulder to the curvy, raven-haired goddess standing in the doorway, balancing a baby on her hip. "Give that feisty shit a go. She'll exorcise your demons and serve you your own balls on a silver platter."

He jogged away, snatched the baby out of the woman's arms, and disappeared.

The woman, however, tilted her head, pinning me with a stare that left no room for challenge. "You good? Do we need to call Lettie?"

I raised a swollen hand. "All good."

"Really?" She cocked her hip, touched a finger to her cheek. "Got a little something there."

I ran the back of my arm over my sore cheek, and yes, there was blood. Already, my vision was blurry, my eye swelling, certain to get worse if I didn't ice it soon.

"You must be Aida."

The woman nodded, coming closer. "You're Dane." She offered a hand, which I didn't refuse. She also didn't comment when I took too long to find my balance.

When I rose to full height, the top of her head barely came to my chest, but somehow her presence filled the room like she was the God damn queen of everything, and I fought the urge to bow in respect.

Arms crossed, she gave me a once-over. "Hear you've been helping James around the grounds."

"Yeah."

"Want a job?"

Aida was Tucker's woman. She knew goodgoddamnwell I was, or had been, a Slayer. Meaning, I worked, or had, only for the club. "Don't need a job."

"Fine," she snapped, unconvinced, then turned around and sauntered to the door. "But if you change your mind, James could use a permanent groundskeeper." She gripped the doorframe and looked over her shoulder. "The guy's a fucking workhorse, but this place is bigger than we'd anticipated, and with summer looming, there's no way he'll be able to keep up with the entire property. We could hire someone from the outside, but that's just more people in our business, and the less people in our business, the better. I'm sure you know what I mean."

"Sure."

"You don't say much, do you?"

"Only when necessary."

"Okay then. If you change your mind, I'll be around."

"I won't."

"Fine."

"Fine."

She raised a hand in the air and flipped me the bird over her shoulder. "Nice to meet you, Dane."

Damn. I liked that woman. "Pleasure. Aida."

"Dane! Grandpa!" Rocky barreled our way, Mim in tow.

"Hey, Rock," James called out from atop the ladder, hammer mid-strike.

Mim came to my side, her shoulder pressing into my thigh. "Hey, Little Lady. You and Rocky having fun?"

Rocky piped in. "Yeah! We helped Grandma make chocolate chip cookies, and Mim spilled eggs all over the floor." Rocky laughed and hell, I couldn't help but laugh, too.

"That true, Mim? Did you make a mess?"

Her arm curled around my leg.

James tucked his hammer into his tool belt and started down the ladder. "Let me guess, Grandma shooed you out of the kitchen so she could clean up."

"No!" Rocky laughed, holding his gut. "That's the best part. Mim and Moriah started cleaning the mess, but Moriah looked at the eggs and threw up all over the floor." He laughed harder. "It was so gross!"

My guts shifted something fierce. My hand went to Mim's back. "She okay? Moriah?"

Mim buried her face in my hip.

James shot me a worried glance. "I'll go check on them. Rocky, you and Mim stay out here in case Dane needs help."

"Sure thing, Gramps." Rocky planted his butt in the grass next to a pile of cedar shakes.

Mim wouldn't budge. "Hey, Mim. You think you can hand me that box of screws?" I pointed to the makeshift sawhorse table behind Rocky. "It's the red box."

Mim did as asked, carefully delivering the box. Her gaze never strayed from the ground, her shoulders hunched, face pale. Christ. I squatted, immediately regretting the painful move, then fell forward onto my knees. I gripped her shoulders. "What is it? You worried about getting in trouble for dropping the eggs?"

Nothing.

"It was an accident. Nobody's mad at you."

"She's not scared about getting in trouble. She's mad."

"Mad?" I glanced over Mim's shoulder to find Rocky inspecting a framing square.

"She said her mom used to throw up all the time when she didn't have her medicine."

"Medicine?" Drugs.

"She said she doesn't want to live with Moriah if she needs medicine, too, because she'll do bad things like her mom."

"Fuck!" My face heated.

Mim ran to Rocky's side and huddled next to him.

"Sorry." Fuck. I'd scared her. "I'm sorry, Little One. I didn't mean to yell."

She lifted her eyes, meeting mine.

"C'mere."

I should've gone to her, but my damn hip screamed in protest. Mim made her way back to me, her steps calculated.

I pushed my anger down, swallowed, choked a bit, but I couldn't let her be afraid of me.

When she stood inches away, I cupped her cheeks and held her steady. "Listen to me. Your mother was addicted to drugs. Very bad drugs. Do you know what that means?"

She blinked, moisture pooling in those big, sad eyes.

"Rocky. Do you know what that means?"

He hopped to his feet and stood by Mim's side. "Yes. We talk about it in school."

"Good."

He took Mim's hand and stepped closer to her. Damn if that move didn't make my chest ache.

"Moriah does not do that shit."

Rocky gasped.

I winced. "Sorry. I shouldn't cuss around you kids." I paused for a calming breath, and scrambled for the right words. "Your aunt is not an addict. She's a good woman, and she's going to take care of you better than your mother ever could. She's going to keep you safe, and love you, and do everything that your mom should've done for you."

A big tear rolled down the side of her face, gutting me, forcing me to curl my arms around her small frame and pull her close.

"Moriah got sick, but it's not the same, Little One. I need you to nod, let me know you understand."

She did, thank fuck, her cheek moving against my neck. I curled my face into her head and whispered, "And anyone tries to hurt you again, I'll kill them. Got me?"

Deep down, I knew speaking that way to a child was inappropriate on every level. But Mim had lived a thousand horrible lives in her few years on Earth. She'd heard worse. She'd survived worse. She needed the truth, no pretty words, no shallow promises. And fuck. What had I just done?

Moriah headed our way, pale, but a smile pasted on her face regardless. She raised a hand to me in greeting.

I turned Mim in my arms, urging her to face her aunt. "See? She's fine. She probably ate too much ice cream last night."

The little girl relaxed under my hands.

Moriah joined us in the grass, sitting cross-legged.

"How's your tummy?" Rocky asked.

"Much better. Thank you." Moriah plucked a blade of grass out of the earth and twisted it between her fingers. "Eggs just gross me out, really bad."

Rocky laughed, then proceeded to tell us stories about kids puking in school, all of them disgusting, all of them making Mim's body shake in silent laughter.

Moriah, however, turned three different shades of green in a two-minute period of time.

"Rocky. How about you and Mim go see if any of those cookies are ready to eat. I'm starving."

"Yeah!"

That was all it took. The kids ran toward the house. Moriah turned and dry heaved into the grass.

"What the fuck, gorgeous?"

I struggled to my feet, made my way to her side.

One more gag, and she stood, turning to look at me. "Oh God. I'm sorry you had to see that."

"What's happening here?"

Moriah took a deep breath. Blew it out nice and slow. Splayed a hand over her stomach. "Stress. That's all."

"Stress?"

She nodded.

"Bullshit."

"I've always had a sensitive stomach. This happened when my dad died, and when my mom was first diagnosed with cancer. It's just how my body reacts to extreme stress. It'll pass."

"You need to go to bed. Get some rest."

"I can't. Mim and I are meeting with the psychiatrist today. I'm worried she isn't ready, ya know? What if she freaks the second I try to take her home? I'm scared that I won't know how to help."

"She's doing better every day."

"I know. It's just...she's doing better because you're here. And Rocky. All of you. But what happens when I take her home, away from this place, probably the only place she's ever felt safe?"

"Then you deal."

"Then I deal?" she asked, brows raised, hands to the sky. "Simple as that?"

"Sure."

"We don't even know what happened to her yet. We don't know her triggers. Physically she's thriving, but emotionally?

We don't have a clue what's going on inside that little head of hers. And what the eff was I thinking trying to take on this responsibility? I mean, seriously, I'm a train wreck, and—"

I grabbed her chin, "Moriah. Take a fuckin' breath. Okay?"

Hard enough to process the foreign emotion rolling through my head, but when that beat-down look on her face had me seeing red, I realized I was in a shit-ton of trouble. I wanted to destroy everyone who'd caused that woman pain. Worse? With every polluted vein in my body, I wanted to take that freckled face in my hands and promise I'd protect her every day for the rest of her fucking life. And fuck. I wanted a forever. Forevers were for normal people. Not assholes. Not career criminals. Not...a trailer trash lowlife.

"C'mon." I grabbed her hand and dragged her back to the house.

When we reached her room, I settled her on the bed, ripped off her shoes, ordered her to lie down, then planted my fists into the mattress on either side of her head. My arms trembled, and I hoped she didn't notice.

"You gonna tell me what happened to your face?" Moriah smoothed a finger under the cut on my lip.

I pulled away, her touch laced with tenderness I couldn't bear. "Tito and I were messing around in the gym."

"You should get that eye looked at."

How could she worry about my sorry ass, when her life was such a mess? I stared down at her, fighting back the slew of profanities I wanted to spew. "Take a nap. You're exhausted. I'll wake you before the meeting."

Allowing no room for argument, I left. I couldn't take another second of that broken voice, or the way my insides responded to her pain. I hated not being in control. Hated that she was leaving and taking that little girl with her. Hated that I fucking cared. Fuck.

The door slammed shut, and I made my way to the kitchen, where Mim pulled out a chair for me at the table, then made me sit, then fed me milk and cookies while she put fucking princess bandages on my face.

"You good up there?" James chuckled.

"Yep."

"Sure you don't need a hand?"

"I'm sure."

I glanced at the mansion one more time, hoping to catch a glimpse through the window. Moriah and Mim had been in that damn room for over two hours talking to that shrink. Couldn't see a thing through the window, the sun's reflection making it impossible. Oh, and the curtains were closed, but still, couldn't keep my gaze from wandering that direction every thirty seconds or so.

"Just saying. I could've had that row down by now."

"Yeah, yeah, old man." I hammered down the last two shingles. Sighed. Then inched my way down the slope to the ladder, where James stood at the base, holding her steady.

When I reached ground level, he pounded my shoulder, said, "Thanks," then handed me an open bottle of pale ale.

"Bottoms up," he said, staring at the finished gazebo. "She's a beauty."

"Yep." I pulled three long swigs of beer and glanced again at the window.

"They're fine. You can quit worrying."

I shot him a glare, warning him to not go there.

Fucker only laughed and pointed a finger toward the window. "That doctor in there. She's the best in the country. Anyone can help those two, it's her. So don't worry."

Something akin to a grunt rose up my chest.

We parked our asses in the cool grass and stared out over the lake, my head a hot mess of agitation.

James cleared his throat. Swirled his bottle. "Can I ask you something?"

Any distraction was welcome. "Shoot."

"What's it like, being in that club? Kurt Sutter get it right?"

"Who?"

"You know...*Son's of...*" He shook his head, his cheeks growing red. "Never mind."

I knew damn well what he was talking about. Better to play clueless. Club business was exactly that. Club business. Wasn't to be discussed with anyone outside of our brotherhood. I'd die before betraying that trust. They'd been part of my life for as long as I could remember. They'd taken me in, yes, because of my father's fuck-ups, but twisted as the relationship was, they'd given me purpose. They'd had every right to end me when my sorry excuse for an old man had betrayed the club. Instead, they'd let me take the reins when it came time to bring him in, and they'd allowed me the final strike when it came time to end him.

Still, club life was hard. Gave you thick skin and roughened any soft edges you might've had. "I wouldn't wish that life on anybody with a moral compass."

James only nodded, eyes squinting against the bright beams of light bouncing off the water's surface.

"You're a good man, Dane."

"I'm not."

"You being here, you doing what you did for Mim, tells me otherwise." He pushed to his feet, tossed his beer bottle into the trash bucket and said, "Come on. Help clean this shit up, then you can check on your ladies."

Seriously. I'd had it. "One." I chucked the hammer. "They aren't my ladies." Hands to hips, I continued. "Two. What makes you think I need to check on them? And three..." I threw my hands to the sky. "Fuck. I don't have a three, but... whatever."

The guy wasn't stupid. He knew not to push. We cleaned up. Headed inside. Before parting ways, James pulled off his dusty cap and wiped his brow with the back of his arm. "You any good with engines?"

"I can manage." I played uninterested, though there was nothing I loved more than dismantling a machine and then putting it back together.

"Good. That old Ford's giving me trouble. Could use some help taking her apart."

My answer should've been *no*, on account of my pending departure, but instead I grunted, "Sure thing."

He hit me in the shoulder with his cap. "Great. See you at dinner."

Yeah. I wasn't joining anyone for dinner.

I wasted no time making my way to the second floor. Voices were audible behind the closed door, but too quiet to catch the gist of the conversation. I considered knocking, or tearing the door from its hinges, which made no fucking sense. I had no business worrying about how either one of those girls were holding up. Instead, I jogged up the stairs, slammed a beer, then cranked the shower to scalding.

They'd been alone for hours, and not once had I been called to comfort Mim. Not one damn time. Seemed she was getting better. Seemed the head doctor was as good as everyone kept telling me. Seemed I wouldn't be needed much longer.

I ducked my head under the water flow and rubbed my left pec. Maybe with some quality shut eye, the ache in my chest would go away.

"Got a minute?"

"Sure." I clutched the open door, towel hanging loose around my waist. I'd tried to sleep. A shower and two beers should've helped. They didn't. So, I'd taken another shower, Moriah on my mind while I jacked off. "Where's Mim?"

"With Rocky." Moriah scooted past, her palm brushing my chest, and damn if her touch didn't give me a swift kick in the gut.

"Rocky showed her how to build forts out of blankets and chairs. They watched movies on my tablet and fell asleep side by side. Lettie's staying with them. She shooed me to bed."

Swear to Christ the woman was torturing me. Thought I'd worked her out of my system in the shower, but those damn jeans, the way they hugged her ass and hips, that soft hair falling in her face, and those sweet fucking lips. I was hard again. And I wanted that woman so God damn bad.

Clueless to my agony, she continued. "The meeting went well. Thought you might want to know."

"Okay." I closed the door. Flipped the lock.

"Dr. Anderson says it'll be challenging, taking Mim home, but we found a good doctor just outside Shelbyville, and she can work with us every day if needed."

"So, you're leaving soon."

Moriah moved around the room, avoiding eye contact. "Yeah. I have to. My life is... My home is..." She swallowed, wincing, as if the words were painful.

"When you leaving?"

"Day after tomorrow."

I wanted to hit something. "She isn't ready."

"Doctor says she is."

I didn't give two fucks what the doctor said. That little girl wasn't ready for the real world. I wasn't ready for either one of them to disappear. "This our last night?"

She didn't answer.

I dropped the towel.

Moriah dropped her shoulders, taking me in. Dark circles rimmed her eyes. She'd lost weight since that night we'd met in the bar. The woman needed rest, but fuck, I needed her, and the way her cheeks flushed, and her lips parted, and her eyes pleaded, I couldn't ignore the fact that she needed me, too.

"Take off your clothes, Moriah." I grabbed my cock and stroked.

An exasperated sigh filled the room. She hesitated.

"I'm not wasting our last night together. Take off your fucking clothes."

She toed off one shoe. I tightened my fist around my hard dick, gave it a good rub.

"You're beautiful," she whispered, kicking off the other shoe.

"I'm ugly, gorgeous." I killed the lights before stepping closer. "You just haven't looked close enough."

Moonlight spilled through the window, highlighting her curves, bathing her face in a hazy glow. The ink on my back was well hidden in the dark, and I made to keep it that way, moving to keep Moriah between me and the window.

Her tongue dragged along her lower lip before disappearing.

"You're taking too long."

Her attention fell to the hand at my waist.

I pumped the full length again, then one more time, because those damn eyes begged for a show.

I took another step closer. Her chest rose and fell. Still, she hadn't removed any of the barriers between us.

"Five."

She gasped, her eyes widening, meeting mine.

"Four."

Her T-shirt landed at my feet.

Another stroke. Another step closer to that bangin' body.

"Three."

She fumbled with her belt buckle, her bottom lip curled between her teeth.

"Two." A heat blazed under my skin.

Moriah shimmied out of her jeans, crying out in frustration when they tangled at her feet.

God damn, she killed me.

"One."

I charged, ducking to catch her over my shoulder.

She squealed.

Whack! My hand met that perfect ass.

"Ow!" She squirmed so hard I damn near dropped her.

Three strides to the bed. The bed that made too much noise for what I had in mind.

I lowered to one knee, then the other, setting her on her feet, squeezing those hips so she couldn't retreat. "Hold still."

She pushed the wild hair out of her face.

Her white cotton panties were sinful in their modesty, but hell if they weren't the sexiest strips of cotton I'd ever seen. Especially after they hung shredded in my hands. "I'm gonna pound this pussy hard, gorgeous. Gonna give you a fuck you'll never forget."

I shoved my nose between her legs, then teased with a swipe of my tongue. The damn woman shivered, a full body blow.

"Gonna ruin you, baby. Fucking break you, then piece you back together so mine's the only cock that can fit in that sweet, tight cunt."

I moved one hand around her back, squeezing her ass, then shoved the other between her legs, rubbing the moisture there, teasing her opening, then rubbing her clit.

Trembling hands landed on my shoulders, those delicate fingers gripping tightly. Her hips curled into my touch, cranking my internal furnace to dangerous levels.

Greedy for her moans and her tits and her skin, I tugged her closer. Following my cue, she straddled my thighs, and lowered herself onto my lap, taking every hot, hard inch of my cock on the way down. She coiled her arms around my neck, I clamped mine around her back, and that sweet thing rode me hard, arching and bucking and bouncing on my thighs, chasing her pleasure, biting my lip, my ear, my neck, then tossing her head back, offering her chest to me.

I devoured those hard buds, sucking, biting, licking. Too damn soon, Moriah pushed me back, grabbing my shoulders, riding my cock, killing me with that hooded, lusty glare, those rosy cheeks and parted lips. When she stopped with the up and down, just rocking her hips, soaking me where our bodies were joined, she snaked her arms around me once again, panted my name, over and over, and came, her whole body going rigid, then limp against me.

Her pussy pulsed around my cock in erratic pulls and fuck, the last thing I wanted was a disconnect, but we hadn't taken time to grab a condom, and I was about to explode. Lifting her by the hips, I pulled out, then stroked my cock, once, twice, and still holding her close, I shot my load between us, and I didn't fucking care about the mess. I snaked both arms around my sweaty, gorgeous girl, tangled my fingers in her hair, stared at the wall, and bit my tongue to hold back the words, *stay, stay, stay.*

But that was fucked. Foolish. We'd enjoyed a few good bangs. I was leaving. She was leaving. I had another day. One more day of bullshit to get through, then she would be gone. Mim would be gone. I could get back to...to what? What the fuck did I have but wasted years, foul memories, and a shit-ton of regret?

I slapped Moriah's ass. "C'mon, gorgeous. Let's get you to bed."

"No. No. Just give me a few more minutes. Let me enjoy the fantasy awhile longer." Her head grew heavy on my shoulder.

"Fantasy, huh?"

"I'm never gonna meet someone with a body like yours. Someone who kisses or touches me like you do. Someone who makes me feel like..."

"Like what?"

"Like a woman. Feminine, and sexy, and..." She dragged her nails up and down my back. "I don't know. Wanted, I guess. I feel wanted, or needed, and it just feels really effin' good." She walked her fingers up my neck and then patted my cheek. "So please, hold me a minute, before we have to go back to reality."

Reality.

What a fucking bitch the real world could be.

"Moriah."

"Yeah?"

"You could stay the summer. Give Mim more time to heal." What the fuck was I asking?

"I can't. I have to get home. Get Mim settled. Find a job. I have to get back to my life."

"Back to the real world," I mumbled into her hair.

She sighed.

I wanted to punch something.

Instead, I begged, "Stay with me tonight."

With a yawn, she replied, "Yeah. A sleepover. I'd love that."

CHAPTER 8

Moriah

"DID YOU GUYS HAVE a fun sleepover?" I pushed my plate away, the scrambled eggs untouched, the pancake missing only two bites.

Mim shot a sideways glance at Rocky. Rocky shoved a forkful of pancake into his mouth, nodding.

Lettie yawned. "They were giggling all night long. It's not fair, really, how they can be so chipper this morning." She lifted her mug to her mouth and winked at me over the rim.

Mim turned her head away, as if trying to hide her smile.

"So." Tango strode into the room, rubbing his hands together, like priming for a secret he couldn't wait to share. "Since today is our last full day together, I thought you guys would like to go out on the boat for a few hours."

Rocky hopped in his seat, dropping his utensil. "Fishing?"

"Well, little man, the fishing boat isn't big enough for all of us. I was thinking *our* boat would be more fun."

He shot his dad a glare. "We don't have a boat."

"We do now." Tucker strode in, his blond hair a tousled mess, his blue eyes blazing, his jeans hanging low on his waist, and a Metallica tee hugging him in all the right places.

Truly, the man belonged in a California tourism commercial. "Dad and Tito are backing her into the water as we speak."

"What's going on?" Rocky lowered his voice, cocking his head.

Tango squatted to Rocky's level. Winked. "We bought a boat big enough for everyone."

"Oh, my God." Rocky clutched his chest. "A fast one?"

"Oh yeah." Tango nodded, fighting a smile.

Rocky tackled his dad. Tucker jumped in, grabbed the boy by his waist, and flipped him upside down, dusting the floor with his black hair.

"Mim! We get to go on the boat." Rocky squealed, then laughed a deep, throaty, infectious laugh.

I was so enthralled by the interaction between the boys, I hadn't noticed Mim scooting closer. But Lord have mercy, did I feel every inch of her when she snuggled against my side and laid her head on my chest, seeking comfort. With me.

Tears bloomed, a few escaping, a slow glide down my cheek before I caught them with my knuckle.

I ducked my head, swallowed the threatening emotional breakdown, and whispered, "Do you want to go on the boat, Mim?"

She fisted the hem of my shirt.

"It's okay if you don't want to go." I curled an arm around her shoulder, afraid she might shrug me off, but she didn't and sweet Jesus I needed to lock myself in the closet and cry for a week. "But you have to let me know, Little One. You have to let me know if it's a yes or a no."

Mim turned her head and watched Rocky wrestle with his uncle on the floor. Rocky threw a punch in Tucker's gut, and Mim buried her face in my boob. It was then I realized she wasn't afraid of the boat, but the roughhousing.

"Hey. Mim." I tucked a finger under her chin and urged her to look up. "They're just playing. See? Rocky's laughing.

He's happy. People do that sometimes. They're pretend fighting. None of those boys would ever hurt each other. And none of them would ever hurt you."

Tango must've overheard our conversation. He tore Rocky away from his uncle, whispered in his ear, then set him on his feet. The little man came our way. "C'mon Mim. The boat is so much fun. And I can teach you how to fish. I only have one fishing pole, but I can share."

Mim studied Rocky with scrutiny only an adult should be able to pull off, the tip of her pinky finger between her teeth. After a long spell, she hopped off the chair, and took Rocky's offered hand.

I scrunched my face, fighting another sob.

Tango stared a hole straight through me.

"Hey, Rocky." Lettie stood and held her hand toward her grandson. "Let's go see if we can help Mim find the right clothes to wear on the boat."

The kids dashed down the hall without a backward glance, Lettie and Tucker following behind.

Tango invaded my personal space in two strides. "You okay?"

I nodded, biting my lip against a wave of nausea. "Did you see? She leaned on me. She let me touch her."

"Yeah. I saw."

"She's gonna be okay."

"I think so." Exotic green eyes narrowed. "But are you?"

Aside from the overwhelming emotions choking me, I'd never been better. "I haven't felt this good in a long time."

As if on cue, the room spun, everything in my stomach clenched, and I dashed to the kitchen garbage, my breakfast making a violent reappearance.

Tango stood in wait, a cold, wet dishtowel in hand, a sad smile on his face.

When I could stand, he asked, "That good, huh?"

"I'm so embarrassed. I'm sorry. I have a sensitive stomach. This happens when I'm under a lot of stress."

"You gonna be okay out on the water? You look a little green."

"I'll be fine, and a day on the lake will be good for Mim."

"Yeah. Something healing about the water." He offered nothing more but shooed me out of the way and tied the bag I'd just barfed into.

"Oh, God. Tango. Let me do that." Mortified, I grabbed for the trash.

With one swift motion, he twisted to keep me from advancing, and lifted the garbage from the container. "We're heading out in about thirty minutes. You go get ready."

I stared at the bag in his hand, my vision blurring.

"Moriah."

Matthew never would've cleaned my mess. He'd have left the room in a cloud of dust. Whenever I would get sick, he'd avoid me for a week, to make sure I wasn't contagious.

"Hey, Moriah."

Ugh. Matthew. I hadn't had time to miss him, but he still hadn't called, and that stung. But the more time I spent in Whisper Springs, the more I realized how blind I'd been to my boyfriend's selfish ways. He was waiting for me to make the first move, to grovel, apologize, admit I'd been foolish to break up with him over the phone. To break up with him at all. Before Mom's funeral, before Mim, I had been that girl. The girl who caved. Admitted fault, even when the fault belonged elsewhere. That girl needed a permanent vacation.

A hand landed on my shoulder, squeezing gently. "You sure you're okay?"

"Yeah. Yeah. I'm fine." I was, for the first time in a long time, and suddenly so much joy filled my heart I feared I would burst.

I had no right touching the man I hardly knew, but there was no stopping the crazy. I threw my arms around his waist and squeezed. "You guys are so nice to me, and I'm so grateful, and happy, and these past weeks have been too much, and..." Oh God. The tears again.

Tango wrapped his free arm around my shoulder and gave me the ol' there, there. Oh, how I needed that hug. But wow, how I wished the arms around me belonged to the man who'd tortured three orgasms from me mere hours before.

We lingered in our awkward embrace for too long, only breaking apart when a throat cleared.

A voice full of jagged glass came over my shoulder, angry, and on the verge of violent. "Slade know you're rubbing all over other ladies, Pretty Boy?"

Tango's arms constricted, holding me in place, more protective than possessive. "Fuck off, Dane."

"I'll fuck off when you get your hands off my girl."

"Your girl?" I squeaked, stumbling back a step.

Tango dropped his arm, releasing me. "The fuck?"

Dane was furious. Red-faced. Eyes dark as death. Hands fisted at his sides. His jaw clenched tight, every vein and sinew in his neck bulging.

He avoided my gaze, staring over my head at Tango, as if assessing the most efficient way to kill the competition. Clearly, those two had history. Although I was curious, I wanted no part in whatever was about to happen.

His girl? Seriously?

Didn't matter. The kids could return any moment, and the last thing they needed to see was two grown men acting like teenagers.

I shoved a palm into Dane's torso. "Get out."

His feet didn't budge, but his chest rose and fell in short, sharp jerks.

I pinched his nipple through his shirt and twisted hard until he aimed his glare my way. "Go cool off somewhere."

He looked down at my offending hand.

"You want Mim to see you like this?"

Swear to the good Lord above, his mountain of muscles caved under my palm. He shot another glance at Tango, then shook his head, shrugged away from my touch, and stormed out of the room.

Tango raked his fingers through his thick hair. "Wanna tell me what that was—"

"Nope. No. None of your business."

"None of my business?" He pointed down the empty hallway. "He damn near ripped my head off."

True. "Wanna tell me why there's so much tension between the two of you?"

"No."

"Then we're done talking."

"Moriah. Listen." He scratched the back of his head. His glare dropping to the floor, then bouncing back to me. "Dane is, uh...well, he's um..."

I threw up a hand to stop his rant. "Doesn't matter. Does. Not. Matter. I'm leaving tomorrow. Dane and I will never see each other again. So, that's that."

"Okay. Yeah. Well." Holding the trash bag high, he announced, "I'm gonna dump this. Meet you outside?"

"Sure."

Mind reeling after Dane's *my girl* comment, I stomped up the stairs two by two. When I reached the top, a wrecking ball hit my gut, the hallway spun, and all air was forced from my lungs. Faster than I could protest, Dane shoved through the door to my room, kicked it shut behind him, turned to engage the lock, then tossed me on the bed.

He crawled over me, his knees bracing my thighs, his face hovering inches from mine. "You were crying. Why?"

That was the last thing I'd expected to hear, and instead of explaining, I mumbled, "What?"

"You were crying. What happened? Do I need to kill that pretty boy motherfucker? Did he say something to upset you?"

"No."

"Good." He dropped a hard kiss on my nose, then pinned me with a cold, hard, assessing stare. "But he touched you."

I rolled my eyes. What else could I do? Everything about the past ten minutes had been beyond ridiculous. "What's the deal with you two?"

He dipped lower, dropping his nose into my hair, and inhaled. "You smell like him now."

"Are you insane?"

Dane straightened, leaning back on his heels, my legs still pinned beneath him. "You fucked *me* last night." He shoved a finger into his own chest. "We shared a bed. How the fuck would I be okay with you smelling like another man?"

Heat blazed in my cheeks. Other places, too, which only added to my befuddlement. "I don't know what's happening right now."

He tugged the hem of my sundress up until my belly was exposed, then laid his hand over my skin, searing me like a cattle brand. "I'm gonna touch you. Rub on you. Fuck you until you smell like me again."

Sweet mother of mercy why did that turn me on?

"The kids are right next door."

He slid his hand lower, then gripped my panties. "Then you better be quiet."

He shifted, rising on his knees, tugged a condom out of his back pocket and held it between his teeth, then yanked my undies to my thighs, grabbed my hips, and flipped me to my stomach.

I tried to scramble away, steal a second to find my bearings. Dane grabbed my hips again, lifting in one hard jerk, forcing me to my knees, my ass in the air, my face smashed into the bedding.

"Another man had his hands on you." The mattress shifted. A sharp sting bit my ass. A hard, swollen cock slid between my wet folds, the stretch so divine I trembled.

My whole body came alive, my skin tightening and tingling, my belly swirling with delicious warmth, my heart and head warring over *you shouldn't let him use you this way*, and *oh God, this man can use me forever*.

"My ass. My tits." He pounded into me, grunting a new proclamation with each thrust. "My pussy. My fuckin' girl. Nobody touches my girl."

Face buried in soft cotton, I couldn't respond. Not that he would've heard a thing I said. Honestly, I don't know what I would've said, because, holy effin' shit the man was relentless and aggressive and touching me everywhere with hands and lips. I loved every volatile, confusing second of his reclamation, or whatever the hell he thought he was doing.

The man was strong, and thorough. He could break me if he were so inclined, but somehow I knew he wouldn't cause any physical damage. He was fierce, but confusing in the way he took me, cherishing my body with light touches, yet holding me captive with possessive grips.

His grunts were heady. His words, filthy. The rhythmic slap of his hips against my ass and his balls against my clit a raw, beautiful anthem to our short story. I came fast and hard, and when my insides tightened around him, he gripped my hair and pulled me upright, holding me tight with one arm cinched around my waist, the other my chest. He bit my earlobe and then grunted, "What are you doing to me? What the fuck are you doing to me?" while he pumped, hard and fast and desperate, the bed scraping across the floor.

He came, grunting into my hair, his arms coiling tighter, his body taut and tense and vibrating.

We fell side by side on the bed, heavy breaths and disheveled clothing. A warm breeze caressed my exposed skin, and I shimmied, pulling my panties back into place, tugging my skirt over my bare ass.

"What was that about?" I rolled my head to find sad eyes roaming the length of me. "Not that I'm complaining. But seriously? What the eff?"

Dane flipped to his back, throwing one arm over his head, while the other lay over his stomach, inches from his still semi-hard cock. "I hate that fucker."

"Yeah, you made that obvious." My first instinct was to reach out, touch him, offer comfort, be the woman to soothe his wounded ego. But I had to stop being that woman. "Doesn't explain what you just did to me, though."

He huffed. "Not hard to figure out, gorgeous." He rolled into the sitting position, then made his way to the bathroom, already removing the condom. "I like you. He touched you."

"Dane."

Silence.

Through the crack in the half open door, I caught sight of a broken man. Posture load-bearing, face a mess and hardened with disgust while he studied his reflection.

There was so much I didn't know about Dane.

A man who clearly carried his own unbearable burdens.

Ugh. What the hell was I doing? I hopped off the bed, wiggled out of my dress and rifled through my suitcase until I found my favorite cutoffs. Mid scramble to get them over my hips, Dane cleared his throat.

"Only three things in this world I've ever cared about," he mumbled, drawing my attention from my button to the bathroom door, where a thousand pounds of brutal male filled the space. "He's taken all of them from me."

That face, all beat to hell, only made him more attractive. What did that say about me?

"That explains nothing." I rifled through my choice of shirts, happy when I found my well-worn Miranda Lambert concert tee, because right about then, I needed some girl power vibes.

I refused to look at him, all brooding and sexy, with his husky voice and *I dare you to fuck with me* glare.

Until he said, "He's not getting you, too."

"Getting me?" I snapped, my nerves on fire. "I'm nobody's to get."

I gave him a minute to counter. When he didn't, I shoved my feet into my Vans.

"Listen. I get it. You don't wanna talk. That's fine." I gestured between the two of us. "This was fun. But it was temporary. Thanks for the orgasms." I paused, waiting for a response, hoping for a reaction, anything to keep me in the game, in his presence for a while longer.

Dane merely dropped his head.

His silence spoke volumes.

The door was maybe three steps away, but the journey seemed impossible, and I wanted a rewind button. I wanted to go back to being naked with those strong arms around me, and that thick, commanding voice grunting dirty words while he made me feel alive and beautiful and wanted.

The door knob was just out of reach when his gruff voice blew across my neck. "Why were you crying?"

Eyes pinched shut to hold the tears at bay, I sucked in a dose of oxygen, and turned, leaning back against the wood. I met his weary gaze.

"Mim let me touch her today. She leaned on me. She almost hugged me. It was perfect, and I had a little emotional meltdown. Then I threw up, and Tango cleaned my mess, and I started thinking about how Matthew never cleaned a puke mess or took care of me when I was sick. And I realized how nice everyone has been to me, and how much I'm going to miss everyone, and well, I had another meltdown."

Dane stared at something over my head, eyes unfocused. His chest rose and fell, his muscles bunching, rolling, almost as if building courage. After holding one deep breath for excruciating seconds, he blurted, "You don't have to leave, you know."

I did. I had to leave. But the words wouldn't solidify.

He braced a hand on the door above my head. Then dipped, catching my gaze. "You could stay here."

"My life is back home. My friends..." I wanted to say family, or job, but neither of those were true anymore. Back home, I had my favorite coffee shop. I adored my doctor, and Frank and Julissa from the bank. My neighbors were great. Sure, I had friends, but soon after Mom got sick, I had lost touch with most of them. Between work, Mom, and Matthew, there hadn't been time to maintain any meaningful relationships.

But still. Shelbyville was home. Familiar. Comfortable. A great town to raise a child.

Dane tucked a finger under my chin, drawing my attention from his massive chest back to his bruised face. "If you had a job here, would you stay?"

"No," came out breathy and spineless. I placed a hand on his stomach, the connection grounding me. "And why are you asking me to stay? You've said yourself that you're leaving the first chance you get." I gave him a wide-open door. *Say something.* I needed him to tell me he wanted me to stay because he wanted *me*. Because he felt the same crazy connection as I did. Because he was as attached to Mim as I was. Because he would miss us.

Instead, the hulking man dropped his arms. Stepped away. Scratched his chin. Grunted, "You're right."

An unbearable ache welled in my chest, spreading through my limbs. "I have to go. They're waiting for me." I turned to leave, then turned back. "Will we see you tonight?"

"Not sure," he mumbled, roughing a hand through his hair.

I lingered too long before finding the courage to leave.

I had one foot over the threshold when "Moriah," came over my shoulder.

"Yeah?" I whispered.

"Turn around."

I did.

Dane kissed me. A kiss I felt from the tingles on my scalp to the curling of my toes.

He stepped back, holding me captive with a glare searing enough to leave a permanent scar. "Have fun today."

"See you tonight?" And then I added, "Please?" And then, so I didn't sound too pathetic, I threw in, "Mim needs to say goodbye. She needs that closure." And for the final hook, "She's going to miss you."

Dane turned his face away from me, gaze aimed out the window. The hard lines of his jaw worked, his muscles flexing. "Yeah. See you tonight," he said, so strained, so quiet, my chest constricted.

The door closed with a quiet click that jolted every nerve ending, and the sting of that goodbye swelled into a sticky ache that would torture me for eternity.

I met everyone downstairs. We had a great boat ride, the sky blue, the sun hot, the company fun and carefree, and I painted on a smile that lasted the whole day.

I pressed my ear against the wall. Dane spoke to Mim, his words mostly a vibration through the barrier between us. He talked. They laughed. I cried. More talking. A few giggles. For two hours I sat on the floor, head to the wall, lulled by the tender, deep timber of his voice. My heart ached for Mim, because that was their goodbye. Their private farewell. She would always remember Dane. He would always be the hero in her eyes. The man she'd measure every other man in her life against.

The room went quiet, and my heart thump, thump, thumped in anticipation. Our goodbye would be next. Our goodbye would be painful, and bittersweet, because I too, in a sense, was ruined for any other man. Nobody would ever hold a candle to the man who made my pulse race. My skin tingle. My soul expand.

I waited on the floor until footsteps moved across the room, down the hall, and stopped outside my door.

I waited for the knock.

The floor squeaked. Heavy breathing.

Soft shuffles.

More footsteps. Retreating.

I sat on the floor another ten minutes before hauling myself into bed, where I cried myself to sleep.

At 6:00 AM, the alarm beeped. I packed my suitcase, cleaned my borrowed room, then tiptoed into Mim's room to pack her few belongings as well. She'd awoken by the time I'd slid the last puzzle box onto the shelf in the tiny closet.

"Good morning, Sleeping Beauty," I whispered, sliding next to her. "Are you ready to start our new adventure?"

Goop-filled eyes blinked at me, filling my heart with trepidation. We lay face to face, and I hated the distance between us. "Are you scared, Mim?"

She reached up, touched my hair, then my eyebrows, then my nose. Then she wrestled her body out of the bedding. Slid to the floor and ran into the bathroom. When she came out, she ran back to the bed, hopped up next to me, and handed me her hairbrush. Then that little girl turned her back to me and waited for me to brush her hair.

She wasn't scared. She was ready.

The entire Slade family waited downstairs for us, gathered around the breakfast table. Tango, Rocky, and Slade were there, as well as Tito and his wife, Tuuli. Lettie held Lucia. Tucker and Aida stood at the stove. James poured a cup of coffee.

After breakfast, Tito took me aside and handed me a large, stuffed envelope. "Everything you need is in here."

I looked inside and thumbed through the paperwork. The lies I would protect until my dying day.

"Birth records. Social Security number. Adoption records. Medical history."

All of it fake. Every scroll of the ink meant to protect my niece.

"If you need anything...anything at all, I've got you. Don't ever hesitate to call."

"You've done so much already."

"That's what I do. That's what we do here. Got me?"

"Thank you doesn't seem adequate."

"Knowing she's going to grow up right is all the thanks we need."

"Well," Lettie started as she came around the corner. "Are we ready?"

I pulled Tito into a tight embrace. Kissed his cheek, then made my way around the room, saying my goodbyes.

Mim and Rocky slid into the back seat of Lettie's truck. We rolled away from the property. I searched for Dane, then tucked that pain away while we headed for the airport, doing my damnedest to ignore my broken heart.

CHAPTER 9

Dane

"YOU HIDING IN HERE?" A booted foot tapped my ankle.

Had it been any other voice interrupting my quietude, as I lay on the cool floor under the old beater, I'd have let the profanities loose. Instead, I grunted, "Nah. Just working."

A loud exhale. "S'pose you're fixing to leave soon, too."

"Soon as we're finished with this engine."

James squatted. I couldn't see his face from my position under the truck, but I felt his glare, sensed his hesitation before he said, "Listen. Dane. It's none of my business, but I reckon a guy like you hasn't had much in the way of stability."

"You're right. None of your business."

He huffed. "You've got something stable here, if you want it."

"Don't need charity, Mr. Slade. I was here for the girl." Girls. God damn those girls.

"And Rocky? What about him? Doesn't go unnoticed the way you track his every move."

Fucker had to go there. "He's an interesting kid."

"He's your only living relative. You okay leaving him behind?"

What the hell was the old geezer's problem? "He doesn't know who I am, and it has to stay that way."

"You saved his life."

"I killed his mother."

"You didn't kill her."

"I didn't stop them."

"But you would've, given the choice." There was no question in his statement, only certainty.

"You don't know that." I dropped the nut splitter and growled, "You don't know shit about me."

"You saved Rocky. Saved my daughter on more than one occasion. Rescued Mim. I know enough."

"What is it with you people?" I scooted out from under the Ford, and, still on my back, pointed a finger in the man's face. "I've put to ground more than a few deserving pricks in my life. I have a criminal record longer than the interstate. Yet, every one of you looks at me like I'm a God damned fallen hero who needs saving."

James face reddened. His lips pinched tight.

I rolled to my knees and then pushed to stand. "Wanna know a secret?"

He didn't answer, but stumbled to his feet as well, leaning against the truck bed with one arm. "Everything that happened with Rocky? Yeah. That was me. The night Tango fucked my cousin and made that perfect little boy? That was my doing. I hated that fucking, pretty boy, entitled asshole and I wanted your daughter. So, I gave Addy the drugs she slipped into Tango's drinks that night. He never would've cheated on Slade without them. I encouraged Addy to do what she did. I made sure Slade found them fucking in his daddy's Mercedes."

Fucking hell, I'd never said those words out loud.

The purge continued. "I watched Slade run away. I followed, watched her crumple in the street—crying, broken, bleeding. And I waited. I waited until she was hollow, and wouldn't turn me away, and then I picked her up and made her all better. Pretty fucking heroic, yeah?"

"Dane," James grunted, slapping a hand to his chest.

"What, James? What? You gonna tell me everything is okay? Because it's not. I set the wheels in motion. Addison is dead because of me. Rocky almost died, because of me. Tango's mother is dead because of me. If my father had succeeded in killing Slade? Yeah, that would be on me, too."

"I'll fucking destroy you," Tango's angry voice boomed.

Jesus H. Christ. Shittiest day ever. Tango had heard everything. I didn't turn to look. I knew what was about to go down—well-deserved retribution. I steeled my spine, waiting for the first strike.

James fell against the truck, struck hard by my admission. Good. He needed to know the kind of scum he was dealing with.

I turned to face Tango's wrath, but a heavy hand clamped my shoulder.

"Dane." James's voice hovered, weak and strained.

His hand slipped from my shoulder, and his body fell against mine before slamming to the ground.

"Dane." Moriah sighed. "I'm so glad you called. I hated driving away without saying goodbye."

"Where are you right now?"

"We're on the freeway. Almost to the airport exit."

"Tell Lettie to pull over. Right now."

"What's going on?"

"It's James. Gonna need you to take over driving. Turn around and head back to town."

"I don't under—"

"No time to explain," I interrupted. "When Lettie's in the passenger seat, give her the phone."

I waited, listening while Moriah gave Lettie instructions. I heard the car doors slam, heavy breathing, worried questions.

"Okay. I'm behind the wheel. What's going on?"

"Give Lettie the phone."

"Dane?"

"Do it!" I snapped, nerves stretched to the breaking point.

Lettie's voice came through, shaky and high-pitched. "What's happening?"

Heart in my fucking throat, I gave Lettie the lowdown, explained that James was on his way to Whisper Springs Medical Center, that Tucker was in the ambulance with him, and everyone else had followed behind.

"We're on our way," Lettie cried before the phone went dead, leaving me alone with the truck, and the silence, and the God damn crushing weight on my chest.

Suppose that would've been a good time for me to make my exit. Give the man a heart attack, then disappear.

I looked around the massive garage, bent to retrieve the tools left on the ground, then fell on my ass, adrenaline draining, brain a jumbled mess.

Hours later, I'd moved from the ground to the front seat of the old beater. I'd tinkered with the stereo. Polished the vinyl. Washed the windows.

Lettie's car rolled up the long driveway just as I headed back to the house. My feet planted to the gravel. Moriah hopped down from behind the wheel. Rocky and Mim followed behind.

The kids dashed off to the tree swing. Moriah came my way, her steps measured, her eyes red, her hair a beautiful, windblown mess.

"How is he?" I asked, the words sticking at the back of my throat.

"Not sure. He's in surgery. I... " She looked down at her feet. Wiped under her eyes. Took two long breaths. "I didn't feel right being at the hospital. It's a family thing, you know?" She looked over her shoulder at the kids, a sad smile breaking through. "I thought it'd be easier for everyone if I brought them back here."

Fuck, the woman was selfless. I couldn't stop from pulling her against my chest. She didn't cry, but she trembled, her arms tightening around my waist, her face buried in my filthy shirt, and God damn how I wanted to make everything better.

"You missed your flight."

"Yeah. We missed our flight."

We stood in silence, wrapped around each other. I wasn't a hugger. I was a fuck 'em hard and get away kind of guy. So why did our embrace feel so necessary, so right?

"You didn't say goodbye," she mumbled into my chest.

Right. Fuck 'em hard and get away.

I dropped my arms and stepped back. "I couldn't."

"Why?"

She stared up at me with those huge, curious eyes, not a lick of judgement in them, only raw honesty, and I could've warned her away. I could've let the bitter, angry asshole loose, scared the shit out of her, so that when she did go back home, she'd go knowing she'd dodged a bullet, because being with a guy like me was dangerous, deadly even. But something held me back. Something in my chest—unfamiliar and uncomfortable.

"I didn't say goodbye, because I didn't trust myself not to fall to my knees and beg you to stay. I didn't trust myself not to pin you to the wall last night and fuck you into compliance.

Didn't trust myself not to throw you into that damn truck and disappear, hide you away in a cabin in the mountains, and keep you locked up, so you'd be mine and I'd never have to share you."

Moriah opened her mouth to speak, but Rocky yelled, "Hey! We're hungry. What's for lunch?"

She held my gaze, her eyes full of questions, her jaw still slack, on the verge of blurting a rejection that would kill me, no doubt. Because a woman like Moriah would never consider a future with a dirty, dangerous criminal.

I took advantage of her hesitation, taking away her opportunity for rebuff, and turned toward the kids. "Pizza sound good? How about we head into town, get some Pete's Famous Pizza."

Rocky yelled, "Yay! Pizza!"

I turned to Moriah still silent, still staring.

"I'm gonna go clean up. Be down in ten." I retreated, jogging toward the house, leaving no room for deeper contemplation.

We'd eat. We'd keep the kids busy. I'd get more time with Moriah before we both had to disappear.

"My grandpa is really sick," Rocky blurted, after his third slice of pepperoni.

The kid had been unusually quiet and sluggish during our ride into town. Fuckin' killed me, that sad expression he wore.

And Mim? Hell, that little angel scooted closer to her buddy, touched his cheek as if testing for tears, then leaned her head on his shoulder like she was put on Earth to be his comfort.

Moriah shot me a sideways glance, one brow raised in surprise, then cleared her throat. "Well, Rocky. The doctors are trying hard to help him right now. And your mom said she'd call us as soon as they know how he's doing."

"He's strong, buddy. He's stubborn, too." I couldn't help myself. I leaned over the table and whispered in his ear. "Maybe he did it on purpose, because he didn't want Mim to leave yet."

Rocky laughed, snorting. "Yeah. Grandpa would be crazy like that."

The smiles returned. We finished lunch. Stopped at the city park on the way home. Then drove back to the mansion.

Rocky grabbed Mim's hand the second we cleared the door. "Can we go to Mim's room and make Grandpa a card?"

"Yeah. Sure." Moriah sighed, breathless and clearly weary.

"I'll head up with them. You must have a ton of calls to make."

"Yeah. Yeah. I need to reschedule my flight." She turned and headed up the stairs. "Call my job contacts. Mom's attorney..."

I followed, mostly ignoring her checklist, until I heard, "Call Matthew back."

I'd have been less surprised, or crushed, if she'd dropped a jet engine on my head.

She jumped when I clamped a hand around her waist, then shivered when I pulled her against me. "What was that you just said?"

"Matthew finally called. Said he wants to talk."

"You told him to fuck off, right?"

Moriah wiggled in my arms, enough to let me know she wasn't about to take my shit, but not enough to make me let go. "Of course not."

"Why the hell not?"

"Why would I?" She lifted her chin. "I'm not taking him back, if that's what you think, but closure would be nice."

"Closure for what? You gave him the only closure he deserves that night we met in the bar."

"Well. Yes. I suppose you're right. I mean. Sure. I ended things. I meant it, too. But he deserves to know why."

"No. No he doesn't. He let you go. End of story. He can't figure out why you gave him the boot, that's on him. Not your responsibility. I mean, seriously, you've been here how long, and he only now calls?"

"Dane."

"The guy's a fuckin' douche, you ask me."

"Dane."

"What kind of prick lets his woman fly clear across the country days after she's lost her mother, to hang out with a bunch of strangers, and bring home a child that may or may not be the daughter of her long-lost sister. The sister she only just found out was dead."

"Dane."

"I get my hands on the pathetic piece of shit, I'll—"

Smack. Moriah landed a hard whack across my cheek, effectively ending my tirade, unwittingly stirring my blood.

I glared at the wall over her head and counted, *one, two, three* before aiming my ire her way, preparing to warn her of all the reasons striking me was dangerous.

Before I could speak, the little minx grabbed my shirt, lifted up on her toes, and short circuited my brain with a punishing kiss. She pulled away for a brief moment, said, "I like you, too, Dane," then attacked again.

I like you, too. That's what she got out of my tirade? I grabbed her waist and spun, pinning her to the wall. Then I took control, showed her how dangerous I could be, biting, sucking, pinching, groping, dry humping her against the wall. And fuuuck, she took my advances like a champ.

Giggles came from the top of the stairs and I dropped Moriah like a hot potato. One deep breath and I looked over my shoulder.

Rocky and Mim stared down at us, bright smiles, and belly laughs, and hell if my face didn't heat like an overworked engine.

"Shoot." Moriah mumbled, wiping her mouth with the back of her hand. "Shoot."

I looked down at her bright eyes, those red cheeks, those swollen lips, and hell if I didn't laugh, too.

"Busted," I whispered, claiming her hand and dragging her to the top of the stairs.

She headed toward Mim's room, but I grabbed her shoulders and aimed her the opposite direction. "Go do what you gotta do. I'll hang with the kids."

With a nod, she turned. Stopped. Whipped around to face me again. "We need to talk about what just happened."

"We need to talk about you staying in Whisper Springs."

"You know I can't."

"We'll see about that."

I nudged her toward her door, smacked her ass, then joined the kids in Mim's room, making myself comfortable on the bed while they dug paper and crayons out of the closet and set them up on the small table.

When I'd had a moment to clear my head, I yanked my cell out of my pocket, pulled up a number I wasn't supposed to have, and hoped to God the man would answer.

"Carlos Rossi speaking."

"Time to pay the piper, old man.

The kids had just finished a cartoon marathon when footsteps fell heavy in the hallway. Tango pushed through the door, his fiery red eyes meeting mine. His glare was not one of anger, though. The guy looked damn near defeated.

I didn't have to ask. The fact he'd come alone, and he wasn't kicking my ass, told me everything I needed to know.

Fuck.

Moriah sat up straight, then started to stand, but Tango stopped her with a head shake. He stepped closer to his son, cleared his throat. Blinked. Cleared it again, then, voice hoarse, he whispered, "Hey, Rockster. I need you to come with me, buddy."

"Dad!" Rocky yelled, jumping off the bed and into his father's arms, wrapping around him like a monkey hitching a ride. That was all it took for Tango to lose his shit. He buried his face in Rocky's neck and sobbed.

Rocky squeezed his dad tighter, and for the first time in my life, I didn't envy that man. How the fuck did you tell your kid his grandpa had just died?

Father and son left the room. Mim watched them leave, then looked at me with a worried expression. Moriah joined Mim on the bed, and while she started to explain, I followed Tango, hanging back out of respect.

Downstairs, Tucker and Aida followed Lettie into her room, her face a ghostly white, her expression blank.

Tango carried his son to the main living room, where Slade waited. The three of them huddled together. Not a chance in hell I was gonna stick around for that show. The kid would be devastated. I couldn't watch while his parents broke his heart.

I turned to leave, made it to the kitchen, when I heard Rocky scream, "No, Daddy. Not Grandpa. No!"

My knees buckled, the weight of his emotion a kick in the gut.

James was gone.

One of the good guys.

Tucker's daughter started to cry, her wails carrying down the hall. I rinsed my face in the kitchen sink, grabbed one of the baby's bottles out the fridge, and made my way back to Lettie's room. Aida struggled with her daughter, who was clearly not happy with all the negative vibes, and although I wasn't family, although I did not belong in that mansion, I could not watch them struggle and do nothing.

I cleared my throat, catching Tucker's attention, held up the bottle, and gestured to the baby. Aida shot me glare. Tucker whispered something in her ear, and Aida passed over her daughter. Fuck me, that little angel smelled sweet, like innocence, and I hoped to God nobody noticed my deep inhale.

"We'll be upstairs," I said.

Tucker nodded in thanks, and I left them to their grief.

The baby cried and fidgeted in my arms all the way back to Mim's room, but the moment I set her on the bed next to the girls, she quieted, hiccupped, then crawled into Mim's lap, snatching the book out of her hand.

Mim smiled.

Moriah smiled.

Jesus. Fuck. Those ladies had my guts all twisted.

My chest collapsed, that large muscle inside crumbling into large, sharp chunks. The room shrank around me. I handed Moriah the bottle, trusting she knew what to do. "You good if I disappear for a bit?"

She tilted her head, her hair falling over her shoulder, soft and touchable. "You okay?"

My throat clogged. I nodded. "Need to get some air."

"We're good here."

I left through the back hallway, avoiding the grief-stricken family, and made my way to the garage. I kicked at the dirt where James had fallen, where I'd pumped his chest, waiting for the ambulance to arrive. Where I'd begged him not to give up. Not to die.

A socket wrench lay by the front tire, taunting me. I scooped the tool off the ground and whacked my head on the rear-view mirror on the way up.

"Fuck!" That shit hurt. But that blast of pain was what I needed. The fuse lit. I screamed at the truck. Threw two punches at the door, then attacked the hood with the wrench. I beat that old beater to shit, cursing the damn thing, giving her the brunt of all my rage.

When I couldn't lift my arms for another strike, or pull in a full breath, I dropped my ass to the ground, scooted under the engine, and continued where I'd left off, fixing that damn engine, like I'd promised James I would.

"Damn allergies," I mumbled, blinking the moisture from my eyes.

CHAPTER 10

Moriah

I SWIPED THE MOISTURE from my eyes. "I need a couple of days to consider your offer." Blink. Blink. I would not cry.

"Take as much time as you need. We look forward to hearing from you."

"Thank you." I hoped to God the nice woman couldn't hear the tremble in my voice.

I pushed the little red button on my phone, my thumb bending at an odd angle with the force of pressure. One deep breath. Then another. "What the actual eff?" I asked no one, tossing my cell on the bed.

Mim bounced out of the bathroom, hairbrush in hand, and bee-lined to her suitcase.

Slumping into the chair, I bent to grab my shoes, then stared at the floor, my mind a swirling vortex of hows, whys, and what-ifs.

A job offer. Monday through Friday. 401k. Full benefits. Starting salary? Twice what I made last year.

"What the eff?" I mumbled again, slumped forward, elbows to knees, face in my palms. The offer was beyond perfect.

Problem was, the job was not in Shelbyville. The job was in Whisper Springs with the Rossi Corporation. I hadn't applied to any jobs outside of Shelbyville. Meaning, one of the Slades or the Rossis were responsible. I mean, seriously, who offers someone a job sight unseen?

Too good to be true? Without a doubt. Was I foolish to consider the offer? Ugh. How could I make a rational decision considering the upheaval I'd already faced?

Or could I? Could I? How could I?

No. No. I needed to get Mim home and settled. Then I could think straight. Make the right decision for both of us.

Right. Home. Why did that word sound so foreign? Taste so bitter?

"Ready, Little Lady?" I asked, shoving my feet into my Vans and pushing to stand.

Mim didn't look up, but she nodded, then pulled the handle on her mini suitcase and dragged it toward the door, her hair bouncing in defiant waves, her chin held high and brave.

I glanced around the room, checking for any items we might have left behind, then grabbed my own luggage and headed out, down the long hallway, then the stairs, out the back door, and around to the front of the house, where the yellow cab waited.

Purposely avoiding the family, knowing they were in no mindset for goodbyes, I left a letter of condolence on the kitchen counter, knowing that would be sufficient considering the circumstances. The family needed their privacy to grieve.

I had also slipped a note under Dane's door, explaining I thought it better to avoid putting Mim through another round of farewells. So, everything wrapped up, I buckled my niece in the cab, tucked our things in the trunk, then rounded the car to settle in for the long drive to the airport.

I reached out to pull the door closed.

"What the fuck, Moriah?" Dane grabbed my hand and yanked me out of my seat, slamming the door behind me.

"Seriously?" He held up the handwritten letter, shaking the paper in my face. "This is what I get? A note? A dear fucking John letter?"

"Dane."

He leaned closer, his breath rank with the scent of whiskey, his eyes red-rimmed and heavy-lidded. "I get that you think you have to leave." He pointed over his shoulder toward the house. "I respect that you're giving them their space. But Jesus H. Christ, woman, this bullshit?" He rocked on his bare feet, drunk, at six in the morning.

"Dane."

His face crumpled, and my guts twisted into painful knots.

He opened his mouth. Snapped it shut. Crinkled the letter in his fist, then shoved the wad into his pocket.

I stared at his bare chest, realizing he must've been awake when I pushed the note under his door.

I swallowed, wetting my dry throat. "You're drunk."

"Rough night." He grunted.

For all of us, I wanted to say, but I knew better than to argue, or attempt a civilized conversation with an inebriated individual. "I have to go. I'll call you when we land."

Hands hung at his sides, he dropped his head back and cussed at the sky. When he met my gaze, he begged, "Don't go."

"I have to go."

"Don't go."

"Dane. I—"

"I'm not a good guy." He took a step back, ducking his head to catch my gaze. "I've got shit to offer. No home. No family. Not even a fucking job." He huffed, shaking his head. "But you stay? You stay here, you own me, body and soul. And I promise you, ain't nobody gonna hurt you or that little girl, ever. I'll kill anyone who tries. Ain't a soul on Earth gonna fight for you like I can. I can give you that. I can give you every dirty fucking piece of me, and I'll spend every God damned second of every day making sure the two of you are happy."

Ouch. His words lashed every inch of my heart. Too bad he wouldn't remember saying them.

I took a step closer. His eyes seemed to lose focus. He swayed, then steadied himself.

"I'll call you when we land." I lifted my hands to his chest, raised up on my toes, and kissed his jaw.

"Don't go."

"Go to bed, Dane. Sleep it off. We'll talk later."

Hardest thing I'd ever done, hands down, was turn my back on that man. But I forced myself to keep moving. I got in the cab, hurried the driver, and didn't turn back as we drove away.

Tears flowed.

Mim curled her fingers around my pinky, and I looked down to find her eyes wet, too. She offered me a brave smile, and she held my hand, for the first time ever, all the way to the airport.

"This will be your room, Mim." I dropped her suitcase on the bed, then squatted to meet her face to face, struggling to ignore the fact that Matthew had not moved his furniture out of my extra bedroom, or any of the rooms for that matter.

"How about we just take it easy today? Tomorrow, we'll sit down, make a list of the things you need, the food you like, and we'll go shopping. Sound good?"

That sweet little angel curled her bottom lip between her teeth and fought a smile.

"Would you like to unpack your suitcase first?" I pushed to stand, pulled open one drawer. Slammed it shut. Opened the next. Then the next, biting back all the ugly words. Matthew had not removed any of his "winter" wardrobe. Sweaters. Jeans. Thermals. The man had more clothes than any woman I'd ever met.

"I'm sorry, sweetie. Let me empty this dresser quick, then we can put your clothes away."

I dashed to the garage, where again I found Matthew's belongings untouched, and rifled through my gardening shelf until I found my box of heavy-duty trash bags. When I returned, Mim hadn't budged, but her eyes worried when I began shoving Matthew's clothes into one of the black bags. "My friend used to live here," I explained. "He was supposed to move all of his things out. Looks like he hasn't done that yet."

Like she was happy to have something to do, Mim came next to me and sweater by sweater, helped me empty the next two drawers.

I wanted to be mad at Matthew. Had every right to be livid, but anger was impossible with my little girl at my side. My little helper. Mine.

God, she was mine.

The reality of the situation hit me hard, a sucker punch to the chest, and despite the challenges that lay ahead, I was happy. So happy, my eyes filled with liquid joy. I tucked that emotion away fast as I could because I didn't want to ruin our moment.

The last drawer took some elbow grease to open, overstuffed with envelopes and papers, pens of all colors and sizes, a couple of old wallets. Outdated cell phones that he hadn't recycled. I shoved those items into a bag as well, but what I found tucked in the very back of the drawer stopped me cold.

A little black box.

Of course I looked inside.

Of course the ring was gorgeous. A white gold band boasting a half-circle of petite diamonds complementing a round-cut centerpiece that had to be close to one and a half carats. The giddy girl in me wanted to try it on and dance around the house, catching the diamond's sparkle under every light source. The woman in me knew I would never wear that ring.

I loved the ring. I loved Matthew. But I was not *in love* with him. Truth be told, he couldn't be in love with me, either. We were comfortable. We were convenient. But we were not passionate. We were not a dent the wall, destroy the furniture, screw each other until the sun came up kind of couple, and until I'd had that with Dane, I hadn't known I had it in me. Hadn't realized I deserved that intense passion. And my, how I craved that feral hunger in Dane's gaze every time he looked my way.

I could never go back to safe. Never go back to Matthew. Not when my soul had been splashed and stained with all the bright colors that made up Dane Reynolds.

I tossed the box into the bag, tied that sucker tight, then dragged Matthew's belongings to the garage.

The rest of his things would follow suit, after Mim went to bed because the rest of the day, and every day after, would be about that sweet little girl.

We'd tucked the last of her clothing into the drawer when my cell buzzed.

"Hello?"

"You made it safe?" That deep gravelly voice sent my heart into a mad sprint.

"Yeah," came out, breathy and desperate.

"How'd she do?"

God, I loved that Mim was on his mind. "She did great. She got the window seat, and she loved flying. I was so proud of her."

"You good?"

"I'm good." But I missed him, desperately and painfully.

His breaths came heavy through the phone. "Can I talk to her?"

Swear to the good Lord above, my chest cracked open and kittens and rainbows and all the beautiful things poured out. "Of course you can."

"Mim." I turned to find her big wise eyes smiling up at me, as if she knew her favorite man was on the phone. "Dane wants to say hi."

My cell in her hand, she hurried to the bed, hopped up, and made herself cozy.

Giving them privacy, I headed to my own room to unpack, my spirits darkening when I entered.

Unmade bed.

Dirty clothes on the floor.

Closet door open.

Matthews suits hanging inside.

"What the eff?" I asked my closet. He hadn't even tried to move out. That smug bastard hadn't left.

I attacked, ripping his clothes off the hangers, throwing his shoes into the hallway, tearing his underwear out of the drawer. When I'd emptied his side of *my* closet, I grabbed the biggest armful I could manage and carried them through the garage, straight to the driveway, and tossed them in his parking spot.

I turned to head inside for another load when headlights beamed and tires screeched. The engine cut. A door slammed.

"Moe?" Matthew said, careful, calculated.

If I turned around, I'd see his "you're acting crazy again" face. The expression he wore every time I brought up any non-agreeable issues involving our relationship. If I dared to look at that face, I'd lose my cool. I didn't turn around.

"I told you we were over. I told you to get out of my house. You can pick up your things tomorrow." I stepped inside the garage, then pushed the button, lowering the garage door, way too slowly for my liking. Regardless, I'd made my point. At least, I'd thought I had, until I heard his keys working the lock of the front door.

I met him at the entryway, face heated, head pounding. "Give me my key. Turn around. Get out."

He wore his favorite navy suit. Tie loose. Eyes sad. "Moriah. Let's talk about this."

"Nothing to discuss."

"We're not over. You can't break up over a text."

"I can. I did."

He huffed. Shook his head. "I'm not leaving." His smile was forced, and not the least bit genuine.

"Get out."

"This is my home, too."

Wrong. My name was on the title. Matthew was aware of that fact, so I didn't bother arguing. "Get out."

"I love you, Moe."

"Last time. Hand over the key and leave."

Matthew pushed past me, running a hand through his thick, blond hair. "If this is about the kid. We'll figure something out." He dropped his briefcase next to the La-Z-Boy. Kicked off his shiny brown loafers. "We'll do right by her, whether she's with us or someone else."

"Someone else?" I shrieked, every ounce of my blood boiling. "Her name is Mim. And there is nothing to figure out. She's mine, Matthew. Mine to protect. Mine to love. Mine! You are in no way involved. Now get the fuck out of my house."

Matthew's head jerked at my use of the actual F word, his eyes widening. Hands to hips, he dropped his head. Licked his lips, then lifted an angry gaze to my watery eyes. "You're exhausted, clearly. Let's sleep on this. We'll talk in the morning."

I searched my pockets for my phone because for damned sure, a call to the police would get rid of him. Only, my phone wasn't in my pocket.

My phone was in Mim's tiny fingers, where she stood right behind me, Dane still on the other end of the line, screaming, "Moriah, baby. What's happening. Fuck! Shit! Moriah!"

Mim's wide-eyed gaze darted from me to Matthew, back and forth.

I dropped to my knees and got right in her face. "Hey, Little Lady. Sorry you had to hear that." I plucked the phone from her fingers and tucked her against my side, holding her tight. Dead set on getting that stubborn man out of my home and away from my niece, I mumbled into the cell, "I'll call you right back," then ended the call without explanation. Then I dialed 911.

The police arrived seventeen minutes later.

Matthew, being an attorney with the most prestigious law firm in Shelby County, convinced them that we were fine, merely having a lovers' spat. After seeing that Mim and I were safe, and in no physical danger, the officers left, leaving me seething, but holding my shit together for Mim's sake.

I could not give her reason to be afraid.

She'd come so far the past two weeks.

Buck up, little camper, I repeated to myself while I made dinner, the little girl clinging to my side. We ate at the table, Mim staring at Matthew, Matthew staring at me, while I wondered how I'd ever believed I could live happily ever after with that man.

A wall-shaking bang jolted me from sleep, and I blinked, trying to find my bearings in the darkness, darting my arm behind me to search for Mim.

Muffled shouts came from the kitchen.

More crashes. Grunts. Curses.

Behind me, Mim lay sprawled across the mattress, soft snores rising from her small body.

Another crash. More grunts. Two voices. Maybe three?

Matthew shouted. Glass shattered. The walls vibrated.

Legs tangled in the sheet, I kicked and shimmied until my feet freed, then bolted out of the room, my heart galloping, mind still ten steps behind.

I rounded the corner, heading for the light switch, and smashed into a lone figure, bouncing, then tripping over my feet and landing, ass to hardwood with a teeth-jarring bounce.

"Jesus. Fuck. Sorry, Moriah," a gravelly voice grunted through the dark. Two hands slipped under my arms and lifted me back to my feet.

"Tito? What the eff?" I cupped my nose, eyes watering from the sting.

I felt for the light switch. Flipped it. Screamed, "Oh my God, Matthew!" Then winced, looking away because Matthew's face was a bloody mess.

Worse? He was pinned to the wall, feet dangling, eyes bulging, fingers raking at the set of hands clamped around his throat. Hands that were attached to ridiculous, powerful arms. Arms that were attached to broad, bunched shoulders.

Matthew's eyes darted to mine. He wheezed my name, a plea for help.

Dane shot me a glance over his shoulder, then focused again on his victim, head tilted just a bit, a menacing study of Matthew's face, which had turned a grotesque shade of purple.

"Dane!" I shouted, storming their way, sidestepping the couch and the broken picture frame.

I grabbed his arm and yanked, my attempt to move the cannon-sized limb futile.

"Gorgeous," he mumbled, glare drilling holes through Matthew's skull. "You okay?"

How dare he. How. Dare. He. "Put him down," I ordered through gritted teeth.

Dane chuckled. Effin' chuckled. His grip loosened a tad, allowing Matthew a deep inhale, then asked, as if a man's life wasn't in his hands, "Where's our girl?"

"She's fine. Sleeping."

"This numb-nuts hurt you?"

"No. God, no. What are you—"

"Let's move back a bit." Tito cut me off, hooking an arm around my waist. "In case things get ugly." His voice, low and menacing, carried a trace of amusement, which only added fuel to my fire.

There was nothing amusing about the situation. Still, Tito was every bit as strong as Dane, and he lifted me with zero effort, moving us safely across the room.

"This isn't ugly yet?" My question fell on deaf ears.

Shell-shocked, I watched the scene unfold, vaguely aware of Tito's hand on my shoulder, acutely aware of Dane in all his violent, virile, menacing glory.

"Moriah told you to get out of her house," Dane snarled, jaw set so tight he vibrated. "So why are you still here, shit-stain?"

Matthew's mouth worked to no avail.

Dane twisted his head as if to listen, knowing damn well Matthew couldn't speak, out of fear, self-preservation, or lack of oxygen, I wasn't sure. What was clear, though, was that Dane was spot on with his intimidation game, with all his bulk, and threatening tone, and brute, bully strength.

"Don't answer that… I hear any half-witted excuses, I might kill you."

Throat dry, blood pressure rising, I managed to rasp, "Dane. Let him go."

Dane brought his face closer to Matthew, studying him with a snarl, like he was about to tear his head off with his teeth.

"I'ma tell you one time. A lady asks you to leave, you leave." He raised Matthew an inch higher. "*My* lady asks you to leave, you tuck tail and flee the motherfuckin' state. Am I clear?"

Swear to all that was holy, that threat in Dane's eyes made my knees buckle, and my body warm in all the wrong places.

Matthew glanced my way, broken, defeated, then blinked a slow blink at Dane.

"Let him go. He hears you."

Dane growled. Growled. Like a freaking werewolf. I half-expected him to howl at the moon and rip his shirt to shreds.

"Don't care where you go. Just get the fuck out. And you sure as hell don't come back. We'll let you know when and where you can collect your things."

Matthew blinked again, all color drained from his face.

Dane wasn't finished.

He slammed Matthew's back against the wall. Once. Twice. Holding an impossible amount of weight. "You even think about calling the cops, you'll be choking on your own cock faster than you can set the phone down, and when you've breathed your last breath, I'm gonna bring you back, do it all over again."

Now that was just overkill. And disgusting. I found my voice. "Enough!" Shrugging free of Tito's grip, I charged Dane, pushing hard. "Enough! He gets it. He's leaving."

Dane dropped his arms but stayed firmly planted where he stood, unwilling to back down. Matthew shimmied along the wall, scooted clear, and without a word, or his shoes, he snagged his keys and left, the house going silent once more.

I shot Dane a glare, ripe with all the ugly things I wanted to say.

He huffed, hands fisting and stretching at his sides.

"Mo—"

I shoved at his chest. "Not a word. Not one word."

Before I could lay into the hulking beast, my stomach clenched tight, a sudden wave of nausea forcing me to the bathroom.

When I finished with the dry-heaving and made my way out of the bathroom, Tito was fast asleep on my couch, and Dane was in Mim's room, shoes off, stretched on the bed, little girl snoring at his side.

Exhausted, and more than over the day, I retreated to my bedroom, and tucked into the sheets that reeked of Matthew.

The thing about shock and awe is that you're blind to the damage until after the smoke fades.

In the light of day, the quietude of morning, with my clear head and fresh perspective, I found the physical damage minimal: small dents in the walls, overturned chairs, broken picture, small bloodstains on the carpet. My heart and my head? Not so bad either. I wasn't a mess, and I wasn't scared. If anything, I was disappointed.

Dane showed his true colors. Exposed his dirty underbelly. The way he'd handled Matthew was nothing short of barbaric. Having glimpsed that brutish side of him, I should have cut and run. Kicked everyone out of my house. Changed the locks. Forget I'd ever met my inked bad boy.

The disappointment was not with Dane, however, but myself, because I'd suffered a morbid thrill, watching him scare the piss out of Matthew. Violence was bad. So why was I turned on? What kind of person did that make me?

Dane had come for me. He'd fought for me. He'd called me *his girl*. I liked being somebody's girl, and oh God, why was I acting like such a girl?

Red flags sprouted everywhere, alarms blaring. What kind of man could wield such violence, destroy another man's dignity, threaten his life, then minutes later curl around a child, protecting her from any threat, and fall asleep?

I crossed my arms, leaned against the doorframe, sipped my coffee, and watched Dane's massive chest rise and fall. Mim's hair covered his face, her right arm thrown over his neck. Both of them snored, Mim's soft and sweet, Dane's deep and rhythmic. The scene was too much, filling my malnourished heart with thick, meaty sustenance.

The front door opened, then closed.

I left my sleeping beauties alone, and found Tito in the kitchen, downing a glass of water.

"Good morning."

"Morning," he huffed, his face wet with perspiration. "Mind if I grab a shower?" His black running gear clung to every dip and valley of his lean, well-cared for frame.

"Use the bathroom down the hall. Towels are in the closet by the door." I set my mug on the counter. "Hungry?" I asked, heading for the fridge. "Eggs and pancakes?"

Tito smiled. "If it's not too much trouble."

"No trouble at all."

He started for the bathroom, then stopped. "Movers are coming today. They'll have Matthew's things out of here by this afternoon. Rented a storage space on the other end of town. I've already emailed him the details, so he has no reason to bother you. You okay being here, telling them what to pack and what to leave?"

I'd planned on leaving Matthew's belongings in the street, but heck, if there were men willing to do the heavy lifting, who was I to argue? "You arranged all of that already this morning?"

"Last night, actually."

"Do I dare ask how?"

"Best if you don't."

"Thank you, Tito."

Our eyes locked, his jaw worked, then his mouth lifted in a smirk and he nodded toward the closed door where Dane slept. "Got movers set up for you, too, in case you change your mind about Whisper Springs."

"Tito, I—"

Hand raised, he cut in, "Listen. Not trying to sway you either way. None of my business. But that guy in there? He's someone I can use on my team. I get the feeling, you stay in Shelbyville, he'll find a way to come to Shelbyville, and he'll be torn, because he has personal reasons for wanting to stay near Whisper Springs. You come to Idaho, that guy can stay where he belongs. If I play my cards right, he'll come work with Tucker and me. I need people like Reynolds."

"Criminals?" No sense beating around the bush.

Tito's brows pinched. He studied me for a moment. Then nodded. "People who do their best work outside the law."

Outside the law. That was the problem, wasn't it? Then again, outside the law was the only reason my niece was safe. Of course, outside the law was the reason her mother was dead.

Words clogged my throat, finding no outlet. Emotions bubbled inside me with no rhyme or reason. I searched but couldn't find a sane explanation as to why I wanted to scream, *yes, yes, take me back to Whisper Springs*. Nonsense. All of it. My stomach lurched.

Pushing past Tito, I dashed for the bathroom.

When I came out, Tito waited for me in the hallway, eyes set hard, arms crossed. "You okay?"

"Stress," I said, waving him off. "Go have your shower. Breakfast will be ready in fifteen."

"You sure that's all it is?"

I nodded, staring at a scuff on the floor to avoid his scrutiny. "Been like this since I was a kid."

"If you say so," he retorted, shaking his head and moving past me. I waited for the bathroom door to close before releasing a huff and heading to the kitchen.

About the time the bacon started to sizzle, Dane came out of the bedroom, targeting me with a heavy-lidded gaze. "Moriah."

"Morning." A whisper was all I could manage, the sight of him sucking me dry. My voice, my confusion, my ire, evaporated, leaving nothing but airy, wispy, head over heels, in too deep, woman.

"Fuck." He smirked, as if he could read my thoughts, then caught my waist in a crushing hug and pulled me up for a kiss that put the sizzling grease to shame, using tongue and teeth in a way that should've been painful but instead polished every rough edge in my body.

"You mad at me?" he asked, while I dangled in his arms.

Yes, should have been my reply. Instead, I wiggled free, mumbled, "Don't know," and turned back to the bacon, giving it a poke, then poured pancake mix into the other skillet. "You hungry?"

"Starving."

"Good." I pulled a mug out of the cupboard and shoved it his way. "Coffee's hot. Help yourself. Creamer's in the fridge, sugar's on the table."

Behind me, the chair scraped against the tile floor, then creaked, accepting Dane's weight. How silly that my first thought was to buy new chairs better suited for a large man.

How inappropriate, the frantic knocking behind my ribs. How maddening my nonchalance.

"Why are you here?" I asked over my shoulder.

"Really?"

"Yes."

A huff. "You didn't call me back."

"And?"

The chair shifted. "You didn't call back."

I turned to face the beautiful, sleepy, frustrating man. "I was busy, getting Mim settled." Figuring out how to deal with Matthew, I left unsaid.

Dane leaned back, crossing his arms, his legs stretched and crossed at the ankles, brows pulled low. "Put yourself in my place. You're two thousand miles away. You're screaming at your ex. You don't call back to let me know you're okay."

"So, your first reaction is to hop on a plane?"

"Yes."

"Again, why?"

His gaze dropped to the table. "I couldn't *not* come."

"You were worried."

"I was scared shitless." Dragging his thumbnail back and forth over his forehead, he huffed. "Moriah, you need to know, nothing scares me anymore."

Cleary that admission wasn't easy, judging by the look on his face.

That confession weighed heavy on my mind, too, for so many reasons, the most blaring, though, was that he cared enough to worry for us. And that was a good thing, right?

Trouble was, I knew so little about the man. If I chose to return to Whisper Springs, I risked a future full of scary surprises. Yet, those unknowns were still more appealing than whatever lay ahead for us in Shelbyville.

"Where's Moretti?" He interrupted my introspect, peeking into the living room.

"Took a shower, then ran to the corner store. Said he needed some pain relievers."

Tito came through the door that very moment, paper bag in hand.

"Perfect timing." I set a plate in front of Dane, then another at the table for Tito.

Mim joined us shortly after. We ate. Mostly in silence. Tito cleared the dishes, then announced he had to hit the road, get back to the family, and disappeared down the hall, to gather his things, I assumed.

Dane and Mim made themselves comfortable on the sofa, Mim pointing the remote at the flat screen until she settled on a loud and colorful cartoon.

"I'm going to wash my hair," I announced, although I was sure nobody was listening.

I bumped into Tito outside my room. He kissed my cheek, said, "I'm off," then whispered, "I hope to see you soon, Moriah."

I started to thank him, then thought, *for what*? For breaking into my home in the middle of the night? For escorting Dane The Destroyer on his mission to mark his territory? Don't think so. Instead, I wished him a safe trip home, then locked myself in the bathroom, dead set on a long, steamy, soul-cleansing shower.

On the sink sat two boxes. Pregnancy tests with a note shoved in-between that read: *If you say so. T*

Tito.

Effin' Tito.

CHAPTER 11

Dane

FUCKING TITO. GOD, I'D never be able to repay the monumental solid he'd done, getting me to Shelbyville on the fly.

Soon as Moriah locked herself in the bathroom, I joined Moretti outside, where he waited by the running yellow cab.

"Moretti," I grunted, lighting a hand-rolled, desperate for a quick hit.

"Reynolds."

I pulled a long drag. Held it. Exhaled. "Appreciate your help."

"Been entertaining to say the least." He handed his duffel to the cab driver, who then opened the trunk and tossed the thing inside. Tito made to get in the back seat, then paused. Faced me again.

"Gonna need you back soon. No fuckin' around with this one." He pointed to the house. "Do what you gotta do, get back. Lettie's in no shape to take care of that big house by herself. Tucker's in no shape to do a run, and I got a shit-ton of leads. Could use you on the road."

Although I respected what Tito and Tucker did on their "runs," their gig was for guys with any sort of a moral code.

I had none. Also, I resented the orders flying my way, so I threw out an, "I'm not up for that shit."

"No?" He came toe-to-toe, snarl curling his lip. "Go back inside, take a long, hard look at that little girl, remember what they did to her, tell me your chest doesn't hurt, your insides don't boil over thinking 'bout other kids suffering the same fate, then tell me you're not up for that shit."

Fucker was right.

Still. I wasn't about to say so. And I sure as hell would not consider leaving without my girls.

Tito dangled another carrot. "You say the word, I'll make sure Moriah doesn't get a job in this town. Give her no choice but to accept Carlos's offer."

Tempting. Would've made things easier if I'd let Tito work his magic, true, but Moriah's fate wasn't mine to manipulate. "Not sure I feel right about doin' her that way."

"Have a little faith, my man. She'll choose right." The prick clapped a hand on my shoulder. Smirked. "Never thought I'd see the day. Dane Reynolds going soft for a couple of girls."

"Fuck off."

He laughed, folded into the cab, said, "See ya in a few days." Slammed the door. Left me alone with my cancer stick.

Minute later, Mim joined me outside, and fuck if I didn't ditch my half-finished smoke for that little nugget. I'd never ditched a cigarette for anyone.

Standing at my side, she blinked big, sleepy eyes at me, and wore a smile brighter than the morning sun. Damn, my chest swelled, threatening to burst. She slid her fingers through mine and leaned into me, giving me the full weight of that little sack of skin and bones.

Fuck all. I was done for. I scooped her up, set her on my shoulders, and mumbled, "I missed you too, Little Lady," then gave her knees a squeeze. "Whaddya say we check out the neighborhood?"

Wasn't expecting an answer, but when she hummed, "Mmhmm," and bounced up and down, that tiny little creature proved herself a Titan, powerful and mighty, breaking through the prison walls that sick fuck had forced her into, and dead set on conquering the mountains of bullshit that I'd built around myself.

Through the open door, I shouted, "Mim and I are taking a walk."

Moriah popped around the corner, her hair wrapped in a pink towel, another one wrapped around her body, her bare legs on full display, and damn. Damn. I'd always been a breast man but consider me converted.

It was because of those toned beauties that it took me too damn long to notice the lack of color in her face. And guilt. I could swear, the woman looked guilty as sin.

"What is it?"

"What do you mean?" she asked, coming our way.

Had Mim not been sitting on my shoulders, I would've plowed through the door and forced a confession.

"Never mind. We're just going around the block. Be back before the movers get here."

"Yeah. Yeah." Her head bobbed. "If you head south"— she pointed beyond the yard— "there's a nice park about two blocks down."

Mim bounced again, her legs kicking under my palms.

"They got swings?" I asked. Mim loved the tree swing at the mansion, and although Rocky was the only person she'd allowed to give her a push, I thought maybe, considering her chipper mood, there was a slight chance she'd allow me the honor of pushing her "high as the sky," as Rocky liked to say.

"Yes. All kinds of good stuff."

"Guess we're heading south, then."

"Have fun." Not a lick of sentiment backed her words. Unfortunately, she pushed the door closed, ending the exchange. And as Mim and I walked away, I could swear she'd been trying to get rid of us.

"That the last of it?" I stood at the door, admiring Moriah's backside while she watched the movers lift her ex's things into the van.

She gave a silent nod, then mumbled, "Think so."

Eye contact had been a no-go since Mim and I had returned from the park. Three hours of cold shoulder. I would've taken a knee to the balls if it meant she'd get over being angry. "Wanna do one last run through before they go?"

"No. I've done three so far," she threw over her shoulder. "Don't want to give Matthew any excuse to come back."

The beefier of the three movers slammed the door shut, gave me the thumbs up, then climbed into the cab with his buddies and waved. The truck rumbled to life, then rolled away.

"He won't come back," she snapped. "You made sure of that." Finally. Finally, she turned to shoot me a glare, meeting me eye to eye, a brief and stormy exchange.

A victory short lived, however, because the little firecracker pushed past me and headed into the house.

Club bitches could be brutal when scorned. Never bothered me. They'd never mattered. But this lady, hell. She had my nuts in a vice. One false move, and bye bye baby makers. Funny thing was, she had no clue the power she wielded.

I gave her a good lead, then followed. Mim lay on the couch, one leg jacked against the back, the other kicked out straight. Her mouth hung open, long lashes dusted her freckled cheekbones, and a soft snore escaped her lips. Moriah stood at her side, staring down at the little beauty, one hand spread across her stomach, the other raised to her face, wiping a tear.

Shit. Crying again.

"Moriah."

"Do you want kids, Dane?" Venom laced her voice.

"What?"

"Do you want to be a daddy?"

"No. Hell no," came my knee-jerk reaction.

"You say you want me, want to keep us safe? Well, newsflash." Her arms flew out to her sides. "You stick around, that's what you're gonna have to be. A father." She stabbed a finger in Mim's direction. "To that little girl." She turned to face me, cheeks red, eyes blazing something fierce. "Insta-daddy. You get that, right?"

"I'll ruin a kid."

"So, there we have it. We've had our talk. Nothing more to say. Have a nice life."

"Wait. What the hell just happened?"

"Don't you see? I'm a mom now. I have a child to raise. I can't do the casual dating thing. I can't do the meaningless sex thing, no matter how good that sex may be. I have to put my niece first. I have to think long-term. And I can't... I absolutely cannot allow a criminal into our lives. Especially a man who gets off on beating people to a bloody pulp."

"Finally, she gets to the point."

"Yes. The point is, you don't want to be a father. I don't want to be a single mother, but I have no choice. You have a choice, and you said, *hell no*. So, the point is, there's nothing more for us to talk about."

"The point is, you've been pissed all day about me getting that loser out of your house."

"No. That's not the point. I mean, yes, it is, well, kind of. The point is, you are violent. I saw that last night. It scared me."

"You weren't scared, Moriah. I had eyes on you. You weren't scared."

"Okay. Fine. I wasn't scared."

"Right. What you are is pissed. You can say it. I get it. You have every right to be angry. I acted like a Neanderthal."

"You did."

"Thing is, I'm not sorry. That asshole should've respected your wishes. He didn't and you're either too nice or too distracted to fight."

She opened her mouth to argue. Sighed. "Right."

"So, I fought for you."

"Dane. Listen. I like you. So much, it scares me. But look at her." She waved toward the couch. "This is about me being in for the long haul. I have no choice but to be one thousand percent committed to her, to being a parent."

Crossing her arms around her middle, she dropped her head and whispered, "You do have a choice. You can leave at any time. As soon as the going gets rough, you can bolt."

"I'm right here."

"Yes. Now. But…"

"I'm right here."

"But you're not ready to be a dad. That's what she needs."

"Bullshit. Mim just needs men in her life she can trust."

Silence. My gorgeous lady dropped her arms, closed her eyes.

"What do *you* need, Moriah?"

"I need time to breathe. Just me and Mim. No Matthew. No you. I need to get my head together, my life back on track."

Shit. My guts twisted. "What are you saying?"

"You need to go, Dane. Please." She swiped at her eyes. "Mim has lived through enough violence. I can't invite more of it into my home, where I've promised to keep her safe."

Moriah needed time to process. I needed time to cool the fuck down. What I didn't need was a reminder of what a fuck up I was. Lived it. Breathed it. Wore it with pride most of the time. My set of questionable social skills were what kept me alive for damn near thirty years. Of course, a woman not born into the life wouldn't understand.

Mim understood, her childhood most likely viler than mine.

Mim had witnessed what I'd done to protect her. I'd die for that girl. I'd die for either of them.

Moriah walked into the kitchen, leaving me standing and unsure how to proceed. She returned with the small bag I'd packed and dropped it at my feet.

God damn, if she'd shoved me balls first into a meat grinder it would've hurt less. "Now?"

"Yes, please. Now."

Fuck. Fuck. Fuck! Every muscle in my body coiled tight. Not happening. No fucking way.

And what the hell with all the dad talk?

I scratched my chin, gave her a cold stare, eyebrow raised, ya know, in case she wanted to change her mind, backpedal with some of the crazy talk.

Lips pursed, she stared back at me, then blinked, then turned to Mim and whispered, "Don't make this harder than it has to be."

Hard? Hard? How about fucking impossible? But shit, how could I tell her no after I'd flown thousands of miles to beat the hell out of the last man who didn't respect her wishes?

She wanted easy? Fine.

I gave her easy.

I snatched my bag off the floor, and I left, leaving my motherfuckingpussyassbleedingheart behind.

Three times around the block.

A detour to the gas station to replenish my smokes.

A breather and a piss at the park.

Two hours. That was how long it'd taken to decide I was not heading back to Whisper Springs alone.

True, I was not, and never would be dad material. Hell, I wasn't boyfriend material. But for damn sure, I was not whole without those two ladies in my life.

Didn't understand, not one bit, why I needed to take care of them. Went against everything I'd ever believed about myself. Made me itchy, to be honest.

But they needed me, and I needed them. There it was. The bare bones. I was taking them back with me, no matter how long it took to convince Moriah.

So, there I stood outside her house, studying the brick entryway, the wrap around porch, the droopy flowers dangling from the overhang, and I scrambled to find the right words, come up with the right argument, to convince her to take a chance on a scumbag like me.

"You fucking whore!" came a deep voice, followed by the sound of glass shattering. "One day? You were gone one day and already fucking that trash?"

I made it to the door in three heartbeats, found Moriah in the kitchen, Mim wrapped around her body, head buried in her hair, and Matthew standing in the corner, face swollen, fists clenched, chest rising and falling in rapid bursts.

"Moriah," I said, straining to keep the violence out of my tone while I moved between Matthew and my girls. "Take Mim out of here, will ya?"

"No. You take her out of here. I'll deal with this asshole."

Before I could argue, Mim jumped into my arms, coiling around me, clinging tight.

Shit. Fuck. Shit.

I tried to set her down, and she tightened her grip. So, I turned to the dead man walking. "You touch Moriah, I'll rip your fingers off one by one. Then I'll ship them piece by piece to your mother in Pittsburgh." Yes, I knew where his mother lived. His sisters, too. I leaned closer and whispered, so Moriah couldn't hear. "And that pretty little receptionist you've been banging? She's the boss's daughter, right? Those videos you thought were safe in your phone will land in Daddy's inbox."

Matthew didn't meet my eyes, but his Adam's apple made a slow bob. I could've stopped there, but what would be the fun in that? Tito was a good man to have in your corner. "Oh, and that sexual harassment case you won last year? The bribes? Know about those too. Yeah. I know all of your dirty little secrets, piss for brains, so again, I'll tell you, don't touch her, or you'll be praying for death by the time I'm finished destroying your perfect world."

Instead of smashing his skull against the wall, I headed down the hall and took Mim into the bedroom because, apparently, I was the bigger man in the scenario.

Shouting started the moment I set Mim on the bed. I dug through Moriah's desk and found a set of headphones. "Put these on, Little Lady. You don't need to hear that shit." I tugged my cell out of my back pocket, scrolled until I found the game app Rocky had made me install, and passed it to Mim. "I'll be right back."

She curled against the headboard, pointed at the door, silently ordering me to make sure Moriah was okay, and pulled the comforter over her head. God damn, that little warrior was amazing.

I stayed in the hall, out of sight, but only a breath away.

"What is it with that guy? What's he gonna give you? Black eyes and Hep C?"

"You know what, Matthew? He's given me more orgasms in two weeks than I got from you in four years. Hell. Now that I think about it, he gave me more in the first night than you ever did."

"Ungrateful little cunt. I gave you everything. This house, your job, fancy dinners, social status in this town."

"This house was my mother's. You only helped me get the hounds off our backs when the medical bills started coming in. And you know what? Fuck you. Yes, I said it. Fuck you! Fuck. Fuck. Fuck you and your fancy, ass-kissing, social-climbing dinners with a bunch of uptight assholes in their pretentious suits with their arm candy wives. Not one of them ever gave a shit that my mother was dying in the hospital. Not one of them ever asked how I was doing, dealing with that nightmare. I didn't want friends like that. I never asked for anything from you. Not once. Except for a place to land when I was falling, and fuck you for not giving me that. Fuck me for being stupid enough to think that one day you'd give me that."

Moriah moved closer to Matthew, her ire vibrating the air.

He swallowed. Tilted his head. "I love you, Moe."

"You love my tits. You love my pretty face, and you love that when we were out together, everybody fawned over what a pretty girlfriend you had, and what a lovely couple we were. You loved that your boss and my father were best friends, and that helped you climb the ladder. You loved that you didn't have to work at our relationship, that it was easy, that I never questioned anything."

"You loved me too. How can you just throw that away?"

"I was comfortable."

Matthew cleared his throat. "Give me another chance, Moe. I can get you your job back."

Silence.

A shit-ton of turbulent, ugly silence.

"How did you know I lost my job, Matthew?"

That fucking slime bag piece of shit. My body coiled tighter than a valve spring.

Moriah's chest expanded. She released a slow breath.

"Matthew. How did you know?"

"Moe."

A hard slam.

"You got me fired?" Glass shattered. Once, twice. "You got me fired. You thought I'd give up Mim if I didn't have a job to come home to. You thought I'd let her go if I didn't have the means to support her."

Dickface cleared his throat. "You need to understand."

"You don't know me at all."

I came around the corner because that girl needed to know somebody had her back.

"Well, Matthew. Guess what?" Moriah marched into the living room, then returned, digging through her handbag and coming up with her cell. She thumbed the screen, put the phone to her ear, and waited.

"Hi. This is Moriah Peterson. "Yes. Yes. Thank you. I would love to take the job. Next week? Yes. Absolutely. I know. I'd have been crazy to turn it down. I'll see you then."

Her phone landed on the counter. Then that little firecracker stood toe-to-toe with the douchebag and pointed in his face. "I got a job all on my own."

My gut dropped to my feet. Oh, fuck. What job?

My world seemed to spin out of control, until she continued, "In Whisper Springs."

Swear to Christ my heart stopped beating, then started up again, triple time.

"You can have this house. I'll have my realtor contact you with the terms of the sale."

Head held high, Moriah shoved past me and headed down the hall. A door slammed, vibrating the walls.

Gloating would've been bad form in the current situation. Also, it would've made me look pathetic. So instead, I grabbed Matthew by the collar and shoved his back against the wall. "You'll pay double what she's asking for this house, or all the dirt I've dug up on you will go public and you'll spend the next fifty years taking it up the ass in a six-by-eight cell. Got me?"

The cocky fucker finally met my glare. "I don't want this house."

"Yes. You do. Trust me. You do."

I dragged him to the back door. Tossed him off the deck, locked shit up tight, then got busy cleaning up the broken glass.

With a fucking smile on my face.

"What are you doing?"

I dropped the armful of empty boxes on the living room floor. "Helping you pack."

"Why?"

"Because you're moving."

"Right. But. Stop. I can do this."

"Jesus, woman. I'm here. Let me help. You've got a lot of shit to deal with. Movers are coming in two days. You need to find a place to live. Need to get your affairs in order. Let me do the heavy lifting here. Besides, I've got Mim to help. She looks like an excellent packer, don't ya think?"

I lifted Mim's arm and squeezed where her bicep muscle should be. "We've got this, right Little Lady?"

Mim nodded, biting back a smile, then slapped her hands on her aunt's ass, pushing her toward the small office.

"Fine. Fine." Hands to the air, Moriah surrendered, her eyes lighting up at Mim's playful gesture. Before closing the door, she shouted, "There are stacks of newspaper in the garage if you need them."

"We got this."

Mim and I started on the living room, which didn't take long. After ditching her ex, there wasn't much left as far as decorative belongings. Fuck. I hated that guy.

By noon, the living room, extra bedroom, and the majority of the kitchen were reduced to stacks of boxes. Taped and labeled in Mim's six-year-old handwriting.

Clearly the little lady had had some schooling in her short, turbulent life.

I ordered pizza for lunch. Paid the delivery guy, made Moriah come out to eat, then sent her off again to do her business.

Mim and I hit the back bedroom. I left her to the bookshelf and made my way into the bathroom to see what damage I could do in there.

I started with the pictures on the walls, then grabbed all but the necessities out of the drawers and off the shelves. When I reached for the trash can, making to empty the thing, I damn near choked on my own heart. Two fucking pregnancy tests stared up at me, like little fucking jokers, blaring the word PREGNANT.

I dropped my ass to the side of the tub.

No fucking way.

No goddamn fucking way.

Fuck my life.

No wonder she wanted me gone.

She was pregnant with her ex's child. Her ex, who didn't want a child.

That explained the daddy talk.

She'd been right to push me away. I wanted Moriah, no arguing that point, but I sure as hell wasn't down with raising another man's child. Not that I had a dislike for kids, so much, but the thought of raising one, of being responsible for their emotional well-being, scared the shit out of me. I wasn't fit to be a dad. I'd fuck up a kid. Violence. Survival. Club life. That was all I knew. And why the fuck did she send Matthew away, take the job in Whisper Springs, if she knew she was pregnant? The man was a shithole, no question, but he had every right to know he was going to be a father.

I hated that guy even more than I had five minutes ago.

Moriah's voice carried through the room. "Hey, Mim. I think we need a break. What do ya say we head to the park for a while? Where's Dane?"

Shit. I moved to stand, my damn hip catching, and I fell back, my ass landing inside the tub, my legs dangling over the side.

Moriah came through the open door. "Hey."

No sense scrambling to get out.

Her gaze lingered on me, a smirk settling on her face, until she noticed the dropped trash bag, and the Clearblue sticks.

"Crap," she mumbled.

"Yeah. Crap."

"Dane, I—"

I choked on my anger, shoving that shit deep. "You need to tell him. You need to tell him today." I didn't try to get up.

I hadn't the energy, physical or otherwise. "You can't move to Whisper Springs if you think there's a chance to fix things between the two of you."

"No. God, no. Wait. What?"

"He's a fucking asshole who doesn't deserve you, but you're having his baby. I hate the fucker, I want to kill him, but he's the father of your child, and he needs to know. You can't keep something like this from him."

Shaking her head, she mumbled, "Matthew never wanted kids, Dane. That's why I dumped him in the first place. He didn't want me to bring Mim home. He wanted me to leave her to the state. I mean, seriously, what kind of human being would abandon any child in need, let alone family? But that doesn't matter—"

"You've gotta be fucking kidding me." Was she seriously considering not telling him? That wasn't the Moriah I'd fallen for, and God damn I was pissed, not just at her, but myself for giving a shit, but God damn.

Pure rage gave me the muscle I needed to get myself out of the tub, and I cornered Moriah, making my distaste for her decision clear. "I was an unwanted child, and fuck's sake, I swore I would never do that to a kid, which is why I'd never considered having any. But you can be damn sure, if I'd been foolish enough to knock-up a chick, I'd want to know. I had a kid out there anywhere, I'd make sure that kid knew his father. I'd make sure he knew he was wanted, whether I believe I'm dad material or not."

Those hazel beauties filled with liquid shame and I hoped to God I was getting through to her.

I planted one arm on the wall above her head, cupped her cheek, and stole a kiss. Our last, most likely, if she chose to do the right thing, because I wanted her, true, but I wasn't one to fuck around with another man's woman.

She tasted like salt and sunshine, and what was meant to be a goodbye seemed more like the beginning of a slow death, because the knowledge that I might never taste her again, feel her skin against mine, or that I may never be the target of that precious smile, or hear that laugh, or share a private conversation in the dark of night, well that shit cut like the drag of a slow blade that would peel my flesh away layer by layer until I drew my final breath.

I kissed harder, pulling her tight to my body, taking my last greedy fill.

Moriah sobbed into my mouth, curling around me, clinging with every muscle in her body, like she, too, understood we were sharing a goodbye.

I pulled away. Studied those fucking gorgeous eyes. Brushed that soft, unruly hair off her face, and whispered, "If circumstances were different, gorgeous..." I choked on my words, unable to speak the truth I'd held in since our first night together.

"What." She blinked up at me, her hands fisting in my T-shirt. "Say it, Dane. If circumstances were different, what?"

Fuck it.

"I'd make you mine. Make sure the world knew you and Mim were mine."

"Dane," she said, barely a whisper, her voice as broken as I was.

My guts twisted something fierce. I'd protected myself from bullshit emotions my entire life. Seemed I'd been right in doing so, because every time I'd thought I'd cared for someone, they'd been taken from me. My mother. Slade. Addison. Rocky. Still, I gave her what she needed to hear, knowing that was the last I'd ever be able to give.

"I'd never let you go."

"Dane, I—"

I jerked away from the wall. "Don't say it. Moriah. Don't. I can't hear it." I would break. In front of her, in front of Mim, I'd crumble, and they needed me whole to get through the next couple of days. Until I knew she was okay enough for me to go.

"Dane. Wait!"

I found Mim at the front door, a smile on her face. "Ready for the park?"

She nodded. I knelt and grabbed her laces, tying the left, then the right shoe.

Moriah came down the hall, face flushed, pulling her hair into a knot on top of her head.

"Dane," she pleaded. "Wait. I...um. Shit." She planted her hands on her hips, dropped her chin. Then chuckled.

I planted a hand on the wall to hoist myself back to the standing position.

"Mim," she said, voice shaky. "Could you grab us some bottled waters out of the fridge?"

I started toward the kitchen. "I'll get them."

Moriah shot an arm out to stop me. "Mim. Please?"

Mim skipped away. I stared at the hand curled around my wrist, unable to meet her eye to eye.

"I haven't had sex with Matthew in over four months."

Because he'd been fucking the receptionist, I thought to myself before her words sank in. I shook my head, the room going blurry.

"What the hell'd you just say?"

"I haven't had sex with anyone but you in over four months." Her voice trembled. "Matthew isn't the father, Dane. You are."

The rug seemed to fall from under my feet, and my knees hit the floor with a sickening crack. I felt no pain. I felt nothing.

"Dane." Moriah kneeled in front of me. "Dane. You okay?"

CHAPTER 12

Moriah

"ARE YOU SURE THIS is okay?" I asked Slade, for the umpteenth time, kissing the top of Mim's head, curling my fingers into her shoulder and pulling her tighter against my side.

Letting go seemed impossible.

"Of course it's okay. I wouldn't have it any other way. Besides, Rocky is so excited. He has the whole day planned out." She leaned back and studied me, her brows pinching. "Mim will be fine. If there are any issues, we know where to find you. I have your number, and the number at the office. And really"—she gestured to Mim—"she seems to blossom around my little guy, and he's not so sad about his grandpa when she's around, so this is a win-win for everyone."

"Thank you, Slade. I mean it."

I turned, meeting Mim eye to eye. "You going to be okay?"

She nodded, her bottom lip sucked between her teeth.

"If you need me for anything, just let Rocky or Slade know, and they'll give me a call. Okay?"

Again, she nodded, then threw her arms around my neck and gave me a long, hard squeeze—her way of communicating that she'd be okay.

Dear God, who knew hugs could be so life-altering.

Mim clung to me until Rocky barreled through the double doors and skidded to a halt, crashing into the table. "Mim! Guess what? I got you a present. Come on, it's in Mom's office."

Without another glance my way, she shimmied out of the booth and disappeared.

Slade slid her fingers through mine, offering a reassuring squeeze. "So, we'll be here for an hour or so, then we'll head to the beach for a bit, then to the mansion. Lettie is excited to see her."

"How's Leticia doing?"

"Putting on a brave face. Tucker hasn't left her side, so that helps. Having the kids around will brighten her spirits. She loves being a grandma. Oh, and Dane's been a huge help, taking care of everything around the house since he came back. Even the grocery shopping."

My heart squeezed at the mention of his name. Dane had gone Defcon 1 after we'd arrived in Whisper Springs two days ago. He'd helped us settle into the apartment I'd rented. Helped direct the movers when they'd arrived, then kissed me goodbye, gave Mim a hug, and said he had work to do. Been a no-show since.

I knew he'd taken the whole, "surprise, you're a daddy," news a bit hard. We'd barely spoken of our recent bombshell on the flight back to Whisper Springs, and honestly, I couldn't blame him for being distant. I hadn't a clue how to handle the situation either. We hardly knew each other.

Slade turned to leave, but I grabbed her arm, desperate for any bit of information. "How well do you know Dane?" I blurted.

Brow quirked, she smiled. "I've known him since we were kids. His cousin, Addy, and I were besties all through high school." She seemed to lose focus, her gaze drifting over my shoulder. "Under that tough shell, he's a big softie. Too bad I'm the only one who's ever seen that side of him."

I'd seen it, too. Still, I asked, "How do you mean?"

She studied the table, then grabbed a napkin and started to twist. "He saved my life once."

"Is that why there's so much tension between him and Tango?"

"You picked up on that, huh?"

"Hard to miss."

Slade gnawed on the corner of her thumb, a contemplative gaze aimed over my shoulder. "Tango and Dane will never be buddies." A loud exhale and her bright blue eyes met mine. "Dane's had a hard life. But he's one of the best guys I know. Mim recognizes the good in him. God, the way she took to him. Blows me away, really. But don't tell him I said that. He likes making people believe he's indestructible."

Slade's words came breathy and light, and I was shamefully jealous of the connection she shared with Dane. With a bitter taste in my mouth, I asked, "Were you two ever a couple?"

"Oh. No. No." She laughed. "Tango and I have been joined at the hip since we were kids. There was never anyone else for me."

"I'm sorry." Not sorry. Not sorry at all. "I just assumed, you know, because I've seen the way he looks at you. His eyes go soft."

"We have history. Not romantic, but epic, nonetheless. But that's a story only Dane can tell."

"Why?"

"Dane is...well... His life is... um..." She huffed. "Listen. It's not my place to say. What I do know, though, is that when he brought Mim here, he had no intention of staying in

Whisper Springs. But then *you* came to town, and boom, he decides to stay. Which, honestly, makes me happy. He needs roots. He needs to settle. He deserves some normal."

"Normal?"

A rosy glow spread across her cheeks. "Oh, God. I've said too much. I'm sorry. Anyway. I should go check on the kids." She scooted out of her seat, leaned my way, and squeezed my shoulder. "Good luck today. You look gorgeous by the way."

I looked down at my chest, brushed a crumb away, then smoothed the skirt on my cobalt sheath dress. "Thanks again, Slade."

I watched her bounce toward the kitchen with that ever-present spring in her step, took one last bite of my hash browns, then made my way out the door. The cowbell rattled a cheery tune, setting the mood for my first day at my new job.

I made it to my rental car when a loud rumble shook the ground. A large, loud, black and chrome motorcycle pulled up to the diner, driven by a man wearing a black leather vest, mean muscles, and a lethal dose of badass vibes.

He shut down his motor, removed his helmet, revealing a bald head, then dismounted his bike. A quick glance around, and he headed inside.

I couldn't make out the words on his vest, but the skull and snake design was clear enough. I'd heard of motorcycle clubs. I'd never paid them much mind, aside from my two months of binge-watching *Sons of Anarchy*, and the sight of that biker, the dangerous vibe he wore, sent a shiver of excitement across my skin.

Oh, God. What was wrong with me?

I shimmied into the car, careful not to dirty my dress or scuff my shoes, and headed off toward yet another new adventure.

The night sky sparkled, tiny dots of brilliant light beaming down at us. Mim lay with her feet dangling over my stomach, her hands tucked behind her head, lips pursed while she studied the tapestry of onyx and gold hanging overhead. Our new deck was the perfect spot for stargazing, and since I had no outdoor furniture, we'd made a comfy bed of blankets and pillows to stretch our legs and enjoy the summer breeze.

My day had been an exhausting whirlwind of introductions, paperwork, and shadowing Carlos Rossi's assistant, Lisa. Tango had checked in every so often, giving me small tasks, and helping me get acquainted with the company software.

Tempted as I had been to come clean about my surprise pregnancy, I wasn't ready to share my personal news with those outside the immediate need to know.

Terrified as I was of pending motherhood, I couldn't deny being over the moon, bursting with joy, knowing there was a life growing inside me.

"Mim." I reached over the pillow and brushed a chunk of hair off her face. "I have to tell you something."

She shifted, her heel digging into my ribs, her bright eyes meeting mine.

I smiled. She smiled.

"I know the timing is terrible, and you and I are only getting to know each other, but we're family, and I love you more than I've ever loved anybody, and I'm so happy we found each other. But. I. Well." I laid my hands over my stomach, right above where her ankles rested. "I'm going to have a baby, Mim. You're going to be a big—"

Mim bolted to the upright position, crab walking backward, away from me. She shook her head, eyes closed, mouthing, *no, no, no.*

I sat up, too, and reached for her, only to have my hand shoved away.

Heart racing, I reached again, then stopped short at the swell of tears in her eyes.

"What is it, sweetie? You can tell me."

Mim pushed to hands and knees, then glared up at me, so broken. So lost. So...angry. With a grunt, she was on her feet, chest rising and falling in short bursts, hands fisted. Hair hung over her eyes, lips curled in a snarl, the girl was feral, sending a shiver through me. She raised her foot, as if preparing to send a swift kick to my gut, and for a split second, I feared she would follow through. Instead, she turned and kicked a pillow, sending it against the glass door.

"Mim!"

Face red, lips set in a tight line, she ran inside, down the hall, and into her bedroom, slamming the door.

I willed my racing heart to steady, took three cleansing breaths, and tried to understand the swift mood change, coming up with nothing. Not a damn thing.

With trembling hands, I gathered our bedding and headed inside, scrambling to find the right words, fearful I'd just undone all the forward progress we'd made.

"I don't know what to do. She won't come out of her room. She won't eat. Won't look at me. If I try to touch her, she freaks. Please. I don't know where you and I stand right now, and that's okay, but please. She needs you." I hung up the phone, praying Dane would listen to my voicemail. The texts I'd sent through the night had gone unread, and I feared without his help, I'd lose that little girl forever.

I paced the living room. Downed a glass of water. Plopped my ass outside Mim's door. Checked my phone.

Checked again. Curled into a ball and cried. Two minutes later, I ran to the bathroom to vomit for the third time.

Of course, when I was at my worst, clinging to the toilet, Dane showed up. His heavy footfalls tracked the living room, the kitchen, then made their way down the hall, paused at the bathroom door, then continued. Mim's door opened, then closed.

Three deep breaths and I forced myself to stand straight, splash water on my face, and run a toothbrush over my teeth. On rubber legs, I made my way to Mim's door, leaned against the wall, then slunk to the ground, wrung out like a dirty dish rag.

Dane's thick voice carried through the walls, a calming vibrato, easing the weight on my shoulders.

Half an hour later, he emerged, closing the door behind him, and bending to scoop me off the ground. "C'mon. You need to get ready for work."

"How can I leave when she's like this?"

"I got her." He set me on my feet in the bedroom.

"Today. Sure. Yes. Thank you. But what about tomorrow, or the next day? You can't come running every time Mim and I hit a bump."

His rough hand cupped my cheek, his weighted gaze boring into my soul. "Tell me what happened."

"We were having a great night. Laying outside. Staring at the sky." I sucked in a sharp breath, nausea rolling through me again. *Buck up, little camper.* "I told her about the baby. I thought it would make—"

"Shit. Fuck. Shit." Raking a hand through his hair, he dropped his chin, falling against the wall. "God damn. You told her?"

"Well. Yeah. I thought it would make her happy."

"God damn." He left the bathroom. Stomped through the house. Came back. Towered over me. "I didn't want to tell you. I should've told you. Fuck. I fucked up."

"Tell me what?"

Hands to hips, glare aimed at the floor, he mumbled, "Your sister was pregnant when she died."

"No."

"I'm sorry," he choked.

"How far along?"

"Far enough you could tell."

"No." I covered my mouth with one hand. "No, no, no, no, no."

"Moriah. You can't fall apart right now."

"My sister." Fisting his shirt, I released a silent scream into his chest, my sanity slipping, my coping abilities dwindling.

Tears didn't fall, but my body shook, as if desperate to rid my skin of all the bad juju. Dane curled his arms around me, one pinning my head to his chest, the other securing my body tight, bearing the weight I could no longer manage.

Lips to my hair, he mumbled, "Mim is scared of losing you, too. That's why she freaked." Soft kisses dotted my head, the affection both exhilarating and maddening.

"We'll hash this out with Mim later. Right now, you have to get ready for work. Focus on that. I've got Little One today. You go make a good impression with Pretty Boy and his old man."

"Yeah. Yeah. You're right." I pushed away, avoiding eye contact, and dragged my feet to my closet, confident and grateful that Dane had everything under control.

Dane stayed close while I dressed. He poured me coffee while I buttered my toast. We didn't talk about the baby, or where he'd been, subjects neither of us seemed ready to broach, but his troubled glare landed on my midsection more than once.

Tension hovered like a black cloud in the room, and I should've filled the quiet with all the questions I wanted to ask or spilled my worries about the pregnancy at his feet or confessed my hurt and anger that he'd stayed away for days.

I remained silent.

Honestly, I was just thankful he'd come, and that I wouldn't lose my job on the second day.

As I made my way out the door, I braved a glance his way. He stood in my living room, features stoic, arms hanging at his sides, brutal and larger than life. Mim's guardian angel. My savior.

Words bubbled up my throat, and I swallowed them back down. He'd come for us, again.

Despite the tension between us, there was no doubt that everything would be okay.

One step at a time. One day at a time. Mim and I would rise above.

I hadn't the heart to watch Dane put Mim to bed, my wounded ego getting the better of me. Instead, I hid my hurt under the impressive spray falling from the giant shower head that hung from the ceiling of my lavish master bathroom.

Store-brand shampoo seemed unfitting in my new surroundings, a space that should have cost more than I could afford, even with my gracious new salary. Later, I'd have to ask Dane how he found the rental at such a steal. Then again, maybe the less I knew, the better. My grandma used to say, "Never look a gift horse in the mouth." So instead of ruminating, I enjoyed my shower, and my bargain body wash.

The bathroom door opened. A throat cleared. I waited.

When the silence became unnerving, I peeked around the glass partition.

Dane paced the small space, his bare feet blazing a loop-de-loop on the gray slate floor.

"Everything okay?"

"Yeah." He worked a hand through his beard and shot me a nervous glance. "Mim's out cold."

"Good. Thank you." I got back to scrubbing, forcing my jealousy and hurt and anger into the background.

Dane continued with the back and forth, his large form casting a daunting shadow, and *oh my god*, how I'd missed him the past few days, and damn him for dropping Mim and me off in our new home and then—poof—leaving me alone to wonder if he hated me or not.

Another throat clear. "How are you...um...feeling?" One of his large hands landed on the glass.

"Effin' great," I shot back, unable to bridle the bite in my tone.

"You decide what you're gonna do?" His voice wavered.

What was *I* going to do? *I*, as in me. Alone. God, that hurt, and I didn't want Dane to have the power to hurt me. "I'm going to shave my legs, then crawl into bed."

"That's not what I meant," he snapped, hard vibes bouncing off the walls.

His irritation grated my unstable nerves. "Oh. What am I going to do about the baby? Is that what you're asking?"

Nothing. Another hand landed on the glass, his head bowing between his arms. Clearly the topic made him uncomfortable, but eff that, and eff him. We were both in the shitter with the baby situation.

And suddenly I was angry. At Dane. At Mickey. At the world. "Hmm. Let's see. Well, apparently, I'm going to puke my guts out ten times a day for the foreseeable future, burst into insane bits of crying for no apparent reason. Maybe lose my job for not coming clean right away about my pending motherhood... Oh, and I'm going to be a single mother who thought she would never be a mother, and I'm going to love the holy living shit out of this baby and Mim because life is short and love is precious, and I'm gonna be the best mom the world has ever seen, and if necessary, I'll be the best effin' father, too."

Silence. His hands disappeared. Back to the pacing.

"How's that sound? That what you wanted to hear? That you're off the hook?"

A loud boom shook the walls. Heart in my throat, I waited for Dane to storm out of my life forever. Instead, he burst into the shower, fully clothed, cheeks red, fists clenched, storm blazing in those green eyes.

"Let's get one thing clear." He towered over me, close as he could get without touching. "You're having *my* kid. Ain't nobody doing the fathering but me."

Sure, I was naked and vulnerable, and Dane was clearly in a mood, but I was woman, goddammit, and I needed to roar.

But when I looked into those turbulent eyes, I lost my steam because despite being big and scary, Dane was also... lost and vulnerable, same as me, maybe more. "Someone interested in being a daddy doesn't disappear for days after—"

"I didn't disappear," he interrupted. "I... I thought you needed time to decide if you wanted to go through with the pregnancy."

"You thought I wouldn't keep the baby? Oh, my God. I would never. I could never..." I couldn't finish the sentence, my body going ice cold. I'd been a mess the past few days, but I hadn't considered what he'd gone through after learning the news.

"The timing is terrible, but I want this baby—"

In a blur, he smothered me between those strong arms and his soaked shirt. "Thank fuck." He kissed the top of my head. "Jesus. Thank fuck." Releasing me, he stepped back, his shoulders hitting the wall, then slid to the ground, knees bent, face buried in his hands.

Killed me, seeing Dane so tormented. I'd bet my right arm he never showed an ounce of weakness. Yet, there he sat, a mess of emotion, fully dressed and sopping wet on my shower floor.

"Dane," I whispered, inching closer. "Talk to me."

His shoulders rose and fell on deep inhales, and with a wet plea, he whispered, "Need a minute."

"Oh. Okay. Yeah." I finished rinsing, turned off the water, and moved to step around him, allow some privacy, but strong fingers curled around my thigh, halting my exit.

"Don't go." That warm hand slid higher, brushing between my legs, then higher still, around to my hip, then upward, resting on my abdomen.

My lungs seized. Chest tightened.

Lifting his eyes to mine, he pulled me closer, then shifted, rising to his knees, dropping kisses on my hip, then my stomach, his hands moving to my ass, fingers digging into my flesh, slowly killing me with his silent worship.

"Promise you won't take my child away. Promise me." Kiss. Kiss. "Whatever I do. However bad I fuck up." Kiss. "Don't walk away. Promise."

His embrace was painful, but I couldn't pull away, the intimacy knotting us together, and although my emotions were muddled, one thing became hauntingly clear. I was forever bound to Dane, and for reasons I didn't understand, my soul was at peace.

CHAPTER 13

A STRANGE SENSE OF peace melded me to the mattress. Moriah flipped her hair, tugging her fingers through the long waves, the blow dryer screaming, that gorgeous ass shaking back and forth causing her tits to bounce under the thin cotton top.

Beneath her soft sheets I was dangerously close to blowing my load, her simple bedtime routine an unbearable tease. Wasn't the time for indulging in dirty fantasies, but hell if I didn't have a firm hold on my cock, working to ease some pressure.

Her bed was a dangerous place for the likes of me, but my clothes still had a good forty minutes in the dryer, and I wasn't about to parade around in a pink robe. So, there I sat, dick in hand, naked, and too damn comfortable.

Good fucking God, a man could get used to that domestic shit.

Moriah came my way, a little hesitant, a red tint to her cheeks, but chin held high regardless. She paused at the foot of the bed. Too far away for my liking.

"C'mere," came out more a plea than the command I'd intended.

Moriah rubbed her hands up and down her hips, lifting those damn pink sleep shorts higher up her thighs. "Dane. We need to talk."

"We'll talk. But let me fucking hold you. Okay?"

She answered with a smile, crawled up the bed, then settled in my lap, straddling my waist.

I breathed, a deep, head-clearing, chest-freeing breath for the first time in ages. "That's more like it, yeah?"

She raked her fingers through my beard, her eyes searching mine, and swear to Christ, that action grounded me, settled in my veins, and rooted my ass to that damn bed, my heart to that woman.

"Are you mad at me?" she asked.

"For what?"

Lips pursed, she leaned back and pointed at her stomach.

A rush of unwanted feelings jostled my nerves. "No, gorgeous. Not mad." Terrified was more accurate, not that I would admit my fear.

"I'm not scared of doing this alone, Dane." Her gaze dropped to my mouth, tongue darting out to wet her lips. "But I don't want to."

I pulled her in for a kiss because...fuck, I needed that connection, wanted her to feel the sentiment I couldn't express with words... *Hear me, feel me, know me.*

When she softened, every rigid muscle relaxed, I pulled away and promised, "You won't be alone."

With a sigh, she asked, "How's this going to work?"

"However you want it to work, Moriah. I'm taking my cue from you." I grabbed her ass and yanked her closer. "I'm not going anywhere. I'm here. I'm in. Just be warned, I'm gonna fuck up once in a while. Probably a lot."

"I'm gonna mess up, too, you know." She shrugged, dropping her arms to her sides. "This is all new and weird, and nerve-wracking, and I'm clueless. You. Me. Mim. A baby." She threw her head back, half-laughing, half-crying. "It's like we're in a bad soap opera."

"So, we'll take it one day at a time."

"Okay. Yeah. Sounds good." She nodded, then yawned, covering her mouth. "One day at a time."

Much as I ached to keep her where she sat nestled over my groin, I ignored my selfish urges. "All right, gorgeous, time to hit the sack." I squeezed her ass, one cheek in each hand. "My clothes should be dry enough to get me home." With a grunt, I hoisted her to my side and pulled the blankets to her chin before she could protest.

We hadn't figured anything out, or made any plans, but she wasn't kicking me to the curb, and damn, what a burden off my chest. The past days had been torture, spent in a perpetual sweat, worried Moriah would realize that having my child was a bad fucking decision. Had I wanted to be a father? Hell no. But damn, when options were taken away, leaving nothing but cold, hard reality, a man learns what he's capable of accepting, and fuck me, but I wanted that kid, whether or not I was deserving or capable.

Without thinking, I dropped my feet to the floor, exposing my naked skin to Moriah.

"What is that?" came from behind.

Shit. I'd been careful to hide the brand I'd been so eager to receive all those years ago.

The bed shifted. "Dane. What is that?" A sharp finger poked at my back making my muscles coil.

"Aww fuck," I moaned, scrubbing my hands over my face. The conversation was inevitable, but that didn't stop me from trying to hide my ugly a little longer. "Not now, gorgeous. You need to sleep."

"Satan's Slayers?" She brushed a finger over the words permanently etched on my skin. "You're in a gang?"

"Something like that."

She traced the outline of the skull and snake. "I don't understand."

"Motorcycle club."

"Oh." Her hand left my body, the bed bounced, then Moriah stood before me, hands fisted at her hips, and said, "Well. Let me hear it. What have I gotten myself into with you?"

"Had a shitty life, Moriah. Junkie mom. Drug-dealing psychopath for a father. Fell in with the wrong crowd. The wrong crowd became my family."

"Satan's Slayers."

"Yes. And before you ask, I can't talk about them."

Eyes narrowed, she studied me, making my guts twist. Then she nodded. "I understand."

She didn't. She couldn't. Eventually, curiosity would get the best of her and that shit would be an open wound that never healed between the two of us.

"Are you still with them?"

"No." My ticker dropped in my chest. I didn't want to elaborate, but I couldn't lie, not to her. "Well. Not really."

"What does that mean, *not really*?"

"It means I left. Walked away. But you're never truly out. Unless you're dead." I hit her with a hard glare, fearing she'd file that info into her *Reasons I Should Stay Away from Dane* folder.

So, when she smiled and said, "I saw a biker at the diner the other morning," my worn nerves began to snap, one by one, sharp needle pricks striking up and down my spine.

"How'd you know he was a biker?"

"Motorcycle. Leather vest."

"He give you any trouble?"

"No." She laughed. "I was across the lot."

Moriah tried to hide a yawn behind her hand, eyes watering, reminding me it was time to hit the road. I pushed to stand, but Moriah gripped my shoulders, holding me down. "Dane." She stepped between my knees. "Please stay. Stay with me tonight." Her fingers snaked through my beard, dusting my jaw. "Please?"

Fuck. I was toast. Burnt and buttered.

I needed to go. Find out why the Slayers were in town. But damn how I needed her invitation, how I needed to just... be. For one fucking night.

I kissed her chest. Her neck. Her chin. Then gave that luscious ass a hard slap. "Get in bed. I have to make a few calls."

"But you'll stay?"

Fuck me, those pink cheeks and sleepy eyes did a number. "I'll never be able to say no to you, gorgeous."

I waited for her to settle under the covers, then dug my boxers out of the dryer, found my phone, and headed to the balcony, dialing Moretti.

"Wow. You were hungry," Tuuli said, winking at Mim while she cleared our plates.

Tito's wife looked like she weighed all of ninety pounds in her Truck Stop T-shirt and khaki pants, apron strings wrapped around her waist at least twice. But that little blonde waitress glowed. She looked far younger than her twenty-plus years, and I suspected that was why Mim took to her so well.

Mim bounced in her seat, nodding, because damn, that girl had chowed, clearing her plate before stealing my bacon. Moriah's breakfast, however, sat mostly untouched.

Tuuli shot me a nervous grin. "More coffee?"

She had witnessed the damage I could do the night I'd taken Erik Meyer off her hands and sent that racist pedophile kicking and screaming to the bowels of hell. She had nothing to fear from me, ever, but she was wise in keeping that fear forefront.

"Please." I tapped the side of my cup.

"Be right back." With a measured grin, she sauntered away.

I searched the diner for Slade or Tango, thankful neither of them had shown their faces. Tango had yet to confront me about my confession to James, but I had no delusions. A shitstorm was headed my way, and rightfully so. I risked bumping into them at the diner, but since I wasn't leaving town, I figured the sooner we dealt with my crimes, the better. Tango and I would never get along, never be friendly, but we were damn well going to share space, and we were damn well going to keep things civil, for our women, if nothing else.

Mim sat to my right, Moriah the opposite side of the table, nails tapping the red Formica. She'd been quiet all morning.

I was about to probe when the familiar, fuckin' beautiful rumble of an engine drew my attention out the window, and despite the knot in my gut, I couldn't help the tug at the corner of my lips. Fuck, I'd missed riding.

Hammer strode through the door like he owned the place, searching the room for threats, before his eyes landed on Moriah. The fucker actually had the audacity to pretend he hadn't noticed I was at the same God damn table, shooting her a menacing grin.

"Trailer." He nodded, coming to my side with a hard clap on the shoulder.

"Hammer." I chanced a glance at Moriah and winced at the blush in her cheeks, and the way she studied the dirty bastard.

Uninvited, Hammer plopped his ass in the seat next to Moriah, wrapping his arm around her shoulder. "Who's this pretty lady?"

Moriah tried to speak, her words catching in her throat. She coughed, straightened her spine, then offered her hand. "Moriah. Nice to meet you."

Hard to tell if she was nervous, or ready to barf, so I slapped the table. "Hammer. Mind movin' your ass. Moriah needs to get to work."

With a grunt, he removed himself from the seat. Moriah wasted no time getting to her feet. She held my gaze, that skin between her brows crinkling. Not a chance in hell I was going to let Hammer witness her effect on me, so I tore my glare from her troubled expression, and focused on the dickhead.

"So—" she started to speak.

I needed her gone, away from my poison.

"Mim will be fine. Don't worry," I offered, tone flat, trusting she understood the severity of the situation.

Moriah's shoulders stiffened, but she played along, blowing her niece a kiss with a, "Bye sweetie." Then, she shot me a warning glare and pushed past Hammer, throwing a casual, "Later, Dane" over her shoulder.

Damn, how I wanted to chase her down and send her off with a goodbye she'd feel for weeks. Instead, I tucked an arm around Mim and settled in my seat, doing my damnedest to appear relaxed.

Hammer raised his chin, eyeing the little girl in my arms. "How's she doing?"

Like he gave a shit.

"What do you think?"

"Well. She ain't screaming like the last time I saw her. Got some color in her cheeks." He winked at Mim, and her tiny body tensed. Then the scary bastard puffed his cheeks and gave her a cross-eyed grin.

She shoved her face under my armpit and damn near fused herself to my body. What the fuck?

I wanted Hammer gone. "How'd you know where to find me?"

"You never could keep your eyes off the chick who runs this joint," Hammer answered, studying Mim like she was a puzzle he needed to solve. "Club's got eyes and ears everywhere, trailer boy, you know that."

Trailer boy. Hammer's way of cutting me down a peg.

"Who's the chick?" he asked, tearing at a napkin, presumably feeling every bit as uneasy with the visit as I was.

"Mim's aunt."

"How'd you find her?"

"I know a guy."

"Shit." He blew a low whistle, turned his head to stare out the window. "You tappin' that ass, 'cause—"

"The fuck you want, Hammer?"

He pounded the table, two raps with his fist, then gestured toward me like I was the crazy one. "Low-Key is moving his mom to a home in Eastern Washington. Had room in the van. Brought your bike."

The asshole had ulterior motives. Not a chance in hell he'd deliver my ride. "Prez know?"

"His idea. Said he was tired of staring at it."

"That fucker don't give without taking. What does he want?"

His attention was back on Mim, who clung to my side, halfway shoved between me and the back of the seat.

Raised my hackles, the way he studied her.

"Club needs your trailer. Coupl'a guys'll be cutting through town the next few weeks. Need a place to crash."

"Haven't been to the river for years. Not sure if that shit's even standing."

"Well. If it ain't, they can pitch a tent. If it is, we expect it to be stocked. Just giving you a heads up. Only reason you own that land is 'cause of your old man. Only reason he owned it was because of the club. We need to use it, we're gonna use it. You know the drill."

The drill. When my old man was alive, the drill meant making sure our trailer was stocked with drugs, booze, women, and food—pretty much in that order. I would not supply shit for anyone.

"That all?"

Hammer tilted in his seat, trying to get a better look at Mim.

"Get your fuckin' eyes off the girl," I warned, his interest in the child unsettling.

He threw his hands up in surrender. "Chill the fuck out, brother. Just noticing the resemblance to her mama. That's all." His eyes met mine in a glare meant to intimidate, but the edge I was used to seeing in Hammer was gone, replaced with something that looked like desperation.

"How well did you know Mick, Hammer? There something you wanna tell me?"

Hammer stared long and hard at the table, then lifted his glare to Mim again, eyes glazed. He made a tsk sound, shook his head in a slow *no*. "Not a damn thing. Come and get your ride, *Trailer Park*, so I can get the fuck outta this shit town."

Low-Key stepped back. Kid was a newer recruit, half the size of Hammer, but twice the man. By the snarl on his face, I guessed he was not happy about being in my presence.

I shifted Mim from my shoulders to the bike, settled her on the worn leather, and waited for her to balance before letting go. She seemed unsure, hands flat on the seat between her legs, body stiff.

One hand at her rear, the other on the handle bar, I blocked her from view of the dickheads standing at my back. "Only been one other girl on my bike, and she didn't look anywhere near as badass as you do right now."

If I could have chosen one moment in time to snapshot and keep forever, that would've been the image, right there, the straightening of her spine, the wide-eyed innocent wonder that spread across her face, the one hundred percent worry-free, shit-free, fear-free smile that cracked her grim expression. Tore me wide open, my innards spilt at her feet. Took nothing for me to place her on my throne, but the girl reacted like I'd given her the world.

Mim ran her small fingers over the leather, then stretched up to study the gauges, and God damn, if I'd known that pride could lift a man so high, maybe I would've considered different paths in my life, because watching that little lady admire my ride, appreciate the beauty, hell, I was suddenly taller than the pines, more majestic than the mountains surrounding us.

I hoisted my leg over the bike and settled behind Mim, gripping the bars and damn near groaning in pleasure. I'd missed my Fat Boy.

"Soon as we get you a helmet, I'll take you for a ride. What do you think about that?"

A gasp escaped her lips, making that wild hair shake across her back, and fast as a blink, the girl turned and had me in a head lock, those tiny arms squeezing tight, and fuck me, but I hugged her back, locking her against me, feeling every nuance of that fragile body against mine, inhaling the fruity scent of her hair, and taking the unrelenting assault on my chest. I never wanted to let go.

God damn my life.

God damn my girls.

God motherfucking damn.

Hammer spoke over my shoulder. "Little shit's got you wrapped around her finger, doesn't she?"

At the sound of his voice, Mim squeezed me tighter, something sharp digging into my neck. I pried her off and that necklace she'd worn the day I found her, and every day since, fell back into place at her chest.

"Hey, whatcha got there?" Hammer asked, reaching toward Mim.

Out of instinct, I blocked his advance, shoving him away.

Mim whimpered, and shoved the necklace under her shirt, where she always wore the damn thing, hidden away, like it was her secret.

An unholy growl tore from Hammer's throat, raising my hackles. He made to reach inside his cut when the diner's cowbell rattled and Rocky burst through the door, barreling our way, skidding to a halt at my side.

"Whoa," he shouted. "Is that your motorcycle?"

Tango followed, hot on his heels, and swear to the asphalt gods, Pretty Boy looked ready to tear me to shreds. Fuck. I knew what was coming, had been expecting a war, but I hoped like hell he would wait until there wasn't an audience.

"Get inside, Rocky. Now." Tango came at me, those unnaturally green eyes deadly sharp and spitting venom. "Take Mim and go to the office until I come and get you."

I dismounted, set Mim on her feet and told her to go with Rocky. She didn't hesitate, grabbing Rocky's hand, and dashing back inside.

The second that cowbell rattled, Pretty Boy swung, and damn, his aim was spot on, his right hook blinding me with a colorful explosion of bright lights. "The fuck you doing bringing your filth to my diner?"

I caught my balance and charged, knocking the surly fucker in his expensive suit to the ground. He had every right to pummel me, and were I a better man, I'd have stood still and let him purge, but I'd wanted to turn that smug mug to pulp since grade school, and damn if I'd give up the opportunity.

Rocks tore at my jeans, dug into my back, then my face. He swung, I countered. My nose cracked, his lip tore wide open.

Tango was faster, but I was meaner, and I had no problem fighting dirty, going for the throat, balls, spleen, hell, I wasn't above hair pulling to keep the upper hand, and the rich boy had plenty of hair to grab.

Blondie, being Tango's kryptonite, yelled, "Jesus fucking Christ Tango! Your son is watching," tearing his attention away from the fight, and giving me the upper hand.

I twisted, grabbing his throat, and laid my full weight over the top of him, then dug my fingers deep, ensuring he knew his next breath depended on my generosity.

Only because Blondie begged, "Dane. Let him go," did I loosen my grip.

"You drugged me," he wheezed. "You sick motherfucker. I never would've fucked Addison that night. You drugged me goddammit. Six soulless, miserable years I suffered because of you. That's all on you!"

Asshole was right. I deserved any punishment he deemed fit. I hadn't only hurt Rossi, I'd hurt Blondie, and that girl didn't deserve the hell she'd gone through. I fell back on my ass. Tango wasn't one to waste an opportunity. Once, twice, he struck my jaw, laid me flat in the gravel, and I didn't fight back. Pretty boy could have his retribution.

No doubt, the guy would've crushed my skull with his fist, had Blondie not warned, "The kids are watching."

Tango trembled, his bloodied face twisted. "Get out of my town."

"Can't," I rasped, blood choking me.

"Like hell," he growled, landing two more licks to my jaw.

"I ain't leavin'."

"Tango," Blondie warned.

Fisting my shirt, he leaned closer. "I'll fucking kill you."

Out of habit, I taunted, "You're too much of a pussy."

"Stop!" Blondie screamed, using the full force of her body to shove Tango. He slumped at my side, heaving, every muscle coiled to strike.

Standing over me, she ordered, "Dane. Get out of here. Get yourself cleaned up. Mim can stay with me today."

Then, turning her venom on her man, she scolded, "Tango, get out of my sight. You two are acting like a couple of pimple-faced, 'roid-raging, high schoolers. Go." She kicked at Pretty Boy. "Get out of here." She marched off, still yelling, "This is my place of business, and you're turning it into a freakin' circus sideshow, and not even a good one."

Tango hopped to his feet, whereas I had to roll to my side, push to hands and knees, then breathe through the pain while I rocked to my heels and eventually crouched. Only through stubborn pride was I able to stand upright, where, what do ya know, Pretty Boy met me bloody nose to bloody nose.

"Get the fuck off my property." He spit, pointed toward Hammer and Low-Key. "And take your trash with you when you leave." Brushing the dirt off his shirt, he turned and stormed toward the back of the diner.

"Pathetic." Hammer huffed.

"Get the fuck outta my sight," I mumbled, though I wasn't sure my jaw worked right.

Hammer advanced, getting right up in my grill. "You got something of mine," he said, voice low and threatening. "Soon as I get it back, you'll never see me again."

"The fuck you talking about?" I stood my ground, though unsteady.

Sirens in the distance drew the bastard's attention toward the highway. Two blue and whites heading our way.

Hammer hung his head, gave it a shake, then tossed a set of keys at my feet. "I'll be in touch."

I stared at the gravel under my boots, watching the earth absorb drop after drop of my blood. After the rumble of Hammer's engine faded, I fired up my baby, and hit the open road.

What do ya know, the tin box from hell still stood, looking like a rotten tooth sprouted in the otherwise untainted landscape. Mother Nature had done her best to hide the eyesore. Yard was overgrown, though that was nothing new. Weeds and wildflowers reached almost to the windows. Years' worth of dead foliage and moss coated the roof.

A quick inspection revealed a broken window around back, most likely caused by a fallen branch, but the shithole didn't look like it'd been ransacked. Front door was boarded over, but easy enough to break through.

The second I stepped inside, prepubescent emotions rolled through me like acid, unwanted memories stinging my pulverized psyche. My sorry ass dropped to the moldy carpet, the polyester fibers clumped and hardened from years of abuse, spilled libations, piss, and vomit.

I'd taken beating after beating in that shithole. Covered my father's crimes. Witnessed and been victim to degradation most wouldn't survive.

Only reason I'd stuck around was for Addy. Wasted energy. My father had ruined her regardless. Looking back, maybe she would've been better off in the system instead of the rotten metal cage and its ever-changing parade of guards.

When my head stopped spinning enough for me to stand, I stumbled to my old room, pausing at the hole in the wall that had marked my turning point, changed my path, branded me abuser. No longer the victim.

The Slayers had come to collect a debt from my father on my tenth birthday. A bastard three times my size had tried to get "friendly," and I'd beaten the sick fuck to a bloody pulp. He'd only stopped me by shoving my head through the wall. The Slayers had threatened to kill me then, but after a private conversation with my father, the club had taken me under their wing. There was never any doubt I was nothing but a grunt. From that day on, until years later when they'd patched me in, I'd been called "trailer boy." A reminder that I was trash, like the heap of tin and sin I'd come from.

After I had proven myself loyal, and indispensable to the club, the derogatory nickname was upgraded to "Trailer."

For a short time, I wore that name with pride. Not anymore.

Face a pulsing, throbbing mess, I rifled through the closets, the cupboards, the hidden compartments under the carpets, coming up with a hefty stack of dear ol' dad's dirty money. I found a few photos of Addy that hadn't been destroyed and shoved them into my breast pocket.

Out back, the tool shed stood crooked, half the roof missing. I collected anything flammable—a canister filled with old gasoline, paint cans, turpentine, motor oil, then dragged that shit back to the metal shack, and made a pyro's version of pick-up-sticks in the center of the living room.

Giving the shithole a final fuck you, I raised my middle finger, made my way outside, lit a cigarette, took a long drag, then ignited the rest of the pack. I tossed the burning Marlboros through the open door, waited for the orange glow of flames, then kicked my bike into gear and left that putrid, piece of shit to burn.

Fuck my father. Fuck the Slayers. Fuck Trailer.

CHAPTER 14

Moriah

"FUCK THAT TRAILER TRASH piece of shit, fucking Reynolds." The stairwell door flew open, scaring a squeal out of me, and Tango barreled my way, face bloody, clothes dirty and disheveled, murderous glower aimed straight ahead.

Before I could muster a greeting, he grunted, "Clear my schedule. I won't make any meetings today."

"Sure." I paused, then before his door slammed shut, blurted, "Are you all right?"

Stupid question.

From behind the heavy wood, I heard, "Not even close."

Awkward situations were nothing new in my profession but having my new boss of two days storm through the building beaten to a bloody pulp was definitely a first. No protocol for that occurrence.

Instinct led me to the employee lounge, where I found hot coffee, ice, and a first aid kit. Then I dug a bottle of pain relievers out of my handbag. I found Tango slumped in his wingback chair, a fancy crystal tumbler full of amber liquid in his hand, attention aimed at the family photo on his desk.

Tango ignored me while I opened the shades, filled a plastic bag with the ice cubes, then got busy with the bandages and antiseptic. He didn't protest while I cleaned his face and winced only once while I dug dirt and pebbles out of his chin. The guy was either a rock, or he was in shock.

"I'm a good listener if you feel like talking."

"What I have to say, you don't want to hear." Shrugging away from me, he tipped his head and downed his liquor. "You know what? Fuck it." His glass landed on the desk, heavy bottom landing with a crack. "Dane is bad news. You and your niece need to stay the fuck away from him."

A punch to the gut would've been less surprising, painful, or nauseating. And because I fought a constant uprising of bile, and wonky hormones, and because I was already on edge from that strange encounter at breakfast, I slammed my hand on the desk and met him nose to nose. "I'm going to keep my mouth shut about that comment, considering the shape of your face. But I would appreciate if you don't talk to me in that tone ever again." A huff. A deep inhale. "I'm grateful for this job, but not dependent on it." Lie. Lie. Lie. "So I would have no problem walking away." I almost gagged on my verbal diarrhea.

Tango had absolutely no grounds to keep me under his employ. I hadn't been with the company long enough to make any kind of impression, and the thin ice began to crack under the weight of my self-righteous rant.

When he didn't order me to pack my belongings and leave, I picked up a cotton swab, squirted goopy gel on the tip, then continued poking his face. After a long silence, I asked, "So, how does the other guy look?"

The *other guy* obviously being Dane, considering Tango's outburst. I worried about his current state of health, assuming he was the reason Tango looked like he'd survived a tangle with a grizzly bear.

"He was uglier than sin to begin with. I might've improved his looks." Tango started to crack a smile, then mumbled, "ouch" under his breath, bringing a finger to the cut on his lip.

"All right. I've done all I can do." I leaned back, inspecting his wounds. "Let me know when you need more ice."

"Thanks, Moriah," he mumbled, pressing the cold bag to his face.

I gathered the garbage and turned to leave. Halfway through the door, I heard, "And I'm sorry for being a dick."

Back at my desk, my phone lit up with a string of unopened texts. All of them from Slade.

Mim is w/ me today. I'll take her to her appointment

BTW Dane is a jackass

Mim and Rocky are so cute together. He's teaching her to use the milkshake machine.

Mim let Charlie pick her up and set her on the counter. I almost cried

Did I mention Dane is a jackass?

Tango is a jackass too

I'm venting. Sorry

I'll bring Mim home after dinner if that's ok

I responded with: That's perfect thank you so much

I didn't question why Mim was with Slade. I trusted her completely. Dane, on the other hand, had some explaining to do. But that would have to wait until after work.

I released a frustrated breath and shook off the bad vibes. Had to be a full moon. Everyone was acting off kilter.

To prove my point, the senior Rossi sauntered toward my desk, all crisp, clean lines, sharp angles, and uber-confidence, singing "Downtown" by Macklemore and carrying a coffee mug that read "Billion Dollar Grandpa." He paused mid-rap and offered a panty-melting smile. "Morning, Miss Peterson."

"Good morning, Mr. Rossi."

"Tango in?" He gestured toward the closed door.

"Yes." I considered the courtesy of a warning, then decided it wasn't my place.

Mr. Rossi paused, sliding his free hand into the pocket of his trousers. "How are you settling into Whisper Springs?"

"Fine, thank you. I love this town. So charming."

"And your niece? She's well?"

"Better every day."

"Good to hear."

"Mr. Reynolds treating you well?"

"Mr. Reynolds?" I asked, my heart skipping a beat.

"I apologize. I assumed you and Dane were an item, considering..." He let the sentence hang. Charm seemed second nature to the handsome man, with those ridiculous good looks, intoxicating emerald eyes, and that dimple he wielded like a weapon, working their magic, weaving a spell that almost made me forget we were having a conversation.

But then I realized, Dane and I had kept our fling private, neither of us ready to put a name to whatever it was that was happening between us. And Mr. Rossi obviously knew something I did not, and judging by that annoying, albeit sexy smirk on his face, I should have known. "Considering what?"

With a deep, throaty chuckle, he offered, "Reynolds and I are old friends." He pinned me with a stare, waiting for me to connect the dots, a gleam in his eye, clearly enjoying himself.

Carlos Rossi and Dane old friends? Seemed unlikely. Still, my insides warmed, the mystery solved. "Let me guess. *Mr. Reynolds* got me this job?" Dane had gone behind my back to keep Mim and me in Whisper Springs.

"Apologies if that was meant to be a secret."

Mr. Rossi did not appear sorry in the least.

I should've been furious, but I couldn't muster an ounce of indignation. Why? Because although dirty and underhanded, Dane had fought to keep Mim and me close. And damn it, sometimes, being fought for felt really effin' good.

"And because he got me this job, you assumed that we're an item?"

He nodded, his grin fading. "Dane wouldn't have called me otherwise."

I wanted to ask why Dane wouldn't have called him otherwise. I wanted to know more, but I was a professional, and I would act as such. However, I wasn't about to let that handsome devil off the hook. "Mr. Rossi. We're both adults here. Let's be honest, you enjoyed letting that little secret leak, didn't you?" I offered a wink.

He countered with a panty-melting smile and a wink back. "Have a good day, Miss Peterson."

I smiled and waved, keeping my glee in check.

A warm, heavy weight lay over my stomach, rousing me from a daunting dream. Blinking sleep haze from my eyes, I slowly filtered my nightmare from reality, drawing measured, quiet breaths in attempt to steady my racing heart.

Though drowned in darkness, I knew who shared the couch with me, whose thighs my calves were perched upon, whose strong finger traced a circle over my stomach. The scent of alcohol, sweat, and night air permeated the room.

"How long have you been here?" I tried to rise, but he held me steady, a firm grip on my ankle with one hand, the other weighing heavy on my abdomen.

"Couple hours," came a clipped reply.

Agitation rippled the air, adding substance to the silence. "What happened today?"

"Best you don't ask."

"I have every right to know." I kicked free of his grip and shoved to the sitting position. "You said you would take care of Mim. You didn't. And I had to hear from Slade that you'd pawned her off."

The couch shifted. "Fuck," floated through the room, more pained than angry.

Weary, and in no mood to fight, I straddled Dane's lap, ignoring the scratch of denim on my bare thighs. I reached for his beard, but he clamped my wrists and pressed my hands to his bare chest instead, his warmth doing crazy things to my libido.

His silhouette revealed cuts and swollen areas, his handsome mug clearly marred. "What happened?"

"Doesn't matter."

"You can talk to me, you know." I kissed his cheek, a featherlight assurance. "I'm on your side. Whatever it is."

His chest rose and fell. "Don't need to talk."

Uncomfortable silence followed, and I knew if I could see his face, I'd find those eyes gone dark.

I swallowed my trepidation. "What *do* you need?"

His fingers tightened around my thighs. One deep breath. A moan that sounded like a growl.

"I need to fuck." With a grunt, he gripped my ass and yanked me closer, slamming my knees into the cushions, grinding me against his erection, stealing my air. "And I need to forget." He forced a hand between us, moved my panties aside, and worked his voodoo. "Can you give me that, gorgeous? Give me a place to get lost?"

Warm lips brushed mine, his rum-laden breath heightening my arousal. Beneath me, the man was coiled tight, a spring ready to snap, vibrating and humming with an undercurrent of violence.

Strange, my strong sense of security. Curious, my desire to ease his burdens.

In my blissful, sleepy state, I rode his hand, my pleasure spiraling, and rasped, "Trailer."

He stiffened, a low rumble rising up his throat, then bit my lip, and plunged those thick fingers deeper between my legs. "Trailer is fucking dead. It's Dane."

The poison in his tone triggered warning bells, breaking the spell. Hands to his chest, I tried to push away. "Are you okay?"

Rough, and unrestrained, he pulled me tighter against his unforgiving muscles, and circled my clit with his thumb. "Does this feel good?"

"Yes." Oh. Shit. Shit. "Yes."

"Then shut those gorgeous lips and let me fuck you."

My stomach lurched, but Dane gave me no time to react, fisting my hair, and forcing our mouths together.

Though my mind protested, my body gave way to his lips, his hands, his raw, violent need. Every sweep of his tongue, or stroke of his finger, made me hungry, desperate for more, for any pain he could share. Whatever filthy, vile, dirty purge he needed to use me for, I was all in. I was game. His puppet on a string. Somewhere in the back of my mind, I knew regret was inevitable, but in the moment of heat and desperation, I let go of reason and gave myself to the monster beneath me.

Dane was everything and everywhere. Breath, sound. Touch, taste, smell. Darkness, pain, and exquisite pleasure, and I was nothing but a woman wanted, a greedy soul wanting more, more, more.

I came on his hand, whimpering, "Yes, yes, yes," into his neck, and before crashing from the high, we were moving, and then he tossed me on the bed, and his jeans hit the floor.

The mattress bounced, and Dane crawled over me, his beard tickling everywhere his lips touched, my skin tightening and tingling.

When I gripped the hard, hot length of him and dragged my nails up his shaft, he moaned profanities, his hips jutting, filling me with a sense of power.

A victory short-lived.

Dane rolled me to my stomach, peeled my panties over my butt, my thighs, then yanked hard, ridding me of the cotton barrier. Tense and heavy, he lay over me. Tucking his arms under my chest, locking me in place, he shoved his face into my hair, his cock between my legs, and filled me, stretched me, claimed me in one brutal thrust.

Unable to move, or draw a full breath, I lay helpless, accepting his weight, his strength, the unforgiving bites on my shoulders and neck, the vulgar words he rasped in my ear, while he rendered me boneless with each merciless stroke. Relentless and brutal, he pounded into me, and when I couldn't take anymore, I begged, "Dane. Dane, wait, I can't..."

His weight left my body. Breathless, I pushed to hands and knees.

"On your back." He gave me room to move, though his tone left no room for argument.

The moment I rolled over, he caged me again, pinning my arms above my head, and sliding into me, forcing a moan, the fullness of him beyond perfect.

"That's right," he grunted, rolling his hips and building a rhythm. "Fuckin' take me, baby." His teeth sank into my neck. Then my breast. His tongue soothing every pinch.

He continued that way, biting, licking, kissing, marking every inch of skin he could claim. I wanted his mouth, ached to feel his heat under my fingers, but he wouldn't let me move, chasing his pleasure, greedy and merciless, never pausing, only pounding, growling, fucking me into the mattress, into oblivion.

I cried his name into the dark, a praise, a plea, and finally, he released my arms, grabbed my hips, and tilted me to accept him deeper. My body arched in pleasure, and I fisted his hair to ground myself.

Grunts, moans, and the slap of flesh hitting flesh filled the room, none of those sounds as erotic as the filthy declarations whispered in my ear. *Your pussy is heaven. So sweet. So fucking wet. Gonna ruin you. These tits are perfect...*

On and on he continued, working me, mind and body, into a frenzy. My spirit soared. As pleasure reached its peak, Dane sat back on his heels, lifting me with him, snaking his arms around my waist and helping me ride his cock, chase the high, claim my release.

Voice thick and strained, he rasped, "You're mine. My fucking salvation."

Those words hurled me over the edge. My thighs burned from exertion, but Dane pumped into me from beneath, and I was done, mindless and boneless, and as he grunted profanities through his own orgasm, I came, too, my pleasure, my emotion spilling over. "Oh, shit. Oh, shit. Yes. Yes. Dane. I love you."

My bad boy stilled.

The world came to an abrupt halt, everything suspended and floaty.

How desperately I wished I could take those words back, chew them up and choke them down.

In the torturous seconds that followed, I debated apologizing for my slip, blaming the heat of the moment. Denying my sincerity would make me a liar. So, I let his silence brew into a poisonous concoction of unspoken truths.

The fact being, I'd crossed a line that Dane wasn't ready to breach.

Dane's breath hitched. He pressed his lips into my hair, lingering for painful seconds, then laid me down, and left the bed.

My body would be bruised after what he'd just done to me, but my heart? My heart. Oh, God.

Crushed. Battered. Shredded.

How could I have been so careless?

I listened, eyes pinched, while he shut himself in the bathroom, ran the water, came back out, shuffled around for his clothes, then stomped out of the bedroom. He paused by Mim's door, then continued, out the front door, dragging my heart and guts along for the ride.

The locks engaged, and I was left alone.

"Dr. Anderson said you did great yesterday."

Mim smiled, a dribble of milk forging a path down her chin as she chewed her Lucky Charms.

"Tomorrow is Saturday. We get the whole day together. What do you think we should do?"

Eyebrows scrunched, lips puckered, she looked to the ceiling, then raised a finger, hopped off her chair, and skipped to the counter to rummage through the stack of junk mail. She returned with a full-page flyer for the mega baby store in town and pointed to a picture of a crib.

My eyes burned, threatening to spill over. "You want to go shopping for the baby?"

She nodded, studying my face with bright, hopeful eyes.

Fireworks erupted in my chest, carving new grooves, making space for all the extra love. "Oh, Mim. That sounds like fun."

Shopping was the furthest thing from my mind, but how could I deny that sweet face? "Maybe we can go to the toy store, too, and find you some new puzzles."

For a brief moment, I allowed myself to think that maybe Dane would want to join us. However, after the *I love you* slip, aside from a text saying he would be out of town for a few days, he'd pulled a Houdini. Honestly, though, what did I expect? We'd only known each other a few weeks. In that short period of time, he'd had a six-year-old girl, an emotionally unstable woman, a baby surprise, and an *I love you* thrown at him like a Molotov cocktail. The whole situation was crazy and unbelievable.

Any sane person would cut and run.

I couldn't blame him. Didn't mean I wasn't hurting. After all, he had begged me never to leave him, no matter how bad he messed up. But the moment I'd blurted my feelings? Poof. Gone. Leaving me to choke on a black cloud of bad boy dust. That was bullshit. And dammit, I had every right to be angry.

The doorbell rang.

I checked the clock. "That must be Rocky and Slade. Hurry and go brush your teeth. They're taking you to see Leticia today."

Mim dashed to the bathroom while I answered the door. Slade wrapped me in a warm and much-needed embrace, while Rocky shouted, "Hi, Moriah. Where's Mim?"

I pointed down the hall, and he disappeared.

"Please tell me you have coffee." The smile I'd grown accustomed to seeing on Slade's face hid behind worried eyes.

"I have coffee."

Slade followed me to the kitchen and made herself comfortable at my small table. "So, how are the two of you settling in?"

"Mim is doing so well." I pulled a mug from the cupboard and shoved a K-cup into the coffee machine. "Much better than I expected. Although I have you and Rocky to thank for that. If I'd had to find childcare, I don't know what I would've done, or how she would've handled strangers."

"Rocky reminds me so much of Tango when he was young. So protective."

"That's what she needs." I set her coffee on the table.

Slade blanched, eyes going liquid. "You know, Dane has always been that way, too. Only, he was subtler about it, almost as if he were ashamed, didn't want to make a show about caring for people."

"I know, right? He gets all grumpy, acts like it's a burden when Mim needs him, but behind closed doors, he's all gooey and sweet with her. He sings to her when he thinks nobody is listening."

"That's Dane. When we were kids, his cousin, Addison, used to get herself into all kinds of trouble. He would get so mad at her, but swear to God, he was always there to bail her out, even when she didn't ask for help, even when she fought him tooth and nail."

"Where's Addison now?"

"She died." Slade turned her head. Rubbed the back of her hand over her cheek. "Almost eight years ago."

"Oh." I finished pouring creamer into my cup, then joined Slade at the table, resting a hand over hers. "Must've been hard losing your friend."

She nodded, teary gaze aimed over my shoulder. "Harder for Dane, I suspect. Although he'd never admit how much he misses her."

Slade took a sip of coffee, set her mug down, then fidgeted, dragging her fingers over the flyer Mim had set down earlier. "Have you heard from Dane? He isn't returning my calls."

God, that question hit like a punch to the gut. "No. Haven't heard from him in a few days."

Slade studied my face, her bright blue eyes reflecting the turmoil that ate at my insides.

"Can I ask you something?" She leaned forward, crossing her arms on the table.

I nodded, unease slithering through me.

"Are you and Dane an item?"

My blood ran cold, eliciting a shiver. Dane and I were something, though I was hesitant to add a label to our unusual relationship. My brain reeled, searching for a suitable answer.

A problem solved by two effin' kids.

Rocky came barreling down the hall, Mim in tow, their hands entwined like long-time best friends. "Mom! Mom! Guess what Mim just told me?"

Much to my horror, he did not wait for Slade to guess.

"Mim is going to have a baby brother or sister and Dane is going to be their daddy!"

Slade's coffee landed on the floor with a dull thud, splashing my feet and legs. Neither one of us acknowledged the spill, sharing a silent stare down laced with tension.

I silently begged her, "Please keep this between us."

She wordlessly communicated disappointment, her eyes narrowing, a red glow spreading across her cheeks.

Unable to bear the scrutiny, I hopped up to grab a towel, then gripped the counter, fighting a wave of nausea.

Behind me, Slade said, "Mim. Go grab your swimsuit and a towel. It's supposed to be hot today."

I waited for the pitter-patter of feet to reach Mim's room before turning, and blurting, because I really needed her to know, "I love him. I don't know how or why, or that I could fall in love with anyone that fast, and I know it sounds crazy, but I love him."

"Oh, Moriah." Slade wrapped her arms around me once again. "I'm so mad at Dane right now, and I wish I could tell you why, but I can't. And I am happy for you. I really am. And I think I'm happy for Dane, too. At least, I would be, if I wasn't so mad at him. But. Oh, God. He's going to be a dad, and you're going to be a mom, and if there's one thing I know about that big jackass is that he'll move heaven and Earth to take care of you and that baby. He will."

She took a deep breath. "But be careful, okay? He hasn't had an easy life. He grew up surrounded by crazy, and you should know what you're getting into." She leaned back, studying me, then brushed a tear off my cheek. "I get it. I do. Underneath all the scary ink and muscle, and his grunts and one-word conversations, he's a good guy. He doesn't believe he's got a redemptive bone in his body, but I've seen it, and you have too, obviously. But if you love him, and want any kind of relationship, you have to know things are not going to be easy. With Dane, you're going to get dark and dirty. You're going to live and breathe all the gritty, ugly details of his life."

"That's the thing, Slade. I think that's what I love most about him. He lives unapologetically. He knows who he is. Doesn't try to hide it."

Slade snatched the towel from my hand and cleaned her mess. I watched, unable to move, considering her words.

Despite her warning, I sensed she had my back. And I could swear she hid a smile as she squatted to mop the spilled coffee off the floor.

"Thank you, Lettie. I would love to come for dinner. Can I bring anything?"

"I've got it covered. Just bring yourself. I've missed you. It will be nice to catch up."

I laid my phone on the desk and finished typing up the proposals Tango had emailed earlier, the knot in my stomach tighter than it'd been all day.

I still hadn't heard from Dane, and I refused to call him. The ball was in his court. Maybe I'd scared him away. So be it. I would survive. Heck, I'd thrive.

Tango came out of his office, his green eyes popping amidst the dark purple bruising around his face, and stood to the side of my desk, head down, raking a hand through his hair. "Hey. Have a minute?"

"Considering you're the boss, all my minutes are yours."

He laughed, shoving his hand in his pockets and nodding to his office. "In there, where it's private."

"Do I need to bring a notepad?"

"No."

I followed him inside his office, and walked to the window, enjoying the view of Lake Willow. Boats of all shapes littered the water, and a parasail caught my attention in the blue sky. "It must've been great growing up in this town."

"No better place to raise a kid, far as I'm concerned." He stood at my side, and sighed.

"What did you want to talk about?"

Tango turned to face me. "I heard." He dropped his gaze to my stomach, then met my eyes. "And don't be mad at Slade for telling me. She was worried about you."

"I won't let it affect my job. You don't have to worry."

"I'm not concerned about your job performance." He stepped back, resting against the window sill. "I wanted to assure you that my feelings for Dane Reynolds will have no bearing on our work relationship."

"I appreciate you saying that."

"That being said," he continued, crossing his arms, "I would never hinder Rocky and Mim's friendship. I know how important they are to each other. But if that piece of shit is going to be part of your life, I'll have to respectfully request that he is never brought into this office, or anywhere near my family."

"Tango, I—"

"And," he interrupted, "if he hurts you, or Mim, in any way, there will be consequences."

Protective instincts bubbled to the surface. Dane would never hurt Mim. He'd never hurt me physically. He could only hurt me emotionally, and only if I allowed him that power, which I had no intention of doing.

Curiosity got the better of me. "What did he do to deserve so much hate?"

Tango dropped his arms, the veins in his hands popping as he clenched them into fists. "That's between me and Dickface. He wants you to know, you'll know."

I nodded, unsure how to respond.

"You and me, we're good." He headed toward his desk. "Your job is secure. That's one thing you don't have to worry about. And if you need anything. Anything. Don't hesitate to ask. We take care of our people, and you're one of us now, okay?"

"Thank you, Tango."

"Oh. And fair warning." A sinister grin lit his face. "Rockster can't keep a secret to save his life. I'm sure everyone knows that you're pregnant by now."

"Perfect." I feigned annoyance, despite the relief lifting my spirits.

"I'm sure Lettie will offer her services."

"I just got off the phone with her. She invited me for dinner."

He laughed. "Yeah. She's gonna work you." He shifted a paper on his desk. "Little advice? Let her be your doctor.

Nobody smarter than that woman. And, it'll do her good to get back to work. Put all that fancy, expensive medical equipment at the mansion to good use."

"Thank you, Tango. I was nervous about dropping the baby bomb on you. You just lifted a thousand-pound weight off my shoulders."

I excused myself. Sat at my desk. Lifted my chin. Put Dane, Mim, the baby, and all my worries to rest.

And vowed to be the best damn administrative assistant the world had ever seen.

CHAPTER 15

"SHE'S THE BEST FIGHTER I've ever seen." Tito rubbed the hem of his shirt over one of the many weapons he had hidden on his person. Have you seen the way she handles a blade?"

"No."

"Just sayin'. Don't piss off that woman."

Jesus. Fuck. I got it. Aida was a badass. Didn't understand why Tito felt the need to keep drilling that fact into my head.

"Remind me why I'm here." I shifted my ass, hoping to encourage blood flow and ease the pinch in my hip. Not easy to accomplish inside the cramped sedan that measured two sizes too small for a guy of my stature.

"Tucker likes to keep his hands clean." Tito turned his shiny blade over for one last inspection, the dim light catching the carvings on the black handle. "I work better in the mud." He tucked the knife back into his boot. "Need some backup for this job. And I know from experience, you don't mind getting your hands dirty."

The smug bastard leaned back, arms crossed, and settled into his seat, like he hadn't a care in the world. "Besides, thought you might want to blow off some steam, have some fun before the baby comes."

The tin can shrank around me, heating a thousand degrees. "The fuck you know about a baby?"

"Mim told Rocky. Rockster told everybody. That kid can't keep a secret for shit."

"Jesus. Fuck." Had I room to move, I would've knocked the smirk off his face. Instead, I closed my eyes, shook my head, and tried to forget how I'd walked out on Moriah after she'd said those three foreign words that had never been aimed my direction. *I love you.*

"Don't know whether to congratulate you or beat your ass for being so fuckin' careless."

"Was an accident." Why the fuck was I explaining myself?

"An accident?" Tito huffed. "What, your bare cock accidentally slipped between her legs?"

I had no comeback. Truth was, I'd been so drunk on whiskey and Moriah, I'd let my guard down, and we'd fucked countless times those first two nights. Maybe I'd forgotten to wrap my dick, or maybe the damn condom had slipped, or broke. The *how* didn't fucking matter. We'd made a baby. The *what next* was what had me in a mood.

Tito quirked a brow, scratching the scar on his face. "You plan on making an honest woman of her?"

His question struck me like a head-on between a two-speed and a Mac truck, pulverizing my weak frame, leaving nothing but twisted metal.

Rings and wedding bells? Fuck no.

But damn, the woman was crazy enough to think she loved me. Jackass or not, I was smart enough to realize she'd given a rare and precious gift. One I would treasure whether we shared a last name or not.

But that was nobody's business but mine. "You gonna be like this all night, Freddie Kruger? 'Cause I got no problem hitching a ride back to Whisper Springs."

Tucker's voice came over our earpieces. "You twats about done? Blue Lincoln. On your five."

A Navigator rolled into the dark lot, lights off, windows black.

"Flashy fucker," Tito growled. "I'm gonna enjoy taking this guy out."

Tucker lit his phone and flashed three quick beams, luring the target to his vehicle.

Tito and I waited in our car parked at the opposite end of the lot. The clock read 1:17 AM. My stomach knotted, pulse raced, and when a young girl, who couldn't have been older than eleven or twelve, stumbled out of the SUV wearing a dress that barely covered her ass, and heels too unstable for her skinny legs, that damn organ in my chest pummeled my ribcage something fierce. The kid was an older version of what Mim might've been. A younger version of what Addy had become.

The girl swayed, struggling to stay upright, her head lolling to the side.

"Fuck. They drugged her. Fuck!" Tito pounded the steering wheel.

Tucker's jagged breaths crackled through the earpiece.

I was seconds from going nuclear myself. "Why aren't we dangling this guy from his balls already?"

"I knew you were the right guy." Tito shifted in his seat, rage rolling off him like a heavy fog.

"Shit," Tucker roared. "She's not gonna make it to my rig. Change of plans." His door flew open. He skipped the vehicle's side step entirely and landed with impressive form before sprinting toward the girl, shouting, "Cover me. Cover me."

"Motherfuckers!" Tito retrieved the blade from his boot, and ripped from the car, sprinting at full speed across the lot.

My feet hit the pavement at the same time the child crumpled.

Up ahead, a large figure erupted from the Lincoln. "Leave her!" he shouted, strutting in Tucker's direction, gun raised, a cocky stride to his steps.

Ignoring all threats, Tucker fell over the girl, blocking her small frame with his massive shoulders.

The pimp pointed the gun Tucker's direction and hurried his pace. "Back the fuck away."

Tito struck before the guy aimed, the two men falling into a tangled ball on the ground.

The passenger door of the Lincoln opened just as I rounded the rear. A skinny shit with a shaved head stepped in front of me, struggling to pull something from the back of his baggy jeans. A throat punch took him down. A kick to the skull ensured he'd stay horizontal. I cleared the vehicle for threats, and by the time I'd reached Tito, the other guy lay bloody and unconscious at his feet.

Tucker hauled the child off the ground, her head and limbs hanging limp. "She breathing, but she needs a hospital."

"Go. Go." Tito motioned toward Tucker's hidden truck. "We got this."

Tucker turned and disappeared into the dark lot.

"Ready for some fun?" Tito asked, squatting next to the shithead on the ground.

I nodded, jonesing for blood.

"Go grab the sedan." He tossed me the keys. "There's rope in the back."

After binding those child peddlers tight and packing them in the trunk of our stolen vehicle, we headed to the on ramp, my mind heavy with thoughts of Mim and what-could-have-beens.

"You saved another kid tonight. Another life. How does that feel?"

Up ahead, the freeway blended with the dark, cloudless sky. "Feeling twitchy, you want the truth."

"You're feeling that way 'cause there hasn't been any closure yet. I mean, the girl is safe. But that's not enough, right?"

Not sure where he was going, so I grunted.

"You see"—Tito tapped his thumbs to a rapid beat on the steering wheel—"these fuckers won't stop unless we take them down."

"Okay."

"Tucker doesn't want anything to do with that side of the business."

Didn't surprise me. Fucking good ol' American boy.

"We got deep-seated issues, you and me. We need to make them pay. Make them bleed." He threw me a sideways glance, brow hitched. "Am I wrong?"

"No." Nothing better than bringing down your enemies. "The bloodier, the better."

"I knew we'd be on the same page." He rolled into the lot of a run-down motel. The sign read, SWEET CREEK LODGE, but there was nothing sweet about the property. The L-shaped, two-story building needed a new roof. The siding had long since served its purpose. Two windows were boarded with warped wood tagged with graffiti. The only bright spot was the red neon NO VACANCY sign hanging in the office window.

Tito threw the vehicle into park, hung his arms over the dash, and pointed to the neglected building. "The owner lets it slide, all the girls passing through these rooms. I suppose he gets a cut. Every day before he leaves, he deletes the security footage." Tito pointed out five different areas on the lot, each where a camera was perched. "I bypassed his feed two weeks ago. That footage is on its way to the Feds."

"That's it?" I rolled my stiff neck. "You do all that work, then trust the Feds to handle shit?"

"No." His chuckle made me shiver. "Room six is where they filmed the girls. Brokered their deals."

"Jesus H Christ." The videos playing in Wilson Kyle's cabin came to mind, the memory of Mim in that dirt hole flooding me with unholy rage. "And?"

"Room six is where we're taking them down."

Thank fuck. "We ghosting them?

"No. Promised Tuuli and Aida, no more killing."

"Then why the fuck are you wasting my time?" I needed to bloody some bastards, my nerves stretched beyond their limit. I reached for the door handle, stopped when Moretti slammed another blade in my lap.

"Trust me. By the time we're finished, they'll wish they were dead."

"You need to start using the doorbell." Moriah's voice sliced through the dark, a little angry, a lot broken, and the sweetest damn sound to ever reach my ears.

When I sat beside her, she flipped on the mattress, offering her back and pulling the sheet up to her chin.

Couldn't blame the woman. I deserved far more than the cold shoulder. And I'd take any verbal lashing she threw my way, as long as there was skin to skin involved. I slid under the soft sheet, and pulled her flush, settling that perfect ass against my groin.

"You need to leave, Dane." Her command held little weight when she snuggled closer.

"Not leaving." Nose buried in her damp hair, I took my fill of her piña colada scent. "I missed you."

Her chest rose and fell. "Three days. Not one word from you."

Because I was a chickenshit. "I know."

"That's it? That's all you've got to say?"

Fuck. I sucked at apologizing. "Had shit to do I couldn't tell you about."

"Illegal shit," she mumbled into the darkness and wiggled away from my touch.

Feeling the sting of rejection, I rolled to my back and roughed a hand over my head, rubbing the dull ache. "I've never lied to you about who I am."

"No, you haven't, and I accept that, but this disappearing act? Not acceptable."

Tension threatened to crack my chest, and damn if I'd let that fissure spread. *I'm sorry*, were the words she needed, and the very words I couldn't form. Grasping for straws, I asked, "You mad at me?"

Pathetic, yes.

Too many seconds passed before Moriah spoke. "I don't know. People keep warning me about you. What am I supposed to think? What am I getting myself into? I'm clueless here. We're not even in a relationship, you know?"

"We're not?" I asked, having no basis for argument.

Another long pause, then she whispered, "Are we?"

"I'm here. I'm not leaving."

The mattress shifted, but I couldn't look her way, afraid of what I'd find.

"And that constitutes being in a relationship?"

"I wouldn't know," I said to the ceiling. "I can only give you what I have to offer."

"And all you have to offer is being here."

"Yes." And all of me. My body. My rage. My hunger.

"Dane. I told you I love you, and you disappeared."

"I'm here."

With a huff, Moriah wiggled free of the blankets, the bed bouncing under her defiance. Hard footsteps marched across the floor, light flooded the room, and my gorgeous woman, with her wild hair, ridiculous freckles, and killer curves, stood hands to hips, and glared. Until she took in the condition of my mug, the bruising now a dark purple, evidence of my fight with Tango.

Sympathy flashed across her face before her brows pinched. "Jesus. He really did a number on you, didn't he?"

"It was long overdue."

"What does that mean?"

"That's between me and Tango."

"Unbelievable." She plucked my shirt from the floor and threw it at me. "Get out." My jeans came next, whipping my face. "Get. Out!"

The pain shooting through my chest was unbearable. I threw the blankets back and dropped my feet to the floor, counting in my head, *one, two, three,* forcing the anger and frustration down. I rose, slow and steady.

Moriah stepped back, chest rising and falling, cheeks red, eyes wet. "I'm having your effin' baby and I'm stuck with you, but that doesn't mean I have to put up with your bullshit."

I stalked closer. "I'm here."

She stood her ground. "You've said that. You're here. But guess what? I'm here, too. I'm here with you. I'm here for you. I'm here when you aren't. I'm here when Mim calls out for you at night."

"What?" My head snapped back like I'd taken a punch.

"Yeah. She cries for you in her sleep. She was calling your name. And you were gone."

"Shit."

"So cut the bullshit. If you're here, then effin' be here. All of you. You hear me? All of you. I need words, Dane. I need to hear about your day. I need to know what's going on in your head. I need to know if and why somebody beat the shit out of your face. I need to know why you disappear for days. And I need details. I don't care how ugly they are. You can't give me that, then get the eff out of my house, and give me back that spare key."

Ultimatums pissed me off, and despite the fact I was in the wrong, I lashed back. "You want ugly details? You want my ugly details? Fine. Years ago, I helped my cousin drug Tango. I helped her because I hated that pretty boy motherfucker. What he had, who he had, what he stood for. Hated him. I helped Addy drug him, fuck him, make a God damn baby with him. Then I tried to take his girl."

Moriah's gaze dropped to my feet, then she raised her chin and met my glare. "That's why he hates you?"

"Oh, no sweetheart, that's not the half of it." I slid a hand around her neck, then fisted the hair at her nape, holding her steady, giving her no room to flee. "Tango left. Slade didn't want me. Addy found out she was pregnant with Tango's kid. Know what I did? Not a God damned thing. I went on with my life while Addison fell apart. While my father and his sick fucking friends abused her. Blondie tried to save my cousin, despite knowing she was carrying Tango's child, and she managed to save the baby. But Addy? She was too far gone. They hurt her, they killed her, and there wasn't a damn thing I could do to stop them."

"Who?" Her voice trembled. "Who killed her?"

"The club. My brothers. My sick fuck of a father."

"Dane," she whispered on an exhale.

"That's only a sliver of my ugly. Want more?"

Her mouth formed, "Yes." Her eyes pleaded, *no.*

"My father went after Slade. Tango took him down, but I killed him. Made him pay for what he'd done to Addison."

Fat tears rolled down her cheeks, and she mirrored my glare, feigning composure and failing. "That all?"

God, I loved her grit, despite her repulsion. "Not even close."

Moriah stared right through me, chin high, challenging. I gave it right back, silently begging her to concede.

Thank fuck, she backed down, closing her eyes and whispering, "No more. I don't need anymore. Not tonight."

I kissed her wet lips, then let her go. "This is who I am, Moriah. I'm sorry you're stuck with me, but I'm not leaving. Not ever. Not letting the best thing that ever happened to me slip through my fingers."

I yanked my boxers off the bed, stumbled into them, and then pulled my T-shirt over my head. "You love me now?" I asked, mocking—a defense mechanism, cruel and meant to hurt.

Moriah flinched, but didn't take the bait. Instead, she asked, "Where are you going?"

"Mim wakes up calling for me, I'm gonna be there. I wanna hear her say my name. Want her to know she never has to be afraid again." I slipped out the door, knowing I'd pushed too hard, revealed too much.

Hell, wouldn't have surprised me if the police came knocking and dragged me away in cuffs after my confession. Would have been the smartest thing she could do.

Only, the police didn't come. Mim called for me in her sleep, her voice an angel's song, and I woke her from her bad dream, whispering promises in her ear, and I let her kiss my cheek, and rake her fingers through my beard, and fall asleep curled against me, clinging tightly.

I'd be her hero. I'd be her everything. Because...God damn my motherfucking, fucked-up life, I loved that kid, and her crazy aunt.

"Authorities have not confirmed whether these attacks are connected with the Rest Area Reaper, but they aren't denying that whoever is behind this bizarre scene wanted to send a warning." On the screen, the camera panned wide, showing a low-budget motel. "Three men were found bound, and strung from the ceiling, with the words CHILD RAPIST carved not only into their faces, but all over their bodies. One source tells us that evidence was found in the room linking these men to as many as seventeen missing persons reports, eleven of those missing persons being children under the age of fourteen. One of those missing girls was admitted to Hopstead General Hospital early this morning..."

"At first they thought the guy was only mugging truck drivers," Moriah said, pulling the butterfly puzzle apart and dropping the pieces one at a time into the box.

Shame. It'd taken Mim and I three hours to put that one together.

"Mmm," I grunted, lifting the beer bottle to my lips and taking a slow sip.

"Now they say the Reaper is targeting people involved in underage prostitution."

"Yeah. I heard that."

"If that's the case, I hope that vigilante makes them suffer." She closed the lid, sat back on the couch, and tucked her feet under her butt. "If I could meet that guy, I'd give him a hug."

Shit. My chest. "So, you think what he's doing is a good thing?"

"Yes. Don't you? I mean, if what they say is true, and this man or woman is hunting child rapists and sex traffickers, then, hell yes. Make them suffer. Make an example out of them."

Hadn't expected that response from little Miss *I Don't Like the F Word.*

"The violence doesn't bother you?"

"Before Mim, I might've said yes. But now? I don't know. Feels good knowing somebody hurt them back." Moriah pointed the remote and shut off the big screen. "It terrifies me, thinking what could've happened to our little girl."

Our little girl.

Moriah didn't catch her slip, but I did, straight in the gut, and God damn I was about to suffocate on the sudden rush of feelings. I didn't do feelings. Didn't like them. So, I pushed off the sofa and made for the kitchen, biding time to pull my shit together.

I suffered no moral conviction. What Tito and I had done to those men was legally wrong, but I'd never felt so right, so justified in carrying out a violent act. That whole night had been euphoric, despite the gruesome nature. Knowing we'd saved another kid? Fucking fantastic. Only two days had passed, and I was already itching to do it again. For Mim. For Addison.

Hated to admit that Moretti had been spot-on. I was the right guy for the job. We were cut from the same cloth, both suffering the innate need to punish, to atone for past sins, to purge.

I wanted more. Only, I couldn't move forward without bringing Moriah into the loop.

"Dane." Her voice seemed far away.

I had to tell her. Had no choice. She wanted truth. All my ugly.

"You okay?" A warm hand landed on my shoulder.

I opened my eyes. Hands planted on the white marble, head hanging, I sucked in a sharp breath.

Fuck. Fuck. Fuck.

I grabbed my girl by the waist and hoisted her onto the counter, then stepped between her knees and gripped her hips. God, the way that soft flesh melded under my fingers drove me crazy. "What did they tell you about the mansion? Its purpose."

"That it's a safe house for troubled kids."

"Nothing more?"

"No. Why?"

"The mansion. Tucker. Tito. Dr. Slade." My throat constricted against the thick lump forming. "The Rest Area Reaper. They're all connected."

"What do you mean?"

I sucked in another breath, then blew out, "Tucker is the Reaper."

Moriah snorted. Slapped my shoulder. Laughed. The twinkle in her eyes faded while she waited for me to concede.

"Is this a joke?"

I swiped at a freckle under her lip, studying her face, chin to brilliant, beautiful eyes, my breath catching. "No. Not a joke. Tucker did it on his own for years. Then he brought Moretti into the mix. Eventually Lettie and James got involved, using the mansion to rehabilitate the kids Tucker rescues."

Brows worried, she waited for me to continue.

So, I did. Throwing everything on the table. "They brought me in last week."

"Brought you in...how?"

"Those men in the hotel. That was Tito and me."

She leaned back on her arms, putting distance between us. "You guys carved those men up?"

"Yes."

"They needed you, why?"

"That was a two-man job, and Tucker's not so keen on getting bloody."

Moriah stared, eyes unfocused at my chest. "But you are."

"It's who I am."

"And the girl at the hospital, that was Tucker?"

"She'd OD'd. Her captors shot her up, trying to keep her compliant. He got her to the emergency room in the nick of time."

"This is a lot of information to take in."

"I know."

"So that explains the tight security at the mansion. The privacy. The false documents Tito produced."

I nodded.

Painful seconds passed. Moriah gnawed on her lower lip, then met my eyes again. "If you hadn't found me, what would've happened to Mim?"

"Those are questions best aimed at Tucker or Leticia. I don't have all the details."

"This is..." She pushed me away and hopped off the counter. "Wow. I um..." She stepped away. Stopped. Turned to face me. "Thank you for telling me." She shoved hair away from her face, stared at the floor, then huffed, backing away. "And thanks for staying with Mim today. But. Um. I need a bath. And I need time to think. And I think you should not stay here tonight.

Warm candlelight cast dancing shadows across the white tiles, licking Moriah's skin with sultry radiance. She lay with her head back, knees up, eyes closed, bubbles to her chin.

I watched from the doorway, unsteady, unsure, unable to tear my eyes from that peaceful, freckled face, or the way those lips moved as she sang along to the music coming from the portable speaker, something about feeling a rush, having a crush, and hoping it's not too much.

The room smelled like fresh cookies, and my insides warmed at the overload of stimuli. I should've respected her wishes. Gave her time alone. I'd tried. Made it out the door. Down the hallway. Had my finger on the elevator call button before an icy freeze washed over me, halting my retreat.

I had nowhere to go. Nowhere I belonged. Sure, I had a permanent suite at the mansion, but I was nothing but a tick in that vast space, desperately searching for somewhere warm and fleshy to land, somewhere to burrow deep and draw sustenance.

Moriah was my place. My somewhere to be. My flesh and blood home.

I toed off my boots outside the door. Caught her attention when I ditched my jeans, T-shirt, and boxers on the bathroom floor. Those hungry eyes scanned every inch of my skin in silent appraisal.

I squatted, dropping a kiss on that lush mouth, expecting a fight, so fucking thankful when instead, she moaned into my mouth, her knees falling to the sides.

I released her lips, holding her wanton gaze, skimmed a palm down her belly, then worked that bundle of nerves between her legs, challenging her to complain, or push me away.

Instead, my gorgeous woman dropped her head back on the ledge, and she rode my hand, curling those hips into my fingers, heavy lidded gaze on mine, silently begging, *more, more, more*. Water splashed. She panted. Too soon, she slapped a hand around my neck, her body arching while she came undone, curling into me, burying her face in my arm, whispering, "Oh, God. Oh, God. Oh, God."

For a long moment she held me, breaths heavy, and I pushed my finger between her folds, a slow tease, letting her know we were not finished.

A new song played over the speaker, slower than the last, haunting almost, a man singing to his lover. Moriah slid deeper into the bubbles.

I stepped into the lukewarm water. Wasn't pretty, settling into the tub, even though the thing was wide enough to hold three people, but I managed. I'd never felt less a man sinking into a mountain of bubbles, but I'd never been more thankful to be a man when Moriah slid her foot up and down the length of my aching cock.

She smirked. "You didn't leave."

"No." I sank lower, bracing her small hips with my feet, and studied her mischievous expression. "You mad at me?"

Fuck. That smile.

She made me wait before saying, "I look mad?" then added her other foot to the rub and tug, gnawing on her bottom lip.

God, her feet were soft. And she knew how to use them, working me to diamond hard and ready to blow. I swallowed a moan.

"What song were you listening to just now, when you came all over my hand?"

Her lips parted, a soft breath escaping. "'Crush.'"

"That's going to be our song."

"We have a song?"

"We have a song."

"Dane." She sat straighter, tucked her toes under my ass, swiped bubbles off her chin. "That's a couple's thing."

"I'm not going anywhere." I reached between my legs and snatched her foot, pulling it to my chest. "Don't make me say it again."

She couldn't hide her grin. "Will you keep working with Tito?"

"They've hired me full-time at the mansion. My official title is groundskeeper." I rubbed the soft spot on her ankle, applying extra pressure where I knew she'd feel the pleasure between her legs.

"But that's not all you'll be."

"No. That gonna be an issue?"

With a sigh, Moriah reclaimed her foot and sat up straight, placing her hands on my knees, hitting me with a hard glare. "I get the feeling it won't matter. You're gonna do what you gotta do, right?"

"There are more Mims out there, gorgeous. Little girls, helpless and hurting. I don't think I could turn Moretti down even if you held a gun to my head."

"You see, that's the thing I'm struggling with most. Everything I've been taught tells me that what you're doing is wrong. It's a police issue. Let them handle those sick bastards." She paused. Swallowed. Licked her lips.

"But?"

The pink glow on her face darkened, her fingers digging harder into my skin. "I don't know."

"Say it, baby."

She dropped her gaze, drawing a circle over my knee with her fingernail. "It turns me on, knowing you're out there, breaking the law."

"You got a thing for bad boys?"

"Apparently so."

"Well, you've struck gold, gorgeous."

I dragged my naked girl up the length of me and settled her against my chest. Not satisfied, I urged her knees up, and grabbed my cock, guiding it home. Without further prompting, she shifted her hips, opening for me, taking me to the hilt in one slow, torturous slide.

"God damn, we're a perfect fit," I mumbled into her hair, fighting a full body shiver.

Moriah planted her hands on my chest and sat up, arching her back, shoving her tits in my face, and I was a goner.

"That's it, ride me baby." I flicked a tongue over her taut, pink tit.

Her whimper set me on fire. When her lips met mine, and she coiled her arms around my neck, I gripped her hips. I took control. And I showed her exactly how bad I could be.

Even covered in bubbles.

CHAPTER 16

Moriah

"DID SHE LIKE THE bubbles?" I asked, moving the purple bottle and giant pink wand aside.

"Oh, Lordy. She had a blast. Had to hose off her and Rocky afterward. They were a mess." Lettie shook her head, laughing.

It was so good to see her smiling.

"How are you holding up?"

Lettie gestured for me to sit. "Won't lie. It's been rough, especially the evenings. Dane and Mim have been a Godsend, though. I haven't had to worry about anything around the house. And Mim's smile. Lord." Slapping a hand to her chest, she looked up, then shook her head. "How can you be sad with those bright eyes beaming up at you?" She sighed, her shoulders dropping. "I miss my James, though, so much."

I collapsed on a stool at the kitchen island. "I feel like I haven't had time to mourn my mom or my sister with everything that's happened. I'm afraid it's going to hit me all at once. Knock me for a loop, ya know?"

"Well." Lettie grabbed my hand with a motherly squeeze. "When that happens, you call me. We'll carry each other through the rough patches. How does that sound?"

"Sounds like a deal."

The house seemed eerily quiet and empty. I looked around the vast, spotless kitchen. "Where are they now?"

Lettie turned to open the fridge. "They went for a long drive today. Came back about an hour ago but haven't come inside." She pulled a large dish off the shelf and set it between us. "They might be in the barn. They've been spending a lot of time out there the past week."

"Hmm."

"Why don't you go find them. I'll get this casserole in the oven. Should be ready in about an hour."

"You sure? I can help with dinner."

"Salad is already made. All that's left to do is set the timer. Go ahead." She shooed me off. "Make sure they're not getting into any trouble out there."

I started the long trek across the lawn, my heels sinking into the soft grass. Halfway there, I kicked off my shoes, the lawn a cool balm to my aching feet.

The barn door sat open, and Dane's voice carried from the far corner. "No, that's a socket wrench. I need the torque wrench. Remember which one that is?" Metal clanged. "Yeah. That's it." A deep chuckle warmed my belly. "Now come here. You gotta crank it this way, nice and tight." A grunt. "There ya go. That's my girl."

I peeked around the side of a beat-up Ford to find Dane perched on a short stool, Mim standing at his side. Both staring at a motorcycle. Not your average motorcycle, though. A kid-sized bike that stood no taller than a few feet.

My heart leapt to my throat. "What's going on out here?"

Dane looked up, shit-eating grin on his face. Behind him, sat another dirt bike I hadn't seen before.

Mim rubbed a dirty hand across her face, leaving a black streak. I'd never seen her smile so wide.

"She's a natural, gorgeous." He patted Mim's shoulder. "We picked these babies up at an estate sale last week. They run okay. But Mim is learning how to make them run better."

My sweet, little, dirty angel waved a wrench at me.

"You let her ride that?"

He reached behind him and retrieved a small helmet, black and shiny. "Like I said. She's a natural. Never seen anything quite like it." He shimmied the helmet onto her head, fiddled for a minute, then said, "Show your aunt. Stay off the grass, though. We don't want Lettie coming after us for messing up her lawn."

Mim threw a leg over the little bike like a pro. Only then did I notice the tall boots she wore.

"This can't be safe."

"She's fine." Dane pushed her out of the barn and onto the driveway behind the house.

Reluctantly, I followed.

He stood, the back of the bike balanced between his thighs. Mim held the handlebars, then kicked twice on a small lever. The engine buzzed to life. Then, off she went, with a slight wobble, before straightening and tearing down the driveway.

"See?" Hands to hips, he watched, and I swear, he stood ten feet taller.

"She can't... We can't let her... Oh no, this is terrifying."

A heavy arm wrapped around my shoulder. "She's so happy right now. Just let her have this."

"Dane. It's dangerous. How could you do this?"

"I know it seems scary, babe. But when I sat her on my bike the first time, she turned into another kid. Her face came alive. After I took her for her first ride, I couldn't tear her off the seat. She sat there for hours, watching me work. I figured the only way to get my Harley back was to give her a bike of her own. And look at her. That little firecracker was born to ride."

"I don't like this."

Dane grunted. Crossing his arms, he settled into a wide stance. "She feels powerful right now. She's in control. What better gift can we give her than that?"

And shit. How could I argue? Dane was right. And whether he knew it or not, he was parenting. He was fathering.

"Who are you?" I mumbled under my breath, so deeply in love with the man at my side.

"I get off on making that kid smile. She's my crack."

Mim made her way up and down the dirt driveway twice before Dane called her back, helped her off the bike and out of her helmet. My little angel ran to my side and threw her arms around my legs, her eyes wet with happy tears.

"You were so good on the bike, Mim. So good. That was fun, huh?"

She nodded, resting her chin on my hip, starry gaze on me.

"Okay. Okay. So, you're a biker chick. We can work with that." I pointed to Dane. "We'll have to lay down some rules, of course." What rules? I had no clue. But eventually they'd come to me. Good thing Rossi Enterprises offered top-notch health insurance.

"Mim. Go inside. Clean up. Dinner's almost ready."

She tore away from me and sprinted toward the house.

The second she disappeared behind the door, I jumped into Dane's arms, hooked my ankles around his hips, and kissed him hard. "We have time for a quickie?"

Dane spun, slammed me against the truck and cupped my ass, grinding against me. "Can't fuck you in here, gorgeous. Not unless you want Tito to watch." He nodded toward the ceiling.

I followed his gaze to the camera perched in the corner.

"Well. That's unfortunate." I cinched my legs tighter around his hips. "I missed you today."

"Yeah?"

"Oh, yeah." I sucked his bottom lip between my teeth, gave it a nip. "Had to take an extra-long break, take care of myself in the ladies' room."

"You sadistic little tease," he half-moaned, half-whispered.

"What can I say, you bring out the bad in me."

The sun's rays beat viciously on my head, warning me to find cover, but I sat on the park bench regardless, enjoying the squeals of children playing in the sand, the colorful array of swimsuits and flotation devices on the shore, the water-skiers in the distance, and the vast, blue sky.

I loved working so close to the city beach. The bustling park had become my favorite place to take my lunch breaks.

"Mind if I join you?"

The rough voice made me jump. I turned to find Dane's friend from the diner standing next to me, wearing a leather vest full of colorful patches, and a scowl that made me shiver, despite the heat.

Before I could answer, the large man made himself comfortable next to me, forcing me to scoot to the end of the bench. "Moriah, right?"

"Yes." Out of habit, I offered my hand. "Hammer, was it?"

"That's me." His grip was strong, and he held me longer than comfortable.

I reclaimed my hand. My body coiled, the compulsion to flee coursing through me. I forced calm into my voice and asked, "Are you in town to see Dane?"

He shook his head, gaze aimed across the lake. "Here on business. Come to the beach every time I pass through."

"Dane know you're here?"

"Nah."

"Hungry?" I grabbed the other half of my turkey and Swiss and passed it over.

He snatched the bread from my fingers. Took a bite. "Thanks." He caught sight of two bicycle cops and waited for them to pass before asking, "So, you're the kid's aunt?"

Nodding, I said, "Her name's Mim."

"Mim." He laughed, taking another bite of sandwich. "Mickey and Mim. That's funny."

Ice filled my veins. "You knew Mickey?"

He gave me a quick glance, then watched two teenagers in bikinis come out of the water. "Yeah. Met her in rehab." He shoved the last bite into his mouth, chewed, swallowed. "She was trying. Real hard. Wanted to get clean, do right by her kid."

My throat closed tight. "You were in rehab together?"

"Coupla times." He licked his lips, gaze still focused on the sun-kissed, barely dressed, underaged girls.

"Were you and Mick...um...close?"

His attention shot my way again. "Why do you ask? She ever talk about me?"

"Oh. No." I paused for a breath, the force of his glare knocking the wind clean out of my lungs. I should've heeded the warning bells, cut and run, but the desire to know more about Mickey kept my butt firmly planted. "My sister disappeared years ago. I didn't know anything about her, until Mim was found."

My answer seemed to appease the man at my side, his shoulders slumping. "I didn't know Mick real well. What I do remember is that she wore this necklace—a heavy, steel chain. Not sure what was hanging off the thing, a heart, or a key, maybe." He huffed. Shook his head. "Played with that thing all the damn time. Rubbed it between her thumb and forefinger like it was a lucky charm or something."

The bulky man stretched his arms across the back of the park bench, his left hand brushing my shoulder before hooking on the wood behind me. A good six inches separated us, but personal space was obviously not his concern.

"You know anything about that necklace?" he asked, although his question sounded more like a threat.

"No."

"Hmm." His bloodshot eyes narrowed, focused on my lips, then dropped to my chest. "You and Dane fucking?"

"What?"

"You heard me," he said to my boobs.

I shoved my book into my handbag.

Hammer's calloused hand curled around my neck, weighing me down. "Take it easy." He scooted closer, bridging that small gap between us, the scent of nicotine making my eyes water, my stomach churn. "Answer my question."

"That's none of your business."

Those fingers tightened in warning. "Dane's a Slayer. Everything he does is my business. That fucker ain't answering my calls. I figure the only reason he ain't answering is 'cause he's balls deep in some sweet pussy. Got his brain scrambled." He leaned closer still, burying his nose in my neck and taking a deep inhale. "I think you know where I can find him."

"I don't," came my breathless reply.

I wanted to ask how Hammer had found *me*, but what did it matter? He'd found me. He wouldn't hurt me in public.

And we couldn't be any more public than the city beach on a hot summer afternoon. "I don't know where he lives. He's very private."

Hammer hooked his arm around my neck and pulled me close, his forehead touching mine, like we were lovers sharing a secret. "I find out you're lying, that little girl's gonna pay." He pressed his lips to my hair. "When you see that trailer trash piece of shit, tell him he better return my calls." He laid his free hand on my thigh, then slid under my skirt, his thumb stretching, threatening to breach my panties. "Oh. And if he is fucking you. That means you're his property. That makes you Slayer property. That means, one of these days, I might get a crack at those sweet lips."

He let me go, and I jumped to my feet, clutching my bag. Before I could scramble away, he grabbed my hand, a wicked smile cracking his weathered face. "What? No kiss goodbye?"

I swung. His head whipped back, dodging my strike, but my hand was free. Without looking back, I headed toward two of the city's bicycle patrol officers near the parking lot, my pulse beating a painful rhythm.

A large engine roared to life. I slowed my pace, like I was making to talk to the men in uniform. Hammer rolled past on his chrome beast, waving goodbye, then merged into the lazy summer traffic.

My stomach heaved, and I lost my lunch to an innocent cluster of azalea bushes.

"You're not eating," Dane growled at me from across the table, the low rumble of his voice carrying a hint of frustration, but mostly concern.

"Feeling a little nauseous, that's all."

"Gotta get something down, gorgeous."

Mim scraped the last of her fruit salad out of the bowl, slurped it off her spoon, then wiggled off her chair, and carried her dishes to the sink.

I'd never asked her to clear her own spot at the table, yet somewhere along the way, she'd learned. Maybe my sister hadn't been too far gone. Maybe Mim had learned from Lettie. Either way, I was grateful, and in awe of that kid.

I couldn't take my eyes off that sweet little angel, and Dane didn't take his eyes off me. When Mim skipped to her bedroom, I acknowledged his questioning glare.

"I'm fine. Really."

He stared, waiting for the truth.

"Okay. Okay. Jeez. I'm not fine. I'm... I'm..." What was I? Scared? Angry? I slumped in my chair, twirled my fork around my plate. "Let me ask you something."

He shifted, wiped his mouth, then balled his napkin before dropping it on his plate, and giving me his full attention. "Anything."

"In the club, do you pass around women?"

"Where the hell did that come from?" His phone buzzed. He ignored it, leaning back, crossing his arms over his chest.

"Just humor me."

"Sure. It happens. 'Lotta women out there looking for the wrong kind of validation. Too many men take advantage of that vulnerability."

"Okay. So, say one of you has a girlfriend. Or a wife. Do you share her? With your guys, I mean."

A vein popped in his neck, his jaw working back and forth. "Moriah. What's this about?"

"How are women treated?"

His phone buzzed again. His gaze never left mine, though he blinked, clearly irritated.

"You can check that. It's fine." I pushed from the table. "Actually. I insist. Check your phone. Might be important." I stacked my full plate on top of his empty and headed for the sink.

After releasing a loud sigh, he asked. "What's going on?"

I dropped the dishes in the basin, turned, gripped the counter behind me. "I bumped into your friend today on my lunch."

"I don't have friends."

"That guy I met at the Truck Stop. Hammer."

Dane turned sideways in his chair, elbows to knees, hands hanging loose. "What do you mean you bumped into him."

"Well. He bumped into me, I guess. I was having lunch at the park, near the water. He made himself comfortable."

"How comfortable?"

"Enough to get in my head, if I'm being honest."

Two heartbeats and he stood before me, feet bracing mine, hands on my hips. "What the fuck did he do?"

I gave the dirty details of my scary exchange with his biker buddy, leaving out the part where I lost my lunch.

Eyes pinched, Dane drew three deep breaths through his nose before saying, "Don't pay any mind to that shit he spewed. He's gets off on messing with people." His words came forced, an attempt to calm my nerves, the tremble in his voice only fueling my unease.

Dane must have read my worry. He sighed. Scratched at his beard. "Hammer told me they'd be passing through town."

"Well...he was upset you haven't returned his calls."

Dane tapped his cell. Thumbed the screen, studying the call records, I assumed.

His face reddened. My guts twisted.

I turned back to the sink. Water on. Rinse. Rinse. Stack.

Warm muscle pressed against my backside, strong arms coiling my waist. Dane scrubbed his beard against my neck sending ferocious tingles through my body.

His hands splayed across my abdomen. When he kissed the sensitive skin behind my ear, my knees buckled.

Holding me steady and upright, he whispered, "I'm sorry he scared you, gorgeous."

"I know."

"I need to take care of something."

I studied the sink. The soapy dish sponge, the tiny dent in the steel, the sugar spoon tipped inside the drain. Blinking the moisture from my eyes, I mumbled, "Okay."

"Thank you for dinner."

He was leaving, and I wanted to beg him to stay. "Will you be back tonight?"

"Not sure."

I arched my neck, accepting another kiss, then watched him say his goodbyes to Mim.

Although warm and fuzzy from his touch, ice cold shivers rocked my body at the sight of Dane retreating, his muscles taught to the verge of snapping.

He wasn't happy.

Good.

Neither was I.

Clearly, whatever Hammer had done wrong, Dane was going to make right.

"Everything looks great." Leticia snapped off her gloves and tossed them in the covered trash can. "Heartbeat is strong." She handed me a towel, then scooted the ultrasound machine back into the corner. "I'd like to see the numbers on the scale going up, instead of down, though."

"I'm eating," I assured the doctor. "I am. It's just that I'm throwing up more."

Lettie nodded. Scribbled some notes on her pad. "I thought Dane would be here for your exam."

"Me, too. Something must've come up." I forced a smile, refusing to show my worry.

She turned and wrapped a stethoscope around Mim's neck. "Want to hear the baby's heartbeat?"

Mim's eyes widened, her mouth dropping open, then curling into a smile while she nodded. She skipped to my side and waited for Leticia to slide a stool next to the exam table.

I laid back down and watched the two of them interact, mindful of the huge change in my niece from when I'd met her. She still hadn't spoken a word to anyone other than Rocky. But she had started to talk in her sleep, mumbles mostly, and I'd heard my name more than once. She had a voice, and I knew, I just knew, when she was brave enough, speaking out loud to an adult would be her final hurdle to healing.

"I know it's early," Lettie said, smiling down at Mim. "But have you guys thought about names for the baby?"

"Mim should be the one to pick a name," came a deep, gravelly proclamation from the doorway. My heart skipped a beat at the sight of Dane, wrapped in jeans, a faded blue tee, and a thousand layers of confident, muscular, absorbing man.

Mim gasped and hopped off the stool, diving into Dane's arms, the baby forgotten.

Lettie laughed. "That sounds like a great idea."

"But," Dane continued, narrowing his gaze on Mim, "if you want to pick the baby's name, you have to tell us, out loud, with your beautiful voice."

Dane strode my way, Mim hanging from his neck. "Sorry I was late." He dropped a kiss on my lips, then surprised me by dropping a peck on Lettie's cheek.

Lettie blushed with motherly joy and patted his shoulder. "You're here now. Anyone hungry? Mim, wanna help me make lunch?"

Dane dislodged Mim, set her on her feet, and tugged her pigtail. "Be good for Lettie."

When Mim grabbed Lettie's hand and dragged her out of the room, I released a sob. That little girl had come so far.

"You okay?"

"Perfect."

"You're crying." He brushed a tear away, staring down at me.

I leaned into his warm palm. "How did I ever think taking her away from you, or Rocky, or Whisper Springs was a good idea?"

"Temporary bout of insanity?" He chuckled, a rare, beautiful sound.

"That was smart, telling Mim she could pick the baby's name."

He stepped between my knees, the rough pads of his fingers dragging a heated path up my thighs. "I can be smart, sometimes."

I curled my arms around his waist, buried my face in his massive chest. He smelled like fresh air and laundry soap. His hard planes, mixed with the thrum of his inhales and exhales, and the soft *thump, thump, thump* of his heart beat, made my insides warm, my breasts ache, the flesh between my legs swell and throb. I hooked my feet behind his thighs, needing him closer.

Warm hands cupped my cheeks, urging me to look up into mesmerizing, hungry eyes.

"Fuck, gorgeous. Look at you." He bent, stealing my breath with a kiss, soft and full of promise, and so unlike any he'd given before. "Is that blush for me?"

Oh. God. "Yes," I said, a breathy whisper, an exhale, a plea.

Dane stepped away, leaving me cold. He turned the lock on the door. Reclaimed his spot between my knees. Rubbing a thumb over my cheek, he rasped, "I missed this face last night. Missed you. Missed us."

His next kiss was a warning, or maybe a promise, that he was going to give me reason to blush, and heat, and swell in his presence. Holding the back of my head with one hand, he worked the other between us, lifting my hospital gown, manipulating the button on his jeans and shoving them down. His cock sprang free. He gripped my hips. I fell back on the exam chair. Dane thrust inside me with a grunt. I arched in pleasure, a moan escaping my lips. I covered my mouth to stifle the sound while the beautiful man took me, fast, hard, unrelenting, over and over, pounding into me, our gazes locked, his fingers digging bruises into my hips, my breasts bouncing in painful waves. Heavy breaths, skin slapping, the table scratch-scratch-scratching on the tile floor. The rhythm was hypnotizing, intoxicating, filthy, and beautiful, and oh... my... Bright light blinded me, my body coiling tight, a toe-curling, unbearable orgasm ripping through me.

Dane rasped words I couldn't understand, his body going rigid before he fell over me, his face in my chest, rapid breaths cooling my overheated skin.

Tangling my fingers in his hair, holding him against me, I prayed we'd always be that way, frenzied and insatiable and gone for each other.

Dane kissed my stomach, lingering, tracing a lazy circle below my navel. "Hard to believe my kid is growing in there."

I could swear there were tears forming in those sad eyes of his.

"Know what I can't believe?" My words came raspy and thick. "I can't believe what we just did on Dr. Slade's brand-new table." I laughed, hoping to lighten the air, and pulled Dane's head off my stomach. "She'll never forgive us if she finds out."

Dane guided me to my feet. Cleaned between my legs. Helped me dress. I wasn't helpless. But there was something so intimate about the way he cared for me, and I savored every stoke of his fingers, every grunt, every selfless act he offered.

Hand in hand we made our way toward the kitchen. Halfway to our destination, I asked, "Where did you go last night?"

Dane stopped. Stared down at me, the light in the hallway enhancing the dark circles under his beautiful eyes. "I went to find Hammer."

"Did you find him?"

"No."

"Did you return his call?"

Dane dropped his head back. Sighed. Rubbed his eyes. "That's the thing, gorgeous. He hasn't called me. Not once."

A shudder ripped through me, and I did the only thing that could ease my tension. I coiled my arms around my man, absorbing his strength, breathing his air, and laid my head on his unbendable shoulder.

CHAPTER 17

Dane

MIM'S HEAD LAY ON my shoulder, drool wetting my shirt, a soft snore filling the silent room. Heels propped on the coffee table, I held her against my chest and relaxed into the soft cushions. She'd grown heavier over the summer. The hollow in her cheeks...filled. Dark circles under her eyes...gone.

Dust from our earlier ride coated her hair. Dirt and sweaty kid. Fuck. Such a satisfying aroma. I pressed my nose closer to her head and just breathed, absorbing every beautiful detail, her scent, her weight, the soft rasp of her lungs. The girl owned half of my soul. Clutched the worthless bastard in her tiny little fist.

We'd spent the past week discovering new dirt trails around the mansion. The little shit didn't want the beach, or the park, or a trip to the ice cream store. Hell no. She wanted to ride.

When we weren't riding, she wanted to hang in the barn, and work on her Cobra, creating problems that didn't exist, just so she could learn how to fix them.

Hell, she was even content sitting on the dirty floor and passing tools to me while I worked on James's old beater or the lawnmower. To fill the silence, I'd explain what I was doing, and what tools worked best for each job.

Some days, Lettie would drag Mim into the air-conditioned house, just to get her out of the heat. I'd find them in the kitchen whipping up a meal, or in Lettie's office, Mim always surrounded by a pile of books.

Not sure how the kid had ever learned to read.

Which reminded me, school started in two weeks. Moriah, Lettie, and the shrink were convinced that Mim was ready. I didn't agree, but I didn't share my hesitation. My girls had enough obstacles to hurdle. I wasn't about to add my aversion to the public school system to their list of worries. What I did share was that I wouldn't take any "jobs" with Tucker and Tito until we knew for certain that Mim would be okay.

When I'd announced that I would drive Mim to and from school, Lettie and Moriah only laughed. Whatever. Any kid took a crack at my angel, they'd have my ugly mug to face after the school bell rang. Those two didn't understand how the bully system worked. I did. And I had no problem scaring the piss out of any kid who dared give my girl grief.

The front door opened and then closed. Familiar footfalls came our way.

"Hey," came Moriah's soft voice. "Oh. She's out cold." She bent to give me a taste of her sweet mouth, those eyes shimmering with emotion I'd come to anticipate, but had yet to acknowledge. "What'd the two of you do today?"

"Whole lotta nothin'."

"Nothing, huh?" Moriah dropped her handbag on the coffee table, then worked at the buttons on her blouse. "That's why she smells like motor oil?"

I couldn't help the grin that cracked my face.

Moriah headed for the bedroom, kicking off her shoes along the way. "Do you mind waking up your sleeping beauty? She's having a sleepover with Rocky tonight. She'll need a shower before we go."

Her loose skirt swung back and forth across her ass as she sauntered down the hall. I hated knowing Mim would be away from us for the night, but the thought of having Moriah to myself hit me straight in the gut, making my blood pump too fast, and too damn hot.

I riled the girl in my arms. Reminded her that Rocky was waiting and marveled at her ability to go from zero to sixty in the blink of an eye.

I headed to the kitchen and pulled the casserole Lettie had sent home out of the oven. My phone buzzed. I ignored the call. The only people I cared to talk with were currently down the hall. Minutes later, my cell buzzed again. I checked the screen, my gut dropped, and I walked to the deck, shutting myself outside before answering. "Prez. What's up?"

"Need you, Trailer."

"Fuck off," nearly fell from my lips, but when I considered my ladies, I said, "I'm not leaving town, so whatever job you've got better involve Whisper Springs."

I was sure he huffed a laugh. "You got a death wish, boy?"

I didn't. Not anymore. With a deep breath, I reined in my anger. "What do you need?"

"Coupla brothers riding through town next week. Need the trailer on your dad's property stocked."

I swatted a bug away from my face. "*My* property," I corrected the bastard. "That dilapidated piece of shit burned to the ground. Didn't Hammer tell you?"

I'd expected Prez to read me the riot act, threaten my life maybe. Instead he growled a slew of profanities, then asked, "Hammer? You been in touch with him?"

Venomous snakes slithered through my gut. "You sent him. With my bike."

"Fuck." Heavy breaths. Muffled shouts. A door slam. "I never sent that shithead. You with him now?"

"No." I gripped the deck railing, rage vibrating my arm. "What the fuck's going on?"

"Hammer's been AWOL for weeks."

"You don't have to be gentle," Moriah whispered, her nails sinking into my shoulders as she rose high, then slammed back down, taking all of me inside her tight, hot core, doin' a number on my sanity.

Fingers clamped into the soft flesh below her waist, I attempted to slow her pace. "I've got all night to make you scream, woman. This is just a warm-up."

Moriah froze, her full weight landing in my lap, her hands moving to my face. Damn if the glare she shot didn't make my dick twitch.

Fierce resolve flashed through those hazel beauties. "Give me hard. I need you out of control," came her words, more a plea than the command she intended.

My chest tightened, remembering our first night together. She'd begged then, too. *Hard. Harder.*

I shifted, sitting straighter, the weight of a worry I didn't understand settling in my chest. "Why do you need it hard, Moriah?"

"Really? she purred, rolling her hips, driving me mad. "You wanna talk right now?"

Fuck. I did. What was this woman doing to me? "Yeah. Talk to me."

"Okay," she conceded, fingers combing my beard in a nervous tick. She searched my face, then sighed. "I don't like rough sex, if that's what you think. I'm not into kink or anything. It's just. Well. When you take me like you did those first two nights, when we thought it would be our only time together, it was raw, and wild, and unapologetic. Just two people needing each other. Taking, giving. No expectations. I didn't worry about how I looked, or if my breasts were too small, my thighs too big, did my breath stink, did I remember to shave? You know. All those things that get in women's heads when we're doing it."

Doing it? Christ, could the woman be any cuter. "You mean fucking," I interrupted.

She laughed. "Yeah, that."

I slapped her ass. "Jesus, babe. Just say it. Fucking."

"Okay. Fucking." She emphasized the F.

"You're so effin' beautiful when you talk dirty."

That earned me another sweet fucking laugh that hit me straight in the gut.

"Anyway. What I'm trying to say is that when you're unleashed, like you can't get enough, I feel wanted and desirable, all the self-doubt gets pushed out of the way. I can enjoy sex like it's meant to be enjoyed. Does that make sense?"

A few months ago, I would've said *no*. Hell, before Moriah, if a woman tried to get personal while I banged her, I'd have sent her packing, blue balls or not.

"Gotta be honest. I hear you, but I can't sympathize. I'm a guy. A woman wants to fuck, that's all the encouragement we need."

Moriah slumped, her cheeks turning a gorgeous shade of crimson.

I pulled her closer and claimed her mouth before continuing. "Listen close. After that first night? I was done for. Couldn't get you out of my head, much less imagine touching another woman, ever."

Bright eyes lifted to mine, shimmering with emotion that cemented us together.

"I've never wanted anyone more than I want you. You hear me? Hard fucking or not, bad breath and hairy legs, or not, know that you're wanted."

I reached between our joined bodies and dragged a finger up and down her wet slit, landing on that hard nub, then rubbing in a slow tease. "Now that my baby is growing inside you? Fuck, gorgeous, I'm way past want. I'm borderline obsessed. That's why I was taking it slow. I'm so fucking out of my mind, I'm afraid of losing control."

"Do it, Dane. Oh, God. Please, lose control," she moaned, her teeth sinking into my earlobe.

Shit. I'd never been so hard in my life. No way was Moriah topping me. She'd given the green light. My engine hit full throttle.

I flipped us around, spread her wide, and *did* her like she wanted. Hard.

Sated and sweaty, I collapsed at her side, then tucked her against me, my gorgeous. My everything. I stared into the dark, Moriah's soft breaths warming my chest, her sweaty skin pressed against mine. The weight of a thousand new worries molded me to the mattress.

Me. Dane Reynolds, a dad. Responsible for three new lives. What if I failed them like I'd failed Addy? Fuck. No. Never again. I'd die for my girls. I'd tear anyone apart who tried to hurt my family.

Fuck. My family. *My* fucking family.

My chest inflated, the pressure painful. The backs of my eyes burned, and when the first pansy-ass tear rolled down my cheek, I'd never felt more a man.

"Dane."

The bed shook. I rolled over, my limbs heavy, trapped halfway between dreamland and reality.

"Dane!" Moriah shouted. Something soft hit my face. My shirt.

I bolted upright, nerves tingling. Light flooded the room.

"We'll be right there!" She tossed her phone onto the bed. "Ohgodohgodohgod," she mumbled, tugging a pair of pants over her hips.

"Moriah?" The fog lifted, my mind going razor sharp. "Talk to me."

"Get dressed." She tripped over a shoe, caught herself on the bed, then bent to shove her foot into the sandal.

"What's happening?"

"Please, God. No. No. No." Like a mad woman, she scrambled around the room, yanked a sweatshirt out of her dresser and tugged it over her head.

"Moriah!"

"The kids are missing."

That got me on my feet. "The fuck you mean they're missing?"

"They're not in the house or the yard. Tango and Slade have looked everywhere. They're gone."

Pants on. Shirt next. "We'll find them. Don't worry." Boots. Wallet. Keys. "Let's go."

The room spun. My head buzzed. A pain I'd never suffered seized my chest. I forced my legs to carry me forward despite the crushing weight on my shoulders. Kids wandered off all the time, right? I had when I was young, every chance I got. They were fine.

They were fine.

They were fine.

We drove in silence, me fisting the wheel, Moriah's hands fisted on her knees, the air thick with worry neither one of us dared voice. We reached Tango's house in under fifteen minutes. Two cop cars already blocked the driveway, parked directly behind Tucker's truck. Flashlights bobbed across the property from every corner.

Tango met us where we parked, shoved beams into our hands, and said, "Follow me."

Without a word, we jogged behind Pretty Boy, violent urges pulsing through my veins. Anything happened to my girl, that pansy-ass piece of shit would suffer unbearable agony, and I would enjoy every fucking second of his misery.

Through the blood rush pounding my skull, I heard, "I'll check the diner. Moriah, you check around back. Dane," Rossi pointed to the tree line. "You check the beach."

I turned to offer Moriah a reassuring squeeze, but she was already off and running, calling for the kids.

The sliver of moon and ebony sky offered little assistance as I navigated the trail leading from the Truck Stop's parking lot down to the hidden beach, where the calls of the other searchers couldn't reach. Waves licked the shore. A bird protested my approach. Nocturnal creatures scattered, rustling the nearby brush.

I waved the light in a pendulum swing, searching left then right on the path before me. "Mim!" I called. "Rocky!"

My voice broke, and I paused, hands to knees, sucking in a deep breath to calm my raging nerves. Moisture blurred my vision, and I swiped at my eyes before continuing forward. "Mim! Mim!"

Swing, swing with the light. Deep breath. Continue. I reached the soft sand and searched for footprints. Nothing. Thank fuck. Next, I jogged north until I reached the end of that stretch of beach. I searched the trees behind me, coming up empty, then headed south until reaching the other end of the alcove. My voice was hoarse, my chest ached from the pressure, and I turned again to search the brush behind me. Slow swing left. Slow swing right. Shadows stretched and bent against the small cliff, inky figures mocking my state of sanity.

Jesus. Fuck. Why did my chest feel so heavy?

A twig snapped to my left. I swung the light that direction, catching nothing but more shadows. "Mim!"

Silence.

I breathed, tuning my ears to the night's noises, shuffling through nature's lullaby for something recognizable.

A giggle.

Jesus. Fuck. My knees buckled.

Another giggle.

I ran toward the sound. That beautiful God damn sound.

Behind a cluster of pines, a blanket stretched across a bush and a fallen tree. A makeshift tent. A blue glow shone through the heavy fabric.

I tore the blanket away, shining the light on two shocked faces, headphones in their ears, plugged into a mini computer. They sat side by side, an empty carton of Pringles at their feet.

Rocky and Mim screamed at the same time, startled by my sudden appearance.

Unable to bear my own weight, I fell to my knees, dropping the flashlight.

"Dane!" Rocky shouted. "Wanna go camping with us?"

I couldn't speak, my head buzzing, my chest...well...shit, was I even breathing? Mim wrapped her arms around my neck and hugged me tight, then let go, plopping right back down at Rocky's side.

Three deep breaths and I forced my angriest tone, despite the relief crashing through me. "Rocky James Mason. Get your ass up that bank right now. Your mom and dad are scared to death."

His smile faded. He shot a sideways glance at Mim, then met my glare. "Ah, man. We just wanted to go camping."

I was not fit to rebuke the kid. I didn't trust my emotions.

"I'll grab your shit. You help Mim up the trail." I handed him the flashlight, but he handed it right back.

"Jeez. I have my own." He reached under the sleeping bag and pulled out two heavy duty Maglites, slapping one into Mim's lap. "C'mon. I think we're in trouble."

Mim ignored me completely, chin in the air, and marched behind her best friend. I wanted to shake her. Yell and scream and make her promise never to scare me like that again. I wanted to hold her in my arms and never let go. Lock her in a cage where I could keep her safe from the world. Where she could never make me feel such fear, so helpless ever again.

Instead, I followed behind, waited at the base until they'd ascended the trail, then listened for the cries of relief. After hearing Tango's angry voice, I staggered backward, dropped my ass in the sand, and let the emotion take over, every muscle in my body trembling something fierce.

My phone buzzed.

Moriah: They're here. We've got them.

Me: I know. Go back to the house. I need a minute.

Moriah: OK

Head in my hands, I released a silent, violent, purging scream. If that was what parenting entailed, I wanted no part of it. No fucking way would I survive twenty years of that shit. What the hell had I gotten myself into? Caring. Worrying. Responsibility.

I couldn't do the parenting thing. I couldn't be a father.

I wasn't built for such bullshit.

Overhead, the sky morphed from purple to blue. At my feet, waves licked the shore in lazy strokes. My wet ass would be numb for days, yet I sat in the cold, damp sand, staring blindly across the bay, emotions waging war with instinct.

Freedom beckoned, the open road a siren's call luring me from the heavy weight crushing my chest.

Through the early morning hours, I battled the urge to flee. Disappear. Leave responsibilities I had no right bearing behind.

Would've been easy.

Then again, leaving Moriah would kill me. Leaving Mim would destroy any chance I had of being anything less than the fuck-up my nurturing had created.

My girls. Fuck. Not sure how I'd fooled those beauties into believing I was someone worth something, but God damn I was done questioning my luck.

Freedom was alluring, true. But a lifetime staring into those freckled faces, hazel eyes beaming at me, bright fucking smiles? Hell, even their frowns were stronger, more magnetic than any innate pull of the wild.

I was no longer a solitary man. Terrifying, true, but empowering just the same.

My phone buzzed against my thigh as I pushed to my feet.

"Hey, gorgeous," came out raspy and weak, my throat and lungs raw from the damp air.

"Morning." A shuttered breath. "You okay?"

"Sorry about ghosting on you last night." I rubbed at the godawful kink in my neck. "Wasn't in any condition to be around people."

"Okay," came her simple reply. No judgement. No irritation. Just acceptance. "We're at the diner. Charlie opened early for us. I ordered your favorite."

God, that woman.

"Be there in a few."

I turned to head up the trail, anxious to hold my ladies. Mindful of my throbbing hip, I took it slow until my gears warmed up. My phone buzzed with a text from Prez.

We're in town. You spot Hammer, stay clear. He's ours.

Ten different responses came to mind, none of them friendly. So, I shoved my phone into my pocket, and made my way up the hill, pausing at the crest.

The Truck Stop lot was empty aside from an older model Civic. I spotted my girls through the window and stopped dead. That damn organ in my chest shifted, settling in an awkward, yet not entirely uncomfortable spot, its thump, thump, thump beating a soothing rhythm.

Another step, and the glint of chrome from the right of the building caught my eye. I stayed to the tree line until a Harley came into view. A bike I knew too well, half-hidden behind the trash dumpster, yet facing the highway, readied for an easy getaway.

Hammer.

I did not want to deal with his shit.

I shot Prez a quick text, then made my way across the lot.

Mim spotted me through the window. Smiled. Waved. Bounced in her seat. Moriah pressed her nose to the glass and made a funny face, making Mim laugh, and damn if that ridiculous sight didn't release a shit-ton of weight off my shoulders.

I joined them, dropping a kiss on Mim's head, then slid next to Moriah, pulling her against me and whispering, "I'm sorry I didn't come back last night. My head was a mess."

That gorgeous, freckle-faced angel only smiled, whispered, "I understand," and passed me a mug of coffee. "I was scared, too."

She lifted her chin for a kiss, and I didn't hold back. Mim giggled, and I gave her a wink before straightening in my seat and scanning the dining room, again, for Hammer.

No sign of the bastard, and that worried me something fierce.

One man sat at the bar, his dress shirt pulled tight across his slim back as he hunched over his plate. The red-headed waitress filled napkin holders, and Charlie, the Truck Stop's infamous chef, whistled a tune through the service window. When he spotted me, he raised a hand in greeting. I offered a chin nod, then studied Mim. She didn't look the least bit worse for wear after her late-night adventure.

Moriah, on the other hand, had dark circles under her eyes, and wore the same clothes she'd had on last night.

"Did you sleep at the Rossis'?"

"Yeah." She nodded, gnawing on her lower lip, her gaze bouncing to Mim. "Well. One of us slept, anyway."

"You should've gone home."

Her warm palm landed on my thigh. "I wasn't going to leave you here. Besides, Slade insisted we stay in her spare bedroom. It was almost morning already."

I stared at the little girl across from me, scrambling for the right words, still shaken by the thought of losing her. Seemed like a good time to offer words of wisdom, but fuck, was that my job, or Moriah's? Was it my place to lecture, to scold?

Before I could voice my thoughts, the cowbell rattled, announcing a customer, drawing everybody's attention to the front of the dining room. Rocky barreled through, a thousand watts of amped energy, rumpled clothes, and a wild head of messy hair. He sprinted our way, his shoes squeaking on the checkered tile when he skidded to a stop at our table.

"Hey, guys!"

"Morning, kid," I mumbled.

Tango followed behind, fresh as a fucking daisy, shirt and slacks pressed, face smooth as a baby's butt. God damn pretty boy.

"Dane." He nodded, skimming over me, and focusing on Moriah. "Morning, Moriah." He shoved his hands in his pockets, glanced at the kids, then met me eye to eye, and cleared his throat. "Can't tell you how sorry I am for the scare last night."

Gave me morbid pleasure watching that entitled asshole squirm. I could've drawn his discomfort out, made him suffer, but shit, I was too damn exhausted. Instead, I grunted, and gave him my best, *you better not fuck-up with my kid again* glare.

The two of us would have to learn to coexist. I wasn't leaving Whisper Springs. Neither was he.

"C'mon, Rockster." He scooped his kid off the ground, leaving no room for protest, and threw him over his shoulder. "Let's go find your mom."

Rocky kicked and squirmed. "Dad. C'mon. Let me down."

Ignoring his son's pleas, Tango turned and strode through the double doors leading to the back of the diner.

Mim slumped in her chair.

Moriah looked up at me with sleepy eyes and smirked. I kissed her, because damn, what else could I do?

"Well. Well. Well. Ain't that precious." Hammer's deep voice came over my shoulder. "The three of you look like one happy little family." He dropped into the seat next to Mim.

Her face paled, and she pinched her lips together, her eyes filling with liquid.

I pushed to stand, ready to drag that motherfucker outside by his neck, then froze when he shoved the barrel of his Glock into Mim's side.

For the second time in my life, I suffered true, terrifying fear.

CHAPTER 18

Moriah

I COULD REMEMBER THREE times in my life when I'd been truly terrified. The first being the time my sister was bit by a Cottonmouth and Mom had been next door helping Old Man Franks carry boxes down from his attic. She didn't hear me screaming for help, and I was sure Mickey was going to die.

The second was in high school, when my boyfriend dared me to spend the night at the Ridge Cemetery that was rumored to be haunted. I'd never believed in ghosts, so I scoffed at his challenge. We snuck out late at night, parked at the gated entrance, and tucked in for the evening. When we saw the first apparition in the distance, I was sure his friends were behind the scare, an optical illusion of some sort. But then we saw the girl, with the red eyes and blackened skin, begging for help and floating, yes floating, through the iron bars, and toward our car. Tyler started to cry. I had to drive home. We broke up the next day and never spoke of that night again.

The third time I'd experienced true horror was the day Mom had told me she had terminal cancer.

Not one of those experiences compared to the limb-shaking, heart-seizing terror I experienced when Hammer forced that gun into Mim's ribs. I froze. Paralyzed.

Mim's wide, tear-rimmed eyes stayed focused on Dane, while I stared at her, the terrified little girl, and silently willed her to stay still. To stay calm.

Dane, although his muscles tensed against mine, kept his voice low and steady, his gaze narrowed on Hammer.

"What's happening, Hammer."

"I want the necklace."

"What fucking necklace?" Dane asked through gritted teeth.

"The necklace her mama gave her to wear."

"Don't know what the fuck you're talkin' 'bout, brother."

Hammer wrapped an arm around Mim, pulling her closer to his side, and bent, lowering his mouth to her ear. "She knows what I'm talking about, don't you, doll?"

Mim flinched and then shrank, but never tore her gaze from Dane.

Hammer continued. "Where's that necklace, little doll? The one your mama gave you to keep safe?" He fisted her hair, then yanked, exposing her bare neck. "Why aren't you wearing it?"

The tears she'd been fighting spilled down her cheeks, her face scrunching. Still, she stared at Dane. Her safe place.

"Hammer." Dane's voice remained impossibly calm, drawing attention away from my niece. "She wore a necklace the day we pulled her out of that pit. I haven't seen it in weeks. But I'll help you find the damn thing. Just let the ladies walk outta here."

"Naw. I'll take the little one with me. She can show me where that key is hidden." The sick bastard kissed the top of Mim's head. "We'll have fun together. Make a game of it, right, little bitch?"

Dane's thigh twitched against mine. "You're not leaving with the girl. You wanna shoot her? Shoot her. She's better off dead than with a piece of shit like you." He leaned forward, challenging. "But you sure as hell will not walk out that door with the kid."

"Aw, Trailer. You ain't foolin' no one. You won't let me shoot this little princess. Any jackass can see you got a thing for this baby girl. After all, she looks exactly like that cousin of yours, the one you couldn't save." He made a tsk sound, shaking his head. "Sweet piece-a-pussy, that Addy. Real tomcat. I mean, take a look. Same hair color. Same damn freckles. Same sweet, fuck me lips."

His sinister smile sparked a violent shiver, and sent a hellacious wave of nausea through me, every muscle in my body clamping tight as I fought to remain seated.

Until the bastard brushed a thumb under Mim's bottom lip. I lost all control, throwing myself over the table, screaming, "Get off her!" at the same time Mim opened her mouth and bit down on his appendage, hard enough to make him howl.

The second Hammer flinched, Mim slid under the table. Dane attacked, and fast as a blink, the men were tangled on the ground, tables and chairs flying. Somebody screamed. I reached down for Mim, but she was gone.

Pinned between the bench seat and table, and two brawling men, I had nowhere to move, but Mim managed to crawl away, scrambling toward the kitchen.

"Mim!" I yelled, but she pushed to her feet, escaping behind the counter.

"The fuck, Dane?" Tango burst through the swinging doors and jumped in to stop the fight, grabbing Dane by his nape, slamming a palm into Hammer's chest, unaware of the weapon, clueless to the danger.

An ear-shattering crack split the air, and I slammed my hands against my ears, against the pain, my body going ice cold. Dane crumpled, releasing his hold on Hammer. Tango fell to his knees, covering his ears, and Hammer pushed to stand, gun aimed at Tango.

A dark pool of crimson puddled under Dane's leg. My vision blurred, and I moved toward my fallen man. Hammer's aim shifted to me, and I froze.

"Nobody fucking move." Hammer staggered, his left eye swollen and bloody. "On the floor. All of you." He gestured toward Charlie. "You, fat fucker in the kitchen, out here. Now."

The man at the bar was the first to obey. He lay on his belly at Dane's feet. I followed suit, then the waitress. Charlie moved slow and steady from his post, and last to comply was Tango, who seemed to weigh his options before conceding.

"Mim!" Hammer yelled, though his words sounded muffled, everything was muffled. "Time to go, little dolly. We have a necklace to find."

Silence.

"Blondie, I know you're back there. Bring me that little bitch, or all these people die." He stepped toward the bar. "You want all of these people to die because of you?"

Still nothing, then again, I could barely hear a thing through the ringing in my ears.

"Okay!" he shouted, waving the pistol from head to head. "Who's first?"

He pointed the gun at my face, flashing another sinister grin. "One." He waited three heartbeats for a response.

"Two." He swung his arm and pointed the muzzle at Charlie.

"Three."

Slade burst through the doors, hands in the air, face pale but determined.

Hammer stepped over the waitress and aimed the weapon at Slade. "Where is she?"

Slade pursed her lips, and slowly shook her head. "You're not laying a finger on those kids."

Movement caught my attention out the window. Unfortunately, Hammer noticed as well.

Rocky and Mim ran hand in hand across the lot, heading toward the hill that led to Tango's home.

Tango had seen them as well. He pushed to his feet and dove at the gun-wielding psychopath. Two seconds too late.

Hammer swung, striking Tango with the butt of his gun, then sprinted out the door, shouting, "Fucking cunts!"

That man would not touch my Mim. Adrenaline fueled my limbs and kick-started my brain. I gave chase.

The kids continued forward, their little legs no match for Hammer's long strides. He gained ground.

"No! God, no!" I sprinted behind, pushing harder than I'd ever pushed. The wind rushed through my pounding ears, my heart protesting the pressure, and I focused ahead, forcing one foot after the other.

Up ahead, Rocky tripped and fell, but Mim continued up the hill.

Hammer stopped in his tracks. Ordered Mim to stop. Then aimed. Not at Mim, but the boy who was struggling to get back to his feet.

"I'll shoot your little boyfriend, you don't come back right now," Hammer shouted.

Mim continued onward, now at the steepest part of the hill, practically clawing at the dirt to gain ground.

I reached Hammer, out of breath, my legs rubber, and when I reached for his arm, hoping to knock the gun from his hand, he swung. Blinding pain stuck my face, knocking me off my feet. I reached for his leg, desperate to stop him from reaching the kids.

The toe of his boot met my gut, the force knocking the breath from my lungs. My body curled in on itself, but not before he landed another kick, harder than the first. I couldn't draw a breath. My stomach cramped, the sky swirling into a nauseating vortex above me.

He aimed again at the scrambling boy. I screamed, "Hammer! Please. Don't!"

A blur dashed past and headed for Rocky. A crazed laugh erupted from Hammer. I watched, helpless, while he squeezed the trigger. *Pop. Pop.* The figure dropped.

No. No, no, no. I tried to stand, to do something, anything. I couldn't get upright, my stomach protesting any movement.

Pop. Pop.

The earth spun in a kaleidoscope of color before fading to black.

"C'mon gorgeous. Wake up for me. Wake up, baby."

My surroundings came back into focus. Blue sky. White clouds. A bloody beard. Sad eyes. Wetness. A sickening metallic scent.

Dane held me in his arms. Rocking. Rocking. Whispering, "Wake up. Please. Please. Please."

"Dane." I raised a heavy arm to touch his bloody face, curling my fingers into his beard. "Mim. Where's Mim?"

Dane's chest vibrated. He let out a half-laugh, half-sob and kissed my cheek, pulling me closer to his hard, trembling body. "She's fine. She's right here."

Sirens wailed in the distance, drawing closer. Angry voices rumbled all around me.

"Trailer. You good? We gotta ghost," came from somewhere behind me.

Dane stiffened. "Get outta here." Rock. Rock. "Make him fucking suffer."

"You have our word," someone growled.

More shouting. Engines rumbled.

"What's happening?" I tried to sit up, Dane's hold tightening.

"Don't move, gorgeous. Hold still for me, okay? You're bleeding. Just don't move. The ambulance is almost here."

I raised my head to examine the damage, bile rising in my throat. My clothes were stained from the chest down. Blood. So much blood. Tears erupted, and I searched Dane's face for explanation, though I already knew the cause. "The baby?"

"You're gonna be fine," he promised. "Everything's fine."

Liar.

Rock. Rock. Rock. His hold was fierce and steady, but cold. So cold.

Not our baby.

"Get those assholes up here!" he shouted, voice hoarse. "What's taking so fucking long?"

Sadness consumed me, erupting into selfish sobs.

Mim dropped to her knees beside me, combing her fingers through my hair in soft strokes. I felt no pain. Only anguish.

Why wasn't I in pain?

Dane pressed a kiss to my head. "They're here, gorgeous. They're gonna take you to the hospital. I'll be right behind you."

His face was so pale. His lids so heavy. His grip loosening.

His words slurred. "Mim. Go with your aunt."

I was lifted out of his arms, laid down.

Our baby. Our baby. Our baby.

"Sir, you've been shot," I heard someone say.

Who'd been shot?

Dane pushed a uniformed man out of the way. "She's pregnant. Take care of her first."

Two men surrounded Dane.

"Get them to the fucking hospital," he roared, rising on shaky legs.

Only then did I notice the blood oozing from his chest. So much blood.

"Dane!" Oh God. "Dane!"

I needed to get to him. I needed to hold him. Why were they taking me away? He needed me.

Slade ran to my side, scooping Mim into her arms. "He'll be fine, Moriah. They'll meet us at the hospital. They'll take good care of him."

I stretched my neck, tried to call out, but my voice failed me, overcome by pure terror. And I watched, helpless, as Dane fell to the ground.

More uniformed workers surrounded him. I squeezed my eyes closed. I prayed. I prayed. I prayed.

All the way to the hospital, I prayed.

While they examined me.

When they told me there was no heartbeat.

While they scraped my uterine walls, I prayed.

When they moved me to a private room, and Mim crawled into the bed with me, we cried, and I prayed.

I wasn't brave enough to ask about Dane. I'd lost our baby. I couldn't bear the thought of losing him, too.

The sleeping girl in my arms kept me from falling apart.

God, I loved her.

"Hey." Leticia caressed my wrist, rubbing a soothing circle with her thumb.

"Morning." I rolled to my side, laying a hand over the dull ache in my abdomen. "How's Mim?"

"She fine. Having breakfast with Slade and Rocky in the cafeteria."

She moved to adjust something on the monitor above my head. "You're okay to go home today. But if you feel like you need more time, the room is yours." She leaned closer, a smirk highlighting her dimples. "Apparently, the Rossis have quite some pull here."

Apparently, they did. My surroundings resembled a five-star hotel more than a hospital room. They'd even brought in a twin-sized bed so Mim could stay with me overnight.

A bitter question burned the back of my throat. I feared the answer, but the longer I waited, the greater my anxiety. I had to know the facts, so I could deal. And heal. And be whole for Mim.

"Is he alive?" The question burst out on a sob.

Leticia grabbed my hand and squeezed. "Yes."

I'd never heard a more beautiful word.

"And he's going to be fine. By some miracle, the bullet missed his heart and any vital arteries."

Oh, God. Thank you. I nodded, swiping at my tears. "Does he know we lost the baby?"

Her own eyes welled. "He's been in and out of surgery. But when he is conscious, his only concern is you."

"I don't know how to tell him."

"There's no easy way, I'm afraid." She brushed a hair from my face and offered a heartwarming smile, those blue eyes comforting and bursting with motherly love. "But the good news is, you're healthy, and there's no reason the two of you can't try again after you both have healed."

Would Dane want that? Would he want me, still, after I'd lost the one thing binding us?

As if reading my thoughts, Lettie offered assurance. "He loves you. Anybody with half a mind can see that. The two of you will get through this. And you'll be stronger because of it."

Her words hit me hard in all the right places, giving me courage, dulling some of the pain. I couldn't voice my thoughts, though, emotion balling in my throat like a lump of paste.

"You wanna see him?" Tango's voice broke the silence. "I've got a sweet ride, and twenty minutes before the nurses hunt us down." He stood in the doorway, hands on the back of a wheelchair, bandage above his right eye, devilish grin on his face.

My stomach lurched, nerves taking hold, but I managed to whisper, "Yes. God, yes."

Leticia and Tango helped me into the chair, my legs rubber, my stomach a hot throbbing mess.

"I'll go check on the kids." Leticia gave my shoulder a squeeze. "See you in a bit."

Tango led me down the hallway, hospital beeps and chatter filling the silence between us. Before we entered the elevator, he squatted at my feet. "I'm sorry about the baby."

I only nodded, curling my lips between my teeth. I didn't want to cry again. He cupped my cheek, kissed my forehead, and called the elevator to our floor.

When the doors sealed us in the small space, I asked, "What happened to Hammer?" I hoped he was dead.

"You remember anything?"

"No. Not really." I remembered chasing after him. I remembered he'd pointed the gun at the kids.

Tango huffed. "He shot at Rocky. But Dane..." His voice broke. He cleared his throat. "Dane took the bullet for my son."

"Oh God," escaped my lips, and I slapped a hand over my mouth, desperate to hold back the sobs.

"The Slayers showed up. Hammer knew he was cornered, aimed the gun at his own head, but someone shot him in the leg, and took him down. They dragged him off before the police or ambulance arrived."

I shivered. "Please tell me the kids didn't witness that."

Releasing a long breath, he said, "Mim had made it up the hill. Rocky was hot on her heels. They didn't see a thing."

Thank you, Jesus.

Another long silence before Tango asked, "What was he after?"

"Mim used to wear a necklace that her Mom had given her. But a few weeks ago, she took it off. I haven't seen it since. He wanted the necklace. That's all I know."

Eyes narrowed, he stared right through me. "I had an unpleasant conversation with their president. Only thing I got out of him was that Hammer had dug himself an early grave. Turned on his brothers."

Surprisingly, the hows and whys didn't bother me, my only concern was that the right people were still breathing on the other end of the horrible ordeal.

The elevator doors opened. We cleared one hallway, then another, my nerves spiking with every room we passed.

Tango stopped at number 411, and I started to tremble. He pushed me inside.

Dane was sitting up, his chest bare but bandaged, rising and falling in slow rhythmic pulses. He had an IV attached to his left arm. He looked peaceful, his eyes closed, jaw slack.

"I want what he's having," I joked, though feeling not an ounce of humor.

Tango kissed my forehead again. "I'll be back in a bit."

"Thank you."

When the door clicked behind me, I wheeled closer to Dane, not trusting my legs to hold me. His hand was warm, a reminder that blood pumped through his precious veins. I kissed his fingers, one by one, then pressed his palm to my face, roughing the calluses over my skin, desperate for his touch.

"Are you mad at me?" came his gruff voice. My hero's voice.

I couldn't contain my joy, a garbled laugh escaping my chest. "How could I possibly be mad at you?"

He groaned, his head rolling to the side, his eyes peeling open. "I brought that piece of shit into your life."

"You saved Rocky's life."

"I put you and Mim in danger."

"You saved us."

He stared, long and hard, eyes glassy, then whispered, "I love you."

His proclamation slammed my chest, a sneak attack, battering my bruised heart. When I should've been celebrating, kissing him dizzy, giving him those very words back—*I love you*—I only avoided his gaze, staring at a smudge on the window.

"Moriah," he rasped.

"I lost the baby."

A sharp inhale. He reclaimed his hand. Swiped at his face.

Painful silence swelled between us, minutes passing with silent tears and sniffs.

"Are you mad at *me*?" I forced the words through gritted teeth.

"Moriah," he sobbed. "Fuck. No. God, no." He offered his hand again. "C'mere. I need to hold you."

I pushed to my feet, crawled into his bed, and tucked into his uninjured side. Then I let the tears fall. His fell, too, wetting my hair. And there was something cathartic and healing, holding each other through our grief.

He fell asleep, his arms around me going slack, but I stayed in his bed, content to hear his heart beating. So thankful that I hadn't lost him. So effin' thankful.

Mim squeezed the blood from my fingers, her grip tight, while she led me across the lawn, a garden shovel tucked into the back pocket of her shorts.

"What are we doing here, sweet pea?"

She shot me a fretful glance and tugged my hand to hurry me. When we reached the willow tree at the edge of the grass, she squatted, then started to dig.

I sat next to her, checking over my shoulder. Dane trailed behind, his movements slow and careful, the scowl on his face more beautiful than ever. He now boasted two bullet wounds. One on his right thigh, a flesh wound, the other his left pectoral.

He was a walking miracle as far as I was concerned. The doctors had agreed.

Mim dug. Dane made his way to my side, hands in his pockets, brows furrowed.

The dirt was loose, and it didn't take long for Mim to find her treasure. A small puzzle box. She brushed off the dirt, turned to sit on my lap, then handed the box to Dane.

I wrapped my arms around the sweaty little angel and rested my chin on her shoulder.

Dane lifted the lid. Dropped his head. Huffed. Quirked a brow at Mim, then lifted a rusty silver chain out of the box. At the end of the chain hung a heart-shaped locket and a key.

"Let me see that." I swallowed the ball of emotion in my throat.

He passed the necklace over, and offered a hand to Mim, raising her off my lap and pulling her to stand at his side, holding her possessively against his leg.

"I gave my sister this locket when she graduated." I never thought I'd see it again.

I popped the clasp, my heart swelling with nostalgia when I found the picture inside. Mickey and me, laughing. Probably at some bad joke Mom had told.

"I'm sorry," came a soft, sweet voice. Pure innocence and beautiful bravery.

Dane and I locked gazes, and I couldn't help the gasp that escaped. Mim curled into his thigh, burying her face as if ashamed.

"Sorry for what?" Dane asked, voice raspy, thick with emotion.

Mim turned to look at me. "I should have told him where I hid the necklace. Then he wouldn't have hurt anybody."

"It wasn't your fault," I choked out. "None of that was your fault."

Eyes filling with liquid, she blurted, "Mommy said I could never tell anyone about the key. She said I had to keep it safe. She said I couldn't talk to grown-ups, ever, or they might find our treasure."

"Treasure?" I wanted to reach for her, pull her close, but I feared I'd break into sobs and halt her confession.

"We found treasures every day." Mim stretched her neck to meet Dane's eyes. "Mommy put it in our box to keep safe. But then the bad man came."

"Hammer was the bad man?" His name soured my tongue.

Mim nodded. "He used to be nice when he came to see Mommy. He used to be nice to her and give her money and other stuff to put in our treasure box."

Puzzle pieces clicked into place. "Mim, did your mom hide the box from Hammer?"

Mim nodded again.

"Where did she hide the box?"

"At the storange fatuity," she said the words with such confidence I bit my lip to stifle the laugh.

"The what?"

"The orange place."

"Storage facility?" Dane asked.

"Yes." She sighed as if irritated by our questions. "Hammer got mad. He hit Mommy a lot, and we tried to hide. The other bad man who worked at the orange place said he would keep us safe. He took us to his house and gave Mommy medicine. Then he put me in the hole. Mommy didn't help me. Sometimes she cried on the floor and asked him to let me out. But he only let me out when he wanted to play. And Mommy was always asleep. She couldn't hear me crying."

Every word out of her mouth gouged my heart, and I couldn't bear the stoic gaze on her face while she spoke of her abuse.

"Mim." I pulled her into my arms and held her close, my own limbs trembling, my veins ice cold despite the summer heat.

I looked to Dane for help because I wasn't sure how to navigate the conversation, to protect her from revisiting those horrors.

Eyes red-rimmed, cheeks blazing, he cleared his throat, wiping moisture from his face with the back of his arm. "Why did you bury the necklace, Little One? Don't you want to wear it?"

"Rocky said we should bury it because I couldn't say goodbye to my mom," she mumbled into my hair, her arms cinched around my neck. "He helped me have a funeral."

"Oh, baby." I kissed her cheek. "I think we should bury it again. Don't you?"

Mim pulled away from me, searching my face. "Would my mom like that?"

"She would."

Arms coiling, she burrowed her face in my hair. Dane slipped the key off the chain and tucked it in his pocket. He then handed the box to me. I laid it in the hole. Mim shoveled the dirt, burying her necklace once again.

Then Dane tugged a knife out of his back pocket and lowered to his knees. He winced, but valiantly hid the pain from Mim. Then that big, beautiful, beast of a man carved a cross into the trunk of the tree. Below the cross, he carved a heart with my sister's initials.

"How's that?" he asked, tapping Mim under the chin. She smiled. He smiled. And the world seemed right again.

With a grunt, he rose to full height and tugged on my little angel's braid. "I love your voice, Little One."

That beautiful, brave girl kissed his thigh, and with the sweetest utterance I'd ever heard said, "I love you, Dane."

Voice gruff, more grizzly bear than man, Dane responded with, "I love you, too."

That exchange already had me in tears, but when she tossed a smile my way and blurted, "And I love you, Auntie MoMo," I lost my composure and sobbed.

"I love you, too, baby girl. So, so much."

Dane shot me a wink, then tapped Mim on the head. "I'm getting sleepy. Need to lay down. Maybe you can read to me?"

She took off running. "I'll go pick the book!"

Dane grabbed my hand. Snorted. "Auntie MoMo?"

"*Fuck* yeah." I laughed, swiping at my face.

He slapped my ass and chuckled. "That's my girl."

CHAPTER 19

Dane

"THERE'S MY GIRL." I sighed, struck dumb by the sight of her.

"You're back," Moriah said, breathy and so God damn sweet.

Fuck, she was beautiful, standing in the hallway. Hair down, my Ride or Die T-shirt falling off her left shoulder. Those bare fucking feet.

Two weeks had been too damn long to be away from those ladies who owned my heart.

"I'm back." My keys hit the floor. My bag followed suit.

She leaned against the wall, glass of wine in one hand, a book in the other. "Successful trip?"

Off with the boots. "We got her. She's with Lettie right now."

"It went well?"

Better than I'd expected. And what do ya know? Those child-pimping bastards had put up a fight and had to be taken down. Two broken noses, one snapped clavicle, three stab wounds, and one torched van later, they were left for the cops to find, along with enough evidence to put them away for thirty years minimum. "Smooth as silk."

Moriah leaned her head against the wall and lifted the glass to her lips, those sleepy eyes assessing and heavy with worry.

What a great, God damn boost to the ego knowing someone cared that I made it home safe.

Eliminating the distance between us, I hooked an arm around her waist, and teased her with a peck on the cheek. "Mim sleeping?"

She shook her head against my shoulder. "Just kissed her goodnight."

God damn, she smelled like berries. And when she turned to face me, that heady gaze meeting mine, swear to Christ, I died a thousand deaths and came back a better man each time. When I leaned down for the kiss I'd craved, she moaned, leaning into me.

That ass filled my hands, and I squeezed before giving those soft cheeks a hard slap. "Get naked and get in bed, gorgeous. I'll be right there. Got something to show my angel."

Moriah went soft and pliant in my arms, and I took her full weight, so damn happy for something solid to hold.

She smiled, gutting me, then righted herself and downed the rest of her wine in one swallow, a playful lilt to her grin. I watched her saunter down the hall, then went back to my duffel and pulled out the box. When I cracked the door to Mim's room, she lay curled on her side, hands tucked under her cheek, eyes blinking open at the sound of the door.

"Dane!" she squealed.

Knocked me dizzy every damn time, that voice more powerful than a bullet to the chest. That little lady sprang from the bed and wrapped around me in one graceful leap. I hoped she would never tire of my ugly mug.

Clutching her small body, I lowered my ass to the bed. "Guess what I found?"

She pulled her face away from my neck, her tiny hands braced on my shoulders, wise eyes searching mine. "What?"

I handed her the box.

"My treasure!" With a penetrating shrill, she wiggled off my legs and slid to the floor with a thunk. That sweet little angel hugged the tin rust bucket to her chest like it was the most precious gift, looked at me, then the lunchbox. Me. The box. That dazed and amazed expression raised me higher than the clouds, made the extra day away from my girls worth every miserable second.

The storage facility had been easy to find, especially with Tito's help. And what do you know, that damn key of Mim's had fit the shitty lock. When we'd lifted the gate, my heart had damn near oozed out of my chest and dripped to the floor. In the center of that cold, vacant room lay a pile of dirty blankets, a small stack of tattered children's books, one dead flashlight, bloody rags, a box of bandages, and a God damn treasure chest in the form of a Scooby Doo lunch box.

That strong little girl had lived through hell, and still, she'd been the one to pull my pathetic ass out of the grave I'd dug.

"You gonna open it or what?" I grumbled, hoping to hide the lump in my throat.

I'd cleared the box of its other contents. Money—dirty, no doubt. And yes, every cent would go to Mim. She'd earned it. I'd also found three thumb drives, each containing records of club dealings, none of them legal. Evidence that could put every member, including myself, away for life.

Mim lifted the lid. As if afraid to disturb their resting place, she dusted a finger over the pieces of broken glass, colorful rocks, bottle caps, and a tattered feather, giving each item equal attention. When she pulled a rusty old hex nut from the box, holding the filthy thing between her small fingers, her breath hitched. She pushed to her feet, and bounced my way, stopping between my knees, and twisting the damn thing back and forth in my face.

"What's this, Little Lady?"

"Your ring."

"My ring, huh?"

"Rocky said when you love somebody, you give them a ring, and they're yours forever."

I swallowed the lump in my throat. "Yours forever?"

Lips curled between her teeth, she lifted those sleepy eyes to mine. "Now you have to be my daddy. This is your daddy ring. And you can never take it off."

Daddy. God damn. That word had always soured my stomach. Coming from Mim, so innocent, so trusting?

Sweet fucking mother of mercy.

My eyes burned. Chest ached. I blinked away the blurry vision and pulled my saving angel tight against my chest.

Seconds passed before speech was possible. "With or without the ring, I'm yours forever, Little Lady. I'll always protect you. Always love you." I cupped her cheeks. Kissed that little nose, then her forehead. "Best present ever, baby girl."

Mim giggled, scrunching her face, and swiping my beard away.

She dropped the nut into my hand. "It won't fit on your finger."

"I'll wear it around my neck, so it won't get dirty when we're working on your bike."

Her smile hit the megawatt mark. My guts? Hell. No describing what happened to my insides. All I know? I was a new man. Resurrected.

And God damn, if she wanted me to be her daddy, I would reinvent the word.

Wasn't shocked to find Moriah in the tub instead of the bed. She liked her bubbles. I liked her naked. So, bed or bath, all the same to me. I clicked the lock, shucked my gear, and made a mess sliding behind her into the perfumed suds.

Whatever scent filled the room reminded me of cookies fresh from the oven, making my empty gut rumble.

"Was that your stomach?" She laughed, settling her back against my front, her ass on my thighs, feet bracing my knees, her knotted hair hitting me from every angle.

Shifting, I tilted her head, then tasted that spot behind her ear that always made her shiver. "I'm starved. Rushed home. Didn't stop to eat."

"There's roasted chicken in the fridge." Pliant, she offered more of her neck. "Mim made a plate for you."

"Mmm. Sounds good." I sucked her earlobe between my lips, nibbled, then got busy feeling her up, sliding a hand over her slippery chest, handling one glorious tit before giving its rosy bud some attention. "Need you first."

Arching into my ministrations, she snapped a hand around my neck and moaned, rubbing that slippery ass against my steel hard cock, a delicious tease, an invitation. Desire became desperation, and I pressed a hand between her shoulder blades, urging her to bend forward. When she complied, I lifted those hips, positioned my dick, then slammed her down, that tight, slick core devouring every inch of my flesh.

I growled a slew of profanities before pulling my shit together and stifling my urge to flip her over the side of the tub and fuck her into oblivion.

Moriah stilled, her body vibrating, acclimating to the sudden fullness. In those quiet, suspended seconds, anticipation a slithering entity, she filled me, too, with need, want, hope, peace. Certainty. Moriah was the poison in my veins, my sweet addiction, a turbulent storm. She was the antidote, my sobriety, a cool, calm breeze.

And damn, she was killing me.

"Fuck me, gorgeous." Digging my nails into her soft flesh, I trembled, my hunger rampant and teetering on the edge of dangerous. "This is gonna be quick. Ride my cock. Make me come, baby."

My lady took over, her trembling fingers curling around my shins, her body rising and falling, rocking and grinding, thrashing in my lap, a water churning frenzy that lasted torturous seconds before I blew my load inside her silky grip, coming like a fucking teenager, fast, fierce, and self-serving.

Soon as blood flow returned to my brain, I flipped that sexy siren around, claimed her mouth, then worked her clit like my life depended on hearing her moan in pleasure. Mouths fused, she fucked my hand, body arching and bowing, chasing her release. With heavy breaths, and more splashing, that woman came undone, her teeth sinking into my shoulder, body vibrating, and fuuuck I could've played her like that for hours.

Collapsing against me, she whispered, "Missed you."

"Ditto." I leaned my head back to get a good look at that sleepy, sated face. Pink cheeks, fresh kissed lips. The woman was mine. No doubt. But damn, I still had a hard time believing my luck. Which reminded me...

I couldn't help the smile.

"What?" Moriah tugged on my beard.

"Had a meeting with the club."

Worried eyes met mine.

"Prez wants me back. Said the club needs me now that Hammer's gone."

I stopped her protest, pinching her lips closed, making her laugh. "I told him no, of course. He tried to tell me I didn't have a choice."

Like I'd stuck her with a pin, she deflated, making to move away. No fucking way would I let her off my lap. One hand at her neck, the other her lower back, I held her still, holding her gaze.

"Thing is...Moretti hands him the thumb drives we found with Mim's treasure box."

"Thumb drives?"

I nod. "Hammer had been busy stealing from the club. Also collecting evidence, most likely to cover his ass if he ever got caught."

Moriah tensed. She didn't speak a word, but I could hear the questions tumbling around that brain of hers.

"Cool as a fucking cucumber, Moretti tells Prez, 'You already know what these are, otherwise you wouldn't have been looking for Hammer. Reynolds is no longer a Slayer. No hard feelings. No retaliation. Got me?' His unspoken threat hung in the air, and I thought for sure he was dead. Swear to fuck, Prez's face turned five different shades of red, all the while he's glaring at me. He takes his sweet fucking time lighting up a hand-rolled. Takes two slow drags. Then nods at me. Fucking nods, like he's conceding. Gives Tito a quick glance, then warns me never to step foot in Montana again."

"And?"

"*And* nothing. That's it. I'm free."

"You're out?"

"Out."

"For good?"

"Looks that way."

Lips pursed, she curled her arms around my neck, smashing those beautiful tits between us. "Does that mean no more bad boy?"

"Gorgeous." I slammed my hands to her ass, ground my hips, just enough to make her squirm. "I'm as bad as they come."

Moriah sighed, her arms dropping, spine straightening. Again, with those fingers curling into my beard, stroking. All the playful lust disappeared from her face while she stared, the sudden mood shift making me twitchy.

"What is it?"

Her fingers twisted in my facial hair, then tugged, pulling me closer, her lips grazing mine before she whispered, "You're the best person I know, Dane Reynolds."

My chest swelled, a painful, unfamiliar expansion, the room, the tub, hell, my skin shrinking, my ego stretching the boundaries of the universe. Words had never held much power. Yet there I sat, surrounded by bubbles and Moriah, and...fuck yeah...smelly candles, too, and her eight little words brought me back to that hungry little boy I once was, starving for a compliment, a reinforcement, a pat on the head, hell, even a, "Hey kid, how was your day?"

Those eight words, strung together, combined with the shimmer in her eyes, and the blush under those freckles, decimated the years of abuse and neglect, because they never would've mattered coming from anyone other than that fucking beautiful woman sitting naked in my lap.

"Dane," she whispered, swiping a thumb under my eye. "Are you crying?"

"Nah." I coughed, a pathetic attempt to hide the emotion.

But that was fucked. I had no reason to hide from Moriah.

She tapped my chin. "What is it?"

"I'm home." I kissed her, then wrapped my arms around her neck and buried my nose in her hair. "It's really fucking good to be home."

"What is this place?" Moriah asked, hopping from the truck, those long legs showcased in a pair of cutoffs and worn-out Vans, her breasts bouncing beneath the thin fabric of her T-shirt. No denying, I loved her work attire, all sweet, sharp and businesslike, but damn, she rocked the down-home dirty girl vibe like nobody's business.

We stood almost dead center of the twenty-plus acres I'd inherited. Land my father had swindled from its previous owners before I was born.

Surrounded by forest, birds chattered over our heads, the river rushed to our right, and speed boat engines droned in the distance.

"This is my..." *home*, I started to say, but that was no longer the case. "This is where I grew up." I hooked an arm around Mim, lifted her from the truck, and set her on my shoulders.

"Is that where you lived?" Moriah pointed at the charred remains of the trailer, a skeletal reminder of wicked ways and wayward deeds.

"Unfortunately."

Mim wrapped her hands around my chin, leaning over my head. "What happened?"

"Burned to the ground," I grumbled.

"Are you sad?" she asked, her soft, sweet voice worried.

"No, Little Lady." I gave her leg a squeeze. "Nothing but bad came outta that hunk of metal. It needed to go."

No further explanation necessary. The reassurance in Moriah's eyes, her nod of encouragement, told me she understood I'd been the one to torch the place, that the act was cathartic and vital.

"Why are we here?" she asked, sliding her hands into her back pockets, settling her shoulders.

"Trails. Excellent for hiking, but even better for riding." We started toward the wooded patch of land beyond the trailer. "Soon as Mim gets better on her bike, we can have some fun out here. It's where I learned to ride."

"Yesssss," came from over my head.

Moriah huffed. "Damn motorcycles. You're giving me gray hairs, you know that, right?"

Mim laughed.

I did, too.

Moriah protested often, though she'd never ask Mim to give up riding. That little girl had blossomed on her bike, the positive effects undeniable.

When we reached my favorite trail, I hoisted Mim off my shoulders. She took off running the second her feet hit the ground.

Moriah and I followed at a leisurely pace. "I'm trying to decide if I want to sell the land, or maybe build a small cabin. Wanted your input."

"It's beautiful here, Dane. So quiet and secluded."

Moriah saw the beauty in everything. Even a lowlife criminal like me. Fucking blew me away, seeing the world through her eyes.

"Lot of shit went down here. Shit I'd rather forget. But for some reason, I'm struggling with letting go."

Turning to face me, my lady slid her arms around my waist, pressed those tits to my chest, and lifted her chin. "Maybe we can make new memories here. Happy ones."

We. I loved the sound of that. "Yeah." I nodded, lost in that hopeful gaze, that assuring smile.

Hand in hand, we explored, until we reached the crest of the largest hill. I grabbed Moriah's shoulders and turned her toward the lake, pointing over her shoulder. "See that?"

Moriah bent and tilted her head, searching through the thick of trees. "Is that the mansion?"

"Sure is." From that spot, if you looked right, the mansion was visible across the lake. "As a kid, I used to come here to get away from my father. At that time, the house was vacant. Run-down, yard overgrown. But I used to stare across the lake and pretend I lived in that big old dusty house, with a mom and dad who cared about me."

"Oh, Dane," she whispered, leaning against me, a comfort I would never take for granted.

Pity was the last thing I wanted. I'd brought her to that spot for another reason.

"Here's the thing," I mumbled into her hair. "Wherever you are, I'll go. I need to be with my girls. But that mansion is fucking huge. Lettie can't take care of the place on her own. I found something I'm good at, ya know? I want to be there for her, for the cause, and for the first time in my life, I feel like I belong somewhere."

"I understand."

"I've talked to Lettie. There's room for all of us. You, me, Mim. She wants you there as much as I do."

Moriah spun in my arms, taking a step back. "Move into the mansion?"

"Yeah."

"Dane. That's a big step."

"Far as I'm concerned, it's the only step." I rubbed a thumb across that unnecessary wrinkle between her brows, then dropped a kiss on her forehead. "Plus, when I go on a run with Tuck and Tito, you and Lettie won't be alone."

With a sigh, she relaxed, tucking her fingers into my waistband, and pulling me closer. "You're in this for the long haul, huh?"

"I'm not going anywhere, gorgeous."

"What about the girls you bring back? How will we explain them to Mim?"

"Gorgeous, who better to help those kids than a kid who's lived through that shit?"

Releasing me, she stepped back and gnawed her lower lip before saying, "Let me think about it."

Fuck. Not the answer I wanted, but better than a *no*. "Yeah. Yeah. Think about it."

"Think about what?" Mim skipped our way, shoved a handful of white and purple wildflowers into Moriah's hand, then tilted her head to look at me and repeated, "Think about what?"

"Dane wants us to move into the mansion with him and Lettie." Moriah bent and made a show of smelling the flowers. "These are so pretty."

Mim clamped a hand around my wrist, squeezing. "Live at the mansion? Like, live there. With my motorcycle?"

I looked to Moriah for guidance. She offered nothing but a shrug.

"Well, that's where we keep your motorcycle, so technically, yes, you'd live at the mansion, with your bike."

"Oh, can we? Please, please, please?" The little angel bounced on her toes and turned to offer her aunt a ridiculous grin.

"Mim. I told Dane I would think about it."

"So," she squeaked, throwing her hands in the air.

"So, let me think about it." Moriah struggled to keep the humor from her voice.

Mim, my little warrior, wasn't ready to give up. "He already spends the night every night."

Moriah rose to full height, fisted hands landing on her hips. "Yes, but..."

Mim mimicked the pose, eyes narrowing. "He makes us breakfast every morning and takes me to school."

"I know, sweetie, but moving in together is a big step."

I gripped the hex nut, AKA daddy ring, that now hung around my neck on a thick silver chain, rubbing it between my fingers, silently and shamelessly urging Mim to continue.

"MoMo!" The little shit stomped her foot in the dirt like a spoiled child. "I had to take his underwear out of the dryer and fold it." Her freckled nose crinkled.

"So?"

On an exasperated sigh, Mim threw her head back. "So, doesn't that mean we already live together?"

I could no longer contain my laughter.

"Okay. Fine!" Moriah threw up her hands. "Fine. You got me. I don't have to think about it. It just seemed like the right thing to say."

Mim squealed. Inside, I may have squealed, too.

Seriously, those girls.

CHAPTER 20

Moriah

"JESUS EFFIN' EFF. I can't believe I'm standing here watching this!" I covered my eyes. Dropped my hand. Huffed. Glared at the starting gate across the dirt track.

"This is insane." Lettie, too, struggled to enjoy herself on the shoddy wood bleachers, which offered zero shade in the hot August afternoon. "I don't know if I can look. I should've stayed in the car."

"Seriously," Tucker piped in, squirming toddler in his arms. "Kids on dirt bikes? What the hell?"

"Dad. Dad! Put me on your shoulders. I can't see," Rocky bellowed.

Aida shot a glare at her husband. "You all need to chill. She's got this. Look at her. She's the smallest little nugget out there, and all those boys and girls are moving out of her way."

Tango snorted. "That's because Dane is right behind her."

Well, that was true. Dane Reynolds parted crowds everywhere he went.

Tito added, "They've seen her race. Those kids know they're competing for second place."

Tuuli, Tito's wife, offered me a reassuring grin.

Tito was right, of course. Mim dominated every track on her practice runs. The girl was a natural, her bike more an extension of her body than a machine she commanded. A beautiful symbiosis.

I, however, was a ball of jumbled nerves, only able to stand because Slade was at my side, holding my hand.

Dane had been right about Mim. She loved to ride, she loved to work on her bike, and she loved to win. On her bike, on any track, Mim was in control, and with that control, under the tutelage of Dane, that little lady was a Titan.

Hence, the team name she wore with pride. Titan Racing. The name decorating the T-shirts we all wore. Even baby Lucia.

Mim and I had moved into the mansion last summer, but in the year that'd passed, with the therapy, her rides with Dane, and the adopted family surrounding us, Mim had conquered her demons, her night terrors gone, her fear of strangers a thing of the past. She'd even advanced a grade in school, and I couldn't have been happier for the little angel.

The announcer's voice blared over the speakers, words I couldn't make out. Motorcycle engines revved. The gate dropped. Mim shot forward, claiming the lead, and keeping the lead. Number 7 challenged her on the third round, but lost ground when she leaned deep, taking a sharp turn, and cutting him off.

Everyone in the stands was on their feet screaming, Rocky the loudest, me in close second.

Slade squeezed my hand so hard my fingers numbed, but I didn't care, because that was *my* little girl crossing the finish line seconds before anyone else, and that was *my* man waiting for her past the checkered flag. And although I couldn't see Dane, I knew there were tears in his eyes, because that big, scary, bad boy of mine had a heart softer and gooier than roasted marshmallows, and he'd bloomed and grown right alongside Mim. And while I jumped and screamed and cried, celebrating for Mim, Slade squeezed my hand hard enough to crack bones, and when I looked to my left, to beg her to let go, my new best friend was holding her big round belly with her free arm, and bending forward, her face red and pinched.

"Slade?"

She made a weird sound.

"The baby?"

She nodded.

The cheering died down, allowing my voice to rise above the whoops and hollers. "Tango! Tango!" Stretching my free arm around Slade, I poked Tango's ribs.

He looked down, his eyes going wide when they landed on his wife. "Oh, shit."

Like he was a hot potato, Tango passed Rocky to Tito, who'd been looking the other direction, thereby nearly dropping Rocky on his head between the bleachers. Thank the good Lord above, Tucker had been standing behind Tito. He caught Rocky by the ankles, sparing him a nasty fall, and possibly a broken neck. Lucia, who had been sitting between Aida and Lettie, laughed at her dangling cousin and pulled his hair, dancing the way only a toddler with baggy diaper butt could dance. Unfortunately, she'd shared a frozen fruit pop with her uncle Tango, and her sticky fingers tangled in her cousin's thick black mane.

Meanwhile, my purple fingertips were about to pop from the pressure, but the moment Tango wrapped his arms around Slade, she relaxed and released my hand.

"It's time?" Tango asked.

"Yep."

"T, it's time!" he yelled over his shoulder, guiding a very pregnant Slade down the three wooden steps.

"Time for what?" Rocky shouted, still upside down, Aida pulling his hair from Lucia's fingers one by one, spewing unpleasant words under her breath.

"The baby! Mom's about to have the baby!" Tango yelled, his voice shaking.

It was then that Charlie, the Truck Stop's jolly chef shouted, "Yeehaw" and barreled down the steps, scooping Slade up like a bulldozer, and heading toward the parking lot.

"Charlie! What the fuck? That's my job," Tango protested, laughing, but yanked his keys out of his front pocket nonetheless and ran ahead.

"I can't get her fingers out of his hair."

Tucker sat, laying Rocky across his lap. Lucia giggled, then punched Rocky with her free hand. "We need to go. Anyone got scissors?

"No! You can't cut my hair," Rocky cried.

"I've got scissors in my handbag." Lettie sat next to her son and rifled through her very large bag.

"Oh, this is ridiculous," Tito piped in. He handed his car keys to Tuuli, who had remained quiet and calm through all of the chaos, then scooped Lucia up by one arm, Rocky by the other, and made his way toward their waiting vehicles.

"Found them," Lettie shouted, chasing after Tito.

Aida patted Tucker on the shoulder, said, "Good job, cowboy," then followed Lettie.

Tucker chuckled and chased after his wife.

Tuuli shrugged her shoulders, laughed, then asked, "You need a ride?"

"No. I'll head back with my crew." I threw my arms around her small frame.

"We'll see you at the hospital?" she asked, hugging me back.

"Wouldn't miss it."

I waited for Tuuli to join her husband, then jogged around the outside of the track, finding Mim still on her bike, and Dane kneeling, her head in his hands, their foreheads pressed together. He wore a smile that not even the astronauts could miss, and Mim had her eyes closed, absorbing his words.

As I approached, a tear slithered down her cheek, then another, then she buried her face in his neck and fell against him, sliding off her bike and falling into his welcoming arms. Those were tears of joy, and those tears, that moment, belonged to Mim and Dane. A father/daughter moment worthy of a Hallmark movie, and I fell deeper in love with both them.

Dane

After seeing Moriah and Mim to the maternity ward, I retreated to the waiting room, unsure if I'd be welcome in Tango and Slade's private quarters. I paced. Then I ducked outside for some fresh air and room to burn off energy. A cigarette would've eased some tension, but I'd promised my girls I'd quit, and I had, hence the pacing.

A warm breeze made a lazy trip across the terrace, cooling my sweaty skin, a temporary relief from the late afternoon sun. I rubbed the ache in my temple, and opted to stand, rather than sit, afraid I'd pass the fuck out if allowed a moment to relax.

I hadn't slept a wink all night.

Not sure why the thought of Blondie in pain made me so uncomfortable, but I sure as shit wouldn't have wanted to be in Tango's shoes for those twelve hours of labor. Had it been me watching Moriah suffer through childbirth? Safe to say, some undeserving object, or person, would've fallen victim to my fists.

Baby Raquel was born five hours ago. Mom and child both happy and healthy. No doubt, that little nugget would be a looker, spoiled rotten, and shielded from all the ugly in the world. She was Pretty Boy's kid after all, and despite my feelings about Rossi, there was no denying, the man took care of his own.

"Reynolds." A heavy hand landed on my shoulder.

So much for my *me* time.

"Moretti," I grunted, offering my hand.

"Hey," came from Tuck, followed by a fist bump. "What's up, man?"

"Needed air."

"Cute kid." Moretti sighed, roughing a hand through his hair before resting his elbows on the railing and scanning the lot below. "Hope she looks like her mama."

"Hope she has Slade's blue eyes." That came from Tuck, who stood with his hands in his pockets and his gaze to the sky.

"Won't matter her eye color, she's gonna be a heartbreaker," I threw in.

"She won't be breaking any hearts, 'cause that little angel isn't leaving the house until she's thirty." Tango strode through the door, dark circles under his eyes, cheesy smile on his face, and not one fucking hair out of place. God damn pretty boy.

"Yeah. Good luck with that, cousin," Moretti teased.

"Congratulations." I threw him a chin nod, then gestured to his head. "That a gray hair already?"

Tito pulled four Cubans out of his front pocket.

"The hell'd you get those?" Tango asked.

"Stole 'em from your pops."

Tucker slapped his hands together and gave 'em a good rub. "Well, now's as good a time as any."

Tito passed those fuckers out. I briefly considered taking a pass, but fuck, who was I to mess with tradition? Moriah would understand.

"So, who's next?" Tango quirked a brow, shooting each of us a pointed look.

"One's more than I can handle," huffed Tucker, throwing his hands up and backing up a step.

Tito blew a smoke ring. "Tuuli's got another six years of school. Truth be told, I'm not ready to fuckin' share her anyway."

All eyes aimed my direction. "Guess that leaves you."

"Nah." I shook my head. "I'm good. We'll leave the baby-making to Pretty Boy."

Hell, my chest was in a constant state of agony, threatening to crack open with all the feels I had for those girls of mine. I wasn't sure I had room for more.

Tango chuckled. Stood taller. "Five sounds like a good number. Think I'll go for five. Three boys, two girls."

"Let's revisit that statement after you've had zero sleep for three months straight," Tucker threw in, cracking a grin and pointing his Cohiba Tango's way.

"So, you coming up to meet my little angel, or what?"

I coughed out a puff of smoke, thrown off by his unexpected invitation. Tango and I shared a hard stare, a silent communication.

We good?

Yeah. We're good

All's forgiven?

Forgiven. Forgotten. Moving on.

I nodded. "Can I finish my fancy smoke first?"

We finished our smokes. We congratulated Pretty Boy again, with manly hugs and grunts. I followed the guys back to the room.

Surrounded by sighing women, and the biggest bunch of badass, pussy-whipped motherfuckers you could imagine, I held that red-faced, bald, tiny little human. Mim crawled up into my lap, staring at that beautiful little girl, and a lump stuck in my throat.

And fuck. I wanted that to be my life.

I caught Moriah's gaze. Her crooked smile, a knowing glint in her eye, like she imagined that I was holding our baby. My chest swelled, everything in me tightening. I nudged Mim off my lap. Carried the baby to her mama.

"Congratulations, Blondie." I dropped a kiss on Slade's forehead. "She's beautiful like her mom."

"You leaving already?" Her blue eyes were sleepy, but so damn content.

"Can I tell you a secret?"

She nodded.

I leaned closer and whispered, "I'm taking my ladies home, putting Mim to bed early. Then I'm making it my life's mission to put one of these little nuggets in Moriah."

Blondie laughed, hooked her free arm around my neck and planted a lingering kiss on my cheek. "I love you, Dane Reynolds."

Jesus Fucking Christ, that woman. I choked out, "Love you too, Blondie."

She slapped my shoulder, and whispered, "Now go, before you make me cry."

I gathered my girls. We said our goodbyes.

After a trip to the park, a quick dinner at the Truck Stop, and a ride with Mim on the dirt trails behind the mansion, I tucked my little angel into bed, stripped my soon-to-be-wife naked, then made a show of disposing of her birth control pills, dropping them one by one into the toilet.

"Dane," she purred. "What are you doing?"

"It's time."

"Time for what?"

"To add to our team of Titans."

Arms crossed, Moriah leaned against the doorframe, one bare foot resting on the other. "I could have a hundred babies with you."

"That's a lot of bikes." I dropped her pill box into the trash can.

Her sweet smile made my head spin. "What if the next one wants to be a ballerina?"

"Then I'll build a dance studio." I ditched my shirt.

Her gaze dropped to my bare torso, then back up. "What about a fireman?"

"Then I'll build that little rugrat a pimped-out firetruck."

Moriah grabbed my belt and worked the buckle loose. "Dane."

"Yeah, gorgeous?"

"Shut up and eff me already, will ya?"

I roughed a hand over her chest, then cupped her tit before rolling her pink bud between my fingers. "Oh, I'm gonna eff you 'til you're begging for effin' mercy."

"I love you, Dane Reynolds."

Good God. My life. The fucking bomb.

"Love you, gorgeous."

And I spent every day loving the eff outta my woman.

And we made a team.

A team of effin' Titans.

THE END

ACKNOWLEDGEMENTS

Mom. My biggest fan. My hug giver. My prayer partner. My favorite crybaby. Thank you for instilling in me the love of writing. And thank you for almost fifty years of relentless encouragement.

SexyBoyfriend. You'll never read this, but I'm saying it anyway. You've been beyond patient with me and my writing career, and that means the world to me. Someday, I will buy that Porsche I promised you all those years ago.

My babies. I love you. You're the reason I get out of bed every morning.

Elaine York. Thank you for always finding time to fit me into your busy schedule. I hope we can meet face to face someday because I have a big hug waiting for you.

Those of you who stuck with me to then end of this series, from the bottom of my heart, thank you! I still can't wrap my head around the fact that people are reading my stories, let alone falling in love with the characters.

And as always, thank you Jesus!

OTHER BOOKS BY
Krissy Daniels

TRUCK STOP SERIES
Truck Stop Tango
Truck Stop Tryst
Truck Stop Tempest
Truck Stop Titan

How To Kill Your Boss

APOTHEOSIS SERIES
Aflame
Aglow

CONNECT

krissydaniels.com

Facebook
www.facebook.com/authorkrissydaniels/

Instagram
www.instagram.com/krissydanielsbooks/
BookBub
www.bookbub.com/profile/krissy-daniels

Book+Main Bites
bookandmainbites.com/krissydaniels/bites

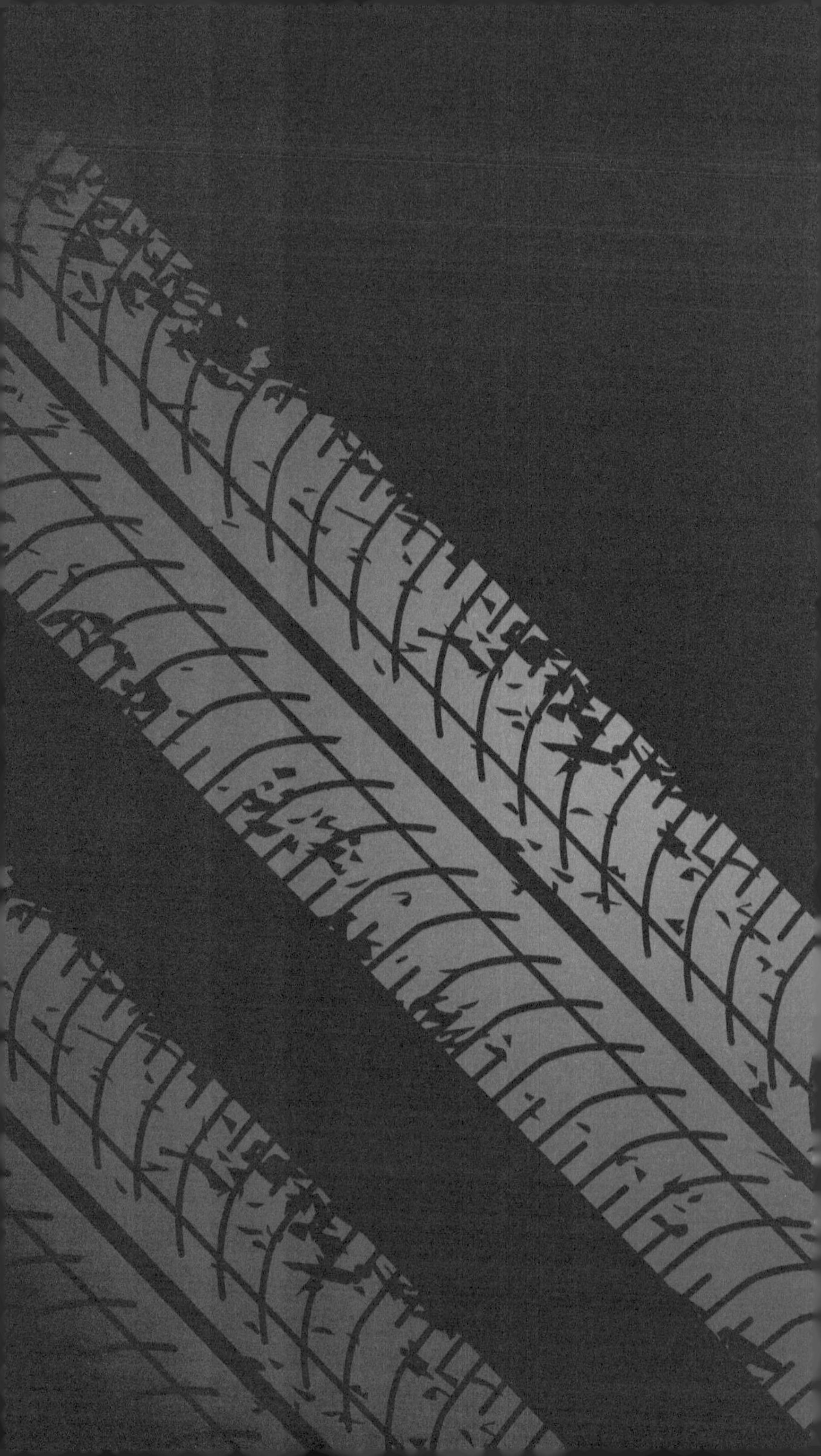